BEST DETECTIVE STORIES

ff

BEST
DETECTIVE
STORIES OF
CYRIL HARE

Chosen with an introduction by
Michael Gilbert

faber and faber

LONDON · BOSTON

First published in 1959
by Faber and Faber Limited
3 Queen Square London WC1N 3AU
Printed in Great Britain by
Whitstable Litho Ltd, Whitstable, Kent
All rights reserved
This paperback edition published in 1986
© This selection Faber and Faber Ltd, 1959

ISBN 0 571 145190 1

CONTENTS

5

Other Crimes

The Children

INTRODUCTION

Cyril Hare

(i)

I became a reader of the works of Cyril Hare in circumstances ideal for their consumption. The year was 1943, and I was one of five hundred inmates of a prisoner-of-war camp on the Adriatic coast of Italy. Further, being under the displeasure of my gaolers, I was serving a term of solitary confinement.

You must not allow my use of this expression to delude you. Dismiss from your mind at once pictures of an underground cell, with dripping walls, a diet of bread and water, and the company of intelligent mice; the *locus in quo* was a private room on the sunny side of the camp. Even "solitary" was a misnomer, for I had another prisoner, a very congenial companion, with me. However, it was undoubtedly "confinement". There was no getting away from that. We had little to do for thirty days but lie on our bunks and devise new methods of irritating our guards.

It was in such circumstances that an orderly delivered to us, one day, along with our lunch of *pasta* and diced meat-loaf, a tattered copy of *Tragedy at Law*. The excitement was intense. The only other reading matter available to us at the time was a week-old Italian newspaper devoted to accounts of Axis victories in Sicily and Pantellaria, and a Complete Works of Milton.

Introduction

We fell jointly upon Cyril Hare with an avidity which you may be able to picture. We rationed ourselves, I remember, to a stated number of chapters a day so that we should not swallow the book whole. And we arrived at a gentleman's agreement, as we read the book alternately, that neither of us would get too far ahead of the other, thus reducing the risk that we should inadvertently disclose to each other its secrets.

This is, of course, the ideal approach to a good whodunnit, and *Tragedy at Law* is not only one of Cyril Hare's best detective novels but a book which bears comparison with any in its class. Julian Symons included it in his recent survey of "best, anywhere, ever", and such a ranking seems to me by no means too high. If I was introduced to this one of Cyril Hare's works in circumstances likely to prejudice me in its favour, I have read it since in more normal surroundings and have been able to confirm my earlier judgment.

For the moment, however, I am speaking of the man himself. It never, I think, crossed my mind that I should meet him, but this happened within four years of the end of the war, when I climbed the stairs of the old house in Kingly Street, behind Regent Street, which at that time housed the club-room of the Detection Club.

I can only say that I had no difficulty in recognising him. "Straight from Forsyte Saga" was his description of himself. I should have said, rather, "Straight from the pages of the *Strand Magazine* and Paget's illustrations of the *Sherlock Holmes* stories". The likeness was remarkable. The thin, inquisitive nose, the intellectual forehead, the piercing eye, the Oxford common-room voice. The matter under discussion when I came in was the gas stove, which had expired, a thing which gas stoves in Kingly Street did with remarkable regularity. No one had a shilling. "I believe," Cyril Hare was saying in beautifully modulated tones, "that a pre-war Italian one lira piece . . ." But fortunately for the reputation of the Detection Club its newest member had a shilling on him.

(ii)

Most people will know that "Cyril Hare" was the pseudonym of Alfred Gordon Clark, barrister of the Inner Temple, Judge of County Courts, and Deputy Chairman of Quarter Sessions.

He was born in September 1900, and his schooldays at Rugby (where, he says, he was starved of food and crammed with learning) coincided almost exactly with the First World War. After leaving Rugby he went up to New College and read, and got a First in History. But there was never any question of his being other than a lawyer. The family traditions were too strong, even had his own inclinations drawn him elsewhere, which they did not. He was called to the Inner Temple, and joined the chambers of Mr. Roland Oliver, a fortunate choice, had he known it, for it was a chambers which was to be concerned in many of the great criminal cases of the twenties. In an article which appeared posthumously in the *Law Journal* Cyril Hare gave an amusing glimpse of these chambers and of their head: ". . . a very great criminal lawyer, who once said to me, then a very callow pupil in his chambers, apropos of a case in which I was convinced that the prisoner had been wrongly accused: 'On the whole—it is—sometimes—not a bad thing—for a young man—to believe in his client's innocence.' I was shocked, as no doubt he intended me to be, by the implication that lay behind his tolerant concession to my enthusiasm. But it did not need a very long experience of defending prisoners to teach me just what he meant."

9

Introduction

The years between the wars were made up of the pleasant, hard-working grind of a junior barrister's life: Common Law and Criminal Law; High Court work, and the South Eastern Circuit. Without amassing a fortune, he was making himself enough to live on, and was making it in the way he enjoyed. Life was shared between Cyril Mansions, in Battersea, and Hare Court, Inner Temple. When he started to write it seemed suitable to him to conjoin a part of each into his own pseudonym.

Cyril Hare's first writings were short stories; flippant pieces, designed for *Punch* and the glossy papers, not many of which have survived the inspiration of the moment that gave them birth. Then comparatively late, at the age of thirty-six, he turned his pen to the detective story.

It was the golden era of the whodunnit; the age of those great ladies, dames of the stiletto, the bottle and the noose—Sayers, Christie and Allingham; the days when the Detection Club was founded and its peculiar rules and ritual laid down; the days when heads of colleges, dignitaries of the Church, judges, and even comparatively unlettered men like cabinet ministers prided themselves on a working knowledge of *rigor mortis* and the symptoms of arsenical poisoning. Competition, in the world of the detective novel, was fierce and the standard was high. To have a manuscript accepted was a considerable feat. To write an outstanding example of the *genre* was becoming more nearly impossible each day.

It was whilst on his feet, in defence of a larcenist, at Maidstone Assizes, that Cyril Hare learned that his first full-length novel, *Tenant for Death*, had been accepted. His son had been born that year. His wife was at that moment in hospital suffering the after-effects of a tonsillectomy. Life must have been complicated in those days. It must also have been great fun.

Introduction

Further novels followed. Then came the upheaval of the Second World War, a tour as Judge's Marshal which produced *Tragedy at Law*; a short spell with the Ministry of Economic Warfare, an experience responsible, no doubt, for the opening chapters of *With a Bare Bodkin*, and a much longer spell in the department of the Director of Public Prosecutions, which produced more good stories than could ever be told.

In 1950 Cyril Hare's legal career was crowned by his call to the County Court Bench. We do not underwork our judiciary. Opportunities for writing became fewer. Novels still appeared, but at longer intervals. There were distractions, apart from judicial work and writing. He was a fine speaker, as anyone who heard him will agree; whether it was the Oxford University or the Cambridge University English Society, the students of Denman College, the delegate conferences of the Women's Institute, the Poetry Society, or even those more flippant occasions of after-dinner oratory at which he excelled.

He died at the height of his career, last year, in *medias res*, full of works, his faculties at stretch. No doubt, when we come to it, this is an excellent way to go; but it is sad for those who are left.

(iii)

In making this collection, I have read, I think, through the complete body of Cyril Hare's short stories, published and unpublished. If it sounds as though this were some form of hard labour, that is very far from the truth. Some writers are difficult to read, even when they write well. Others are easy to read at all times. To call it a matter of style is to beg the question. I should prefer to call it a matter of voice.

11

Introduction

Cyril Hare, as I have said, had a most attractive speaking voice. Even his bad short stories—everyone writes bad short stories from time to time, jokes which do not amuse, conjuring tricks which do not deceive, bubbles which burst—even these stories are most readable, from the smoothness and technique with which they are presented.

It is a technique which must have derived a good deal from the profession of advocacy.

The training of advocate used to be a routine part of upper-class education. There is so much to learn in this technological age that it probably could not be made so today. But I cannot help thinking that it should be a compulsory part of the training of every detective story writer—not in order to give him expertise in his court scenes, although this might not come amiss, but to make him adept at presenting a complicated plot neatly and agreeably.

C. E. Montague quoted with approval Sheridan's saying: "Your easy reading is damned hard writing." He pointed out that any fool can make a passage difficult to understand; any dabbler can muddy the waters. What needs hard thinking and hard writing is to do the reader's preliminary work for him, to present him with a complicated set of facts arranged in such a way that he cannot fail to understand them; moreover, to perform this feat not as a mere pedagogue but with tact and discernment.

But is not this what an advocate does, for his fees, professionally and on every working day of his life? The intricacies of his case are known to him, because he has spilled midnight oil over them. Now, on the floor of the court, in the short time available to him, he has to make matters as clear to judge and jury as they are to him. If he be ambiguous, the opposition will profit. If he be tedious, you may be sure that his client will pay for it, cent per cent, before the end of the day.

The plots of short crime stories are of necessity complicated. It is in this, if in anything, that they differ from short stories on other topics. It is not pretended that they form a class apart. The rules of construction and presentation, which govern all short stories, govern the crime short story equally. But they have this additional prerequisite: that they are, by their nature, complicated. Each story must set out, in sufficient detail, some criminal act. It is not always murder. You will find, within these covers, assault and robbery, breaking and entering, confidence trickery, blackmail, forgery and treason.

And the criminal act has not only to be described. It has also, in some manner, to be worked out. A crime cannot be narrated and left hanging. Some attempt must be made to deal with the criminal. The attempt will not always be successful. In *The Story of Hermione*, which is the shortest in the book and one of the best (the American editor Stewart Beach once described it to me as one of the finest "shock" stories he had ever read), the criminal escapes altogether. In others, such as *The Old Flame* and *A Present for Christmas*, the aftermath of retribution is foreshortened, or only suggested. But the law must always be there. It is the *tertium quid* in every crime story.

The other way, it seems to me, in which the crime story differs from its more lawful kin, is that it is often presented as a conjuring trick. The narrative is but a piece of entertaining patter, designed to fix your attention upon the conjurer's right hand, whilst his left hand is palming the black-jack with which he plans to hit you in the final line.

To my mind Cyril Hare had very few equals at this. His careful training in full-length detective novels, where the incautious giving away of a single clue may jeopardise the whole work, had undoubtedly trained him in this aspect of his craft. If you would like an example of what I mean, turn to the simple little story on page 142 called *The Rivals*. Refrain from cheating. Cover the final paragraph. Now try to make up your mind which of the two young men in question was telling the truth and which was lying. And, when you have read the final paragraph, look back and observe how the clue was planted; how, since it was something which could not be glossed over, it was, in fact stressed, but stressed in so different a context that it did not appear to have any connection with the puzzle. That is what I mean by a conjuring trick.

(iv)

The thirty stories which make up this book have not been dragooned into any very logical order. They come in all shapes and sizes. Some were written with a particular market in view. Some, like The *Rivals* (which I mentioned above), are pure puzzles. Others are straightforward pieces of narrative.

Broadly speaking they fall perhaps into three categories —and are very roughly so arranged. There are stories with a legal background, stories dealing with murder, and stories dealing with other criminal excursions. But even here the dividing line becomes blurred. The *Name of Smith* concerns the little appreciated functions and possibilities of a judge's summing-up and is therefore a legal story. It is also, undoubtedly, a murder story. And into what category would you put *The Markhampton Miracle*?

A large number of the stories are told in the first person. The speaker is rarely particularised, although in one, at least (*Miss Burnside's Dilemma*), she appears to be an elderly lady of unpredictable temperament. But in others

Introduction

there is little doubt about it. The narrator is Cyril Hare himself; standing, as I have so often seen him stand, in front of the fireplace at Kingly Street, hands in pockets, head thrust forward—or prostrate in one of its unspeakable leather armchairs—demonstrating to his hearers that law and life, humanity and inhumanity, probability and improbability, were alike grist to one careful observer's mill.

MICHAEL GILBERT

"Where There's a Will——"

Julian Symondson reached the crest of the hill and stood for a moment looking across the valley at the agreeable little house for which he was making. It was a gusty day towards the end of October, a day of fleeting sun and shower, luminous with all the colour of autumn and keen with a foretaste of winter. It was exactly the type of day that sends energetic young men every Sunday marching in their hundreds over the more picturesque parts of the country. It was exactly the type of day that Julian most cordially detested. It is only right to add that he also disliked the country, whether picturesque or not, walking, and, above all, Sunday.

If Julian had been asked to say what, next to himself, he really cared for, he would certainly have replied, "Life!" "Life" to him did not include the countryside, or bracing October afternoons, or the rich mud which squelched lovingly beneath his over-thin shoes. "Life" meant London, and London meant half a dozen restaurants and not more than three night-clubs (they changed from year to year, but there were never more than three), two bars, ten streets and the faces of a handful of friends. It was not much, but it had been enough to make Julian completely happy—enough, too, to make him, from being rather better than well off, in three years from his coming of age completely penniless. It had seemed unbelievable at the time, but a day came when the restaurants ceased to give credit and the clubs to cash cheques, when the handful of friends shrank into a group of embarrassed people who avoided his eye at meal-times and remembered pressing engagements when he tried to raise the delicate question of a fiver or so to tide him over the weekend. On that day Julian remembered that he was not entirely alone in the world. Blood was thicker than water. He possessed an aunt.

Now he wondered a little wearily, as he descended the slope with the stiff steps of a townsman, whether it would not be truer to say that his aunt possessed him. She owned the cottage in which he lived rent-free, she paid the wages of the servant who looked after him, and the allowance which just kept him in whisky and cigarettes. She had been kindness itself to him—the kind country neighbours whom she had introduced to him had repeated the phrase till he could have screamed; she had certainly saved him from poverty, dire and complete; and in return she exacted—what? Merely that he should live in the country, away from the temptation of that wicked place London, and walk over to tea with her every Sunday. (*Walk*, mind you, not even use the little two-seater which her bounty allowed! Her window commanded a great stretch of country and she could see a mile off if there were any attempt at shirking.) He was not, he told himself for the hundredth time, an ungrateful man—far from it. He was profoundly thankful to Aunt Agnes for what she had done. He was even fond of her in a way. She was a good sort, really, though incapable of understanding what a young man really wanted in this world, as pious widows who live in the country are apt to be. But he had by now endured three years of this thraldom, and as he climbed the final ascent which led him to the house he caught himself wishing that she were dead.

18

Nephews—and particularly those who are entirely dependent on their aunts—have no business to entertain, even for a moment, wishes of this kind. Julian was not so depraved as to be unconscious of this, and he had hardly formed the wish before he repented of it, and resolved to atone for his ingratitude by being particularly considerate to his aunt that afternoon. Julian's good resolutions were not often very effective; and it so happened that this one was even less so than most, for the simple reason that at the moment when it was made Mrs. Thorogood had already been dead for something like half an hour. She had died very quietly in her arm-chair by the drawing-room window, looking out over the view that she loved so much, at about the same time that Julian appeared on the distant horizon. So quiet had been her passing that the maid who brought in the tea-tray had thought that her mistress was dozing, and had gone out for the afternoon as usual without suspecting that anything was wrong. Thus it was that when Julian entered the drawing-room he and the cat were the only living creatures in the house.

There was nothing uncommon in finding the old lady asleep in her chair. He was not sorry when he did so, for thereby he was saved so many minutes of rather painfully righteous conversation. On this occasion, with the deft quietness of one who knows his way about, he lit the lamp beneath the silver urn, brought the water to the boil, made the tea, poured out two cups (weak with milk and two lumps of sugar for her, strong and black for himself) and then turned to wake her up.

His first reaction when he realised that Aunt Agnes would not wake up again, ever, was a feeling of extreme faintness. Not for the first time, but more keenly than ever before, he regretted that Mrs. Thorogood's principles did not allow her to keep any spirits in the house. For want of a better stimulant he drank both cups, one after the other, and found his nerves beginning to grow steadier. For a time, however, he felt quite incapable of any action. He sat still, staring aimlessly at the motionless features, hardly less animated than his own. Poor old Aunt Agnes! This was (he told himself) a blow—really a much worse blow than he had ever anticipated. He had scarcely realized how dependent on her he had been. After all, for three years she had done everything for him, paid for him, looked after him, thought for him. It was thanks to her that he had been saved from heaven knew what fate, even the ultimate degradation of working for his living. He had never really been as grateful to her as he should, he reflected sadly. And now it was too late. He felt suddenly very much alone in the world.

He rose unsteadily to his feet and looked round the pleasant, well-ordered room. It was very much a respectable widow lady's room, he reflected—so prim and neat and on its best behaviour! There came back to him the recollection of all the hours of boredom that he had endured in it, and a feeling of relief grew stronger and stronger in his breast. That was over, at all events! No more Sunday afternoons of interminable chatter—he was his own master now! Then he grinned sardonically as he realised that the room and all that it contained was now his own property. His aunt had said so more than once. "When I am gone, Julian," she had told him, "all this will be yours. You love the place, don't you?" "Yes, Aunt," he had assured her, and she had purred in satisfaction. Oh! he had played his cards pretty well, all these years! Love the place, indeed! To his mind there was only one attraction in it, and that was that it was certain to fetch a good price in the market. He knew that she had refused half a dozen offers for it. It wouldn't

take him long to get it off his hands, and that done—
London and all its joys spread themselves before his
imagination.

It occurred to him to wonder whether she had left a
will. Besides the house, which she had promised him, there
must be a considerable amount of property, for she had
made no secret of the fact that she was a fairly wealthy
woman, in spite of her modest way of living. He had only
heard her mention the subject once, soon after his establishment as her protégé, and Julian, who had a memory
for such things, remembered her words exactly. "I shall
really have to think about making my will now," she had
said. "Not that it could make much difference to you,
dear boy, as you are my only heir in any case. But there
are some things I should like to arrange before I go." She
had never explained exactly what things she meant, but
he imagined that she had in mind small legacies to servants and so forth. It would be interesting, at all events,
to see if she had done it.

He went across to the writing desk, where, he knew,
his aunt used to keep all her business papers. Quietly,
almost furtively, though he knew that there was nobody
who could possibly disturb him, he ran through the neatly
filed and docketed receipts, bills and correspondence which
filled it.

It was not long before he lighted upon a long envelope
occupying a pigeon-hole to itself and marked in Mrs.
Thorogood's firm, prim handwriting, "My Will", followed
by the date, "December 1910". This had been struck out,
and "January 1956" substituted.

With his heart beating considerably too fast for comfort, Julian drew out the contents. First came a long
document in a clerkly hand, the ink somewhat faded
with the years. It was the will of Miss Symondson as she

then was, dated some twenty years before Julian was born. He glanced at it without interest, put it on one side and then turned to the other. This was quite short and entirely in his aunt's handwriting. Julian read it from end to end.

Mrs. Thorogood bequeathed to her nephew her house, together with its grounds and furniture and the sum of £500 a year—an amount which, she added, had always sufficed to keep it in proper repair, and should with due economy enable him to do the same. The residue of her property was to be divided between the Charity Organization Society and the Society for the Propagation of Christian Knowledge. The will concluded with the words: "Should my nephew cease to occupy the house or attempt in any way to part with the possession or ownership of it by lease, sale, mortgage, or otherwise, he is to forfeit all benefits under this Will."

There are some disasters too great to be understood at once, and Julian must have read the last sentence through half a dozen times before he grasped its meaning. At last the full horror of it broke in upon him. So this was what the old woman called being her "heir"! After all, she meant to tie him down still from the grave, and keep him in this dead-alive place for the rest of his life! This was all he got in return for what he had done, for all his detestable Sunday walks, for his—his—he was unable to think for the moment of anything else which he had done for his aunt, but this did not in the least moderate his growing fury. He looked out of the window to where the sky was darkening towards sunset, and felt that he had never seen anything so forbidding as the view which he was condemned now to put up with for ever. The thought made him cold, and, going to the fire, he poked it into a warmer blaze. He was still holding the will, and in the firelight the writing flickered as though it were alive. Confound the old woman! Why couldn't she have left well alone and died intestate as she had half promised to do? With the poker in one hand he absently read the fatal document through once more, down to the names of the witnesses: "Martha Thwaites, Spinster" and "Louisa Peck, Widow". Who on earth could they be? Then he remembered his aunt's two "treasures" of maids, Martha and Louisa. They had both been killed in a motor accident on their holiday a year before and she had been quite inconsolable. Then very slowly, for his brain still felt numb with the shock it had received, an idea began to dawn upon him.

Once upon a time, while his parents were still alive, it had been suggested that Julian should become a lawyer, and to that end he had actually gone so far as to make some pretence at studying that dismal science. The pretence had not gone far, and if anybody had asked him how much he knew of the law he would have answered, in all sincerity, "Nothing". Now, as he stood by the fireside, a fragment of his forgotten learning drifted back into his mind. "Marriage invalidates a will." He remembered hearing it droned out by a tedious lecturer and copying the words wearily into a shiny red note-book. "Marriage invalidates a will." Therefore his aunt's first will, made when she was still Miss Symondson, simply didn't count. If she had never made the second one—this horrible thing that he held in his hand at this moment—she would have been—what was the word?—intestate. *And* Martha and Louisa were dead. Therefore . . .

Julian would never afterwards admit, even to himself, that he did more than release his grip on the sheet of paper for an instant. But there was no denying the fact that after it had fluttered down into the flames he pressed the poker very firmly upon it until it was a crumpled heap of ashes. That done, he pulled himself together and telephoned for the doctor.

Next day Julian drove the little two-seater over into the neighbouring county town. He made his way to the offices of Messrs. Coltsfoot and Proudie, Solicitors, and sent in his card. The lad who took it in returned almost at once.

"Mr. Coltsfoot will see you, sir," he said.

Mr. Coltsfoot was an elderly tired-looking man, with a bald head and immense bushy eyebrows which gave his occasional stare a peculiarly disconcerting quality.

"Mr. Julian Symondson," he said, looking up from the card which he held in his hand. "You are the nephew of the late Mrs. Thorogood, I understand?"

"Exactly," answered Julian. "Her only nephew, to be accurate—in fact, I think I am her only relative of any kind. And understanding that you were her solicitor——"

"We have acted for her in the past," interjected Mr. Coltsfoot, "but latterly she seems to have preferred to manage most of her affairs herself."

"—well, I thought you were probably the right person to see. Considering that I seem to be the heir and so forth, you know."

Julian's voice trailed off uncertainly under the purposeful glare of Mr. Coltsfoot's eye.

"Surely Mrs. Thorogood left a will?" he demanded.

"Certainly not," answered Julian, completely taken aback. "Absolutely not, in fact. Not in the least, I mean."

"You have made a thorough search, I suppose? Old ladies sometimes leave these things in odd places."

"Oh, complete, yes, rather! Looked everywhere, you know, and there's simply not a thing to be seen. She was

24

a very tidy old lady, too. But if you've any doubt about it," he added with growing boldness, "I wish you'd come over with me and have a look. I want to be perfectly fair about it, I can tell you."

"I am not suggesting that you are not being perfectly fair, as you call it," replied the solicitor drily. "But, on the whole, I think it would be as well if I did."

Julian could hardly restrain himself from chuckling aloud as he drove Mr. Coltsfoot back to the cottage in his car. Everything was working out just as he had hoped. It was too easy! In due course the old will would be found, pushed away under a mass of papers, enclosed in an envelope which he had artistically dirtied that morning to give it the appearance of age. (The original, with the damning date of 1956 upon its face, he had, of course, destroyed.) After that, his sincerity in the matter would be apparent; and Coltsfoot could burrow and rummage as much as he pleased before he found another. Julian had made sure of that.

Things proceeded according to plan. The invalid will was duly discovered, and Julian uttered carefully rehearsed little expressions of surprise. A long and thorough search then ensued—and Mr. Coltsfoot was surprisingly thorough—which produced precisely nothing.

"Odd!" said Mr. Coltsfoot, as he stood exhausted in the drawing-room, his curiosity at last satisfied. "Very odd!"

"What is odd?" asked Julian, by now somewhat impatient.

"This will," said the solicitor, tapping his left hand with the document in his right, "was prepared by my firm for your aunt many years ago. It was lodged for safe keeping in our strong room. Quite recently—no more than two or three years ago—she asked us to return it to her, as she desired to make a fresh one. She did not—h'm—she did not favour us with her instructions on that occasion, however. But I am certainly surprised to find that she never carried out her intentions."

"She changed her mind, that's all," said Julian shortly. "Nothing surprising in that, is there?"

"At all events," said the solicitor deliberately, "it is somewhat unfortunate. That is to say, although I know nothing definite"—his eyebrows fairly scintillated discretion—"yet from what she let fall in my last interview with her I rather gathered that the document I hold in my hand did not altogether represent her final intentions. As it is——" He fumbled for his pince-nez and began to read it to himself.

"Now look here, sir," said Julian rudely. "I know something about the law, I may tell you, even if you don't. That will was made before my aunt married. Marriage invalidates a will. So——"

He broke off. Mr. Coltsfoot had looked up from his perusal, and Julian did not like his expression.

"Marriage invalidates a will!" the solicitor repeated. "Just so! Tell me, Mr. Symondson, did you ever know the late Mr. Thorogood?"

"Good Lord, no! He died years ago, before I was born."

"Quite. Well, I'm afraid that he didn't, in all respects, live up to his name. . . . At the time he met your aunt, and for many years afterwards, he had a wife living in an asylum, and the divorce laws were stricter then than they are now. Your aunt was very young, very much in love . . ."

"You mean that she——?" Julian managed to get out.

"I mean that she committed an indiscretion, as we used to call it in those days, and although she certainly atoned for it in after years by a life of the most exemplary

26

Christian piety, she had no more right to call herself Mrs. Thorogood than I have. I can quite understand that your family did not speak about it, and I am afraid this must be somewhat of a shock to you. She had often told me of your devotion to her. You must try to forget it," he added kindly.

"But the will!" cried Julian.

"Is, of course, perfectly unassailable in law. The whole estate goes to charity, I see. Dear me, Mr. Symondson, you really look ill. I'm afraid this has been a shock for you!"

Miss Burnside's Dilemma

I t's the fact that it's the vicar that makes the whole
business so *difficult*. I simply don't know what to do
about it. Those were his very words to me when I taxed
him with it after matins last Sunday. "Well, Miss Burnside," he said, "and what do you propose to do about it?"
He smiled at me as he said it, I remember—just a friendly,
amused sort of smile over his shoulder as he locked the
vestry door, and then he took off his hat in that courteous
way of his and walked back to the vicarage, leaving me
standing there without an answer. That was nearly a
week ago. And I don't know what the answer is. And he
knows quite well that I don't know. I can see it in his
eye whenever we meet. And in a small place like this it
does make for a really impossible situation.

My first thought was to go to the police about it. In
fact, if it had not been for the chance that my nephew
John was staying with me at the time I think I should have
done so. I call it chance, but looking back on it now I feel
that it was rather the hand of Providence. Because if I
had obeyed that first impulse I can see now what a terrible
scandal there would have been. And much worse than a
mere scandal, indeed! It so happened that on that Sunday
evening John—he is studying for the Bar and is a very
clever boy indeed—was talking to me about a big law
case there had been recently in which a poor woman was
made to pay enormous damages for—what did he call it?—

28

Malicious Prosecution. That made me think a great deal of the danger of acting rashly in the matter, and in the end I told him all about it and asked his advice. After all, he is very nearly a lawyer, and as he is not one of the village it didn't seem to matter. John was tremendously interested—more interested than shocked, I'm afraid, but I suppose that is only natural—and he spent nearly the whole evening considering the matter when he ought to have been studying the Law of Real Property, which is his next examination, and in the end he told me that he could not find that any crime had been committed. Well, that may be the law, and of course I believe what my nephew tells me, but it does seem to me very wrong that the law should permit such things to be done—especially by a minister of the Church of England.

Of course, I could write to the bishop about it. Indeed, I have considered very seriously whether it is not my *duty* to write to the bishop. But it is a step that one shrinks from. In some ways it seems almost more serious than informing the police. I mean, it does seem almost equal to invoking the help of a Higher Power—I trust I am not being irreverent in putting it in that way. But I do not think the seriousness of it would deter me if I were only sure that the bishop would be able to do anything about it, and of that I cannot be sure. I asked John, but he could not help me. It appears that Church Law is not one of the subjects they examine him in, which seems a pity. However, he was very kind and helpful in explaining all kinds of points about the Law of Wills and so on, so that I do at least understand the whole of the dreadful story now quite clearly. Not that that is very much comfort to me, indeed! Rather the reverse. And situated as I am, there is literally *nobody* to whom I can turn for guidance. It is just the sort of problem that I could have set before the vicar himself until this terrible thing happened. But now——!

I want to be perfectly just to the vicar. In all the time that he has been in the village nobody, I am sure, has had a word to say against him, except indeed old Judd, and he, I fear, is irreclaimably ill disposed to every influence for good in the village. Of course, one might say that he— the vicar, I mean—has merely been a hypocrite all these years and that we have all been woefully deceived in him. But I prefer to think of him as a man suddenly exposed to a great Temptation and being carried away, as might happen to any of us. True, I cannot forget the way in which he brazened it out with me on Sunday, but neither can I believe that I have been utterly mistaken in the man, after knowing him so well for nearly ten years. That is the time that he has been in the village, and I remember quite well how good an impression he made when Mrs. Wheeler presented him to the living. It was quite soon after Mrs. Wheeler settled down among us, and bought the Hall and with it the patronage. I do not myself altogether approve of such a thing as a cure of souls being in the gift of a private person and I am very glad that Parliament has done something about it, though I can never understand quite *what*, but it seemed impossible to quarrel with Mrs. Wheeler's choice, and the fact that he was her godson as well as her nephew made it so peculiarly appropriate. Certainly, we all agreed that it was a mercy that the old vicar had survived until after Sir John sold the place, for Sir John's intellect was beginning to fail, and what with that and his dangerously Low Church tendencies one shudders to think what his choice might have been.

Altogether, there is no denying that the double change, at the Hall and the vicarage, was all to the good of the neighbourhood. Everybody liked Mrs. Wheeler. Even

Judd had hardly a word to say against her. True, she lived very quietly, as was after all only proper for a widow who was no longer young; but until last year, when her health began to fail, she took her full part in all the village activities, and whenever help was needed she was unfailingly generous. As indeed she could well afford to be—not that I consider that that detracts in any way from her kindness of heart, but it was common knowledge that Mr. Wheeler, whoever he may have been, had left her very well provided for. The all-important thing was that she used her wealth for the good of others.

But if it is true to say that we respected the new vicar and admired Mrs. Wheeler—and I think it is—there is no doubt that we loved Miss Dalrymple. She, I should explain, was Mrs. Wheeler's companion. There is a lot of nonsense talked about the companions of rich old ladies who have no daughters of their own to look after them. They are always represented as poor abject creatures, perpetually bullied and down-trodden by their employers. Miss Dalrymple was not at all like that. She was a very cheerful, active young woman—not really young, of course, only in comparison with Mrs. Wheeler she seemed so—and there was nothing in the least abject about her. Of course, she kept herself well in the background when Mrs. Wheeler was present, but that is no more than one would expect. And there was no doubt that they were very fond of each other. They were indeed just like mother and daughter—or, rather, like what mother and daughter should be but so often, alas, are *not*.

The only person in the place who did not seem absolutely devoted to Miss Dalrymple, strangely enough, was the vicar himself. It was strange, because in many ways they had so much in common. At one time, indeed, I had hopes that the pair of them would make a match of it. It seemed so extremely suitable, and I know that I did my little best to bring it to pass. Certainly, I have always felt that a bachelor vicar, however excellent, is out of place in a parish like ours—though I know that Saint Paul thought otherwise. But it was not to be, and as the years went on it was impossible not to notice a certain coolness—I wouldn't go so far as to call it hostility—between him and Miss Dalrymple; although, of course, they always remained scrupulously polite and acted together quite harmoniously on committees and bazaars and at other parish functions.

That was how matters stood when Mrs. Wheeler came to the village, and that was how they remained for a very long time. Nothing changes very much with the years in a quiet place like this, except that we all grow a little older, and I think it was quite a shock to most of us to realize last year how very much older and more infirm dear Mrs. Wheeler had become. She went out less and less, and Miss Dalrymple, too, withdrew almost entirely from our little activities owing to the necessity of having to look after her. Mrs. Wheeler had some objection to a nurse, so that all the burden fell upon poor Miss Dalrymple. It was really very hard upon her, though she never complained, and I must say that she was quite as good and careful as any professional nurse could be.

A month or two ago, however, it became sadly evident that Mrs. Wheeler was seriously ill. Dr. Perry—who was always, I think, just the least bit afraid of her—plucked up the courage to insist that she should have a night nurse permanently on duty, and this gave Miss Dalrymple a little more freedom to come out and see her friends. One evening, shortly after the nurse had been installed, she came round to see me. I had expected her to be tired and anxious, but I was not prepared to find her quite so depressed and utterly unlike her usual cheerful self.

Naturally my first question was after Mrs. Wheeler.

"She is very ill indeed," she told me. "Dr. Perry thinks that it is most unlikely that she will recover."

It is always difficult to know what to say on such occasions. I said, "Oh dear!" which, I am afraid, was rather inadequate, but I tried to put as much sympathy into my voice as possible.

Miss Dalrymple said nothing for a moment or two but sat there looking very low and miserable. Finally she said, "The trouble is, Miss Burnside, that she doesn't realize how ill she is."

"Surely that is all to the good," I said. "After all, if she is going to die, it is better that she should not be troubled with any forebodings about it. It isn't as if she was a Roman Catholic," I added, "and in need of making a confession or anything of that kind. Not that a dear, good woman like Mrs. Wheeler could have anything to confess, in any case."

"It isn't that," she answered, looking more miserable than ever. "You see, Dr. Perry says that she might die at any minute, and I happen to know that she has not made any will."

I confess that I could not help feeling a little shocked— disgusted even—that Miss Dalrymple should be thinking of such things at such a time, and I thought then—as I have thought many times since!—how mistaken one can be, even about somebody one has known for a long time. Of course, I knew, like everybody in the village, that Miss Dalrymple had absolutely nothing of her own, and I knew also, because Mrs. Wheeler had told me so, that her employer had intentions of making some provision for her after her death. I could quite understand Miss Dalrymple feeling disappointed at having to go out and look for another post at her age. But at the same time I could not but think that it was rather improper to be thinking of such matters, much more discussing them, while the person in question was still alive.

I must have shown something of my feelings in my expression, although I certainly did my best not to, for Miss Dalrymple immediately said, "Please don't imagine that I'm thinking of myself, Miss Burnside."

Naturally, I said, "Of course not!" though I wondered very much of whom else she could possibly be thinking. But what she said next surprised me very much indeed.

"It would be a lamentable thing," she went on, "and, absolutely contrary to Mrs. Wheeler's own wishes, if all that money of hers were to go to her son."

Now this was the very first time that I, or anybody else so far as I was aware, had ever so much as heard that Mrs. Wheeler had a son, and that only goes to show how very reticent she had always been about her own affairs, and how very loyal a companion Miss Dalrymple had been, never once to have mentioned the fact to any of her friends in the village.

"Her son, Miss Dalrymple?" I said. "Whatever do you mean?" And then she told me all about him.

It appeared that Mrs. Wheeler had a son who, as is, I am afraid, so often the case with the children of the most excellent, religious people, had turned out very badly indeed. It crossed my mind that perhaps young Charles Wheeler—that was his name, apparently—took after his father, but this was really very uncharitable of me, for, of course, I knew nothing whatever about the late Mr. Wheeler except that he had made a great deal of money, and that, after all, was nothing against his character—rather the reverse. At all events, as the result of his misconduct (and although Miss Dalrymple, most properly, entered into no *details*, I gathered that it had been very grave indeed), the young man had for many years entirely cut himself off from his family. Miss Dalrymple did not so much as know where he was living, except that it was somewhere abroad, and the only communication that his mother had received from him recently was an application for money a little time before she was taken ill, which she had, of course, refused to consider in any way.

And now there was a possibility of Mrs. Wheeler's money being diverted to this wicked person, to be turned by him to the most disreputable purposes! I could well understand Miss Dalrymple's agitation at such a thing, although I may as well admit that I did not *wholly* credit her assertion that she was not thinking at all of her own prospects, because, after all, we are all *human*. Speaking for myself, I felt particularly alarmed when I reflected that Mrs. Wheeler's property included the right of presentation to our living and that this might well fall into the hands of an outright rascal.

I was sadly perplexed in my mind as to what advice I should give Miss Dalrymple on this difficult question, for though I am always prepared to listen to other people's troubles, and my friends have told me that I am a particularly good listener, giving advice is a responsibility which I do not care to undertake. At last it occurred to me to suggest that she should consult the vicar, who, from his position, was particularly suited to bring Mrs. Wheeler to a sense of the danger which she was in, and who was himself really interested in the matter in another way. I mean, until this moment everybody regarded him as Mrs. Wheeler's nearest relative, although presumably he was well aware of the existence of his ill-behaved cousin.

I could see that Miss Dalrymple did not altogether like

the prospect of confiding in the vicar, but she agreed to think it over, and a little later she went home, feeling, I am sure, all the better for having had a good chat. There is, I think, nothing better than a good chat with the right sort of person to make you look on the bright side of things.

Next morning, as soon as I had breakfasted, I put on my hat and went round to the Hall to enquire. I had done this many times since Mrs. Wheeler had been taken ill, of course, but on this occasion, though I am not, I trust, superstitious, I did feel a certain sense of foreboding as I did so. And sure enough, as I came round the bend in the drive, I saw that the blinds of the house had been drawn, and knew at once that our dear friend had passed away. I was about to turn round and go home again, when the front door opened and Miss Dalrymple came out. She saw me and came straight up towards me, so that, without feeling that I was in any way *intruding*, I was able to get the very first information about what had happened from her instead of having to rely upon village gossip, which is always rather undignified, in my opinion, and has the added disadvantage that one does not know what to believe!

Dear Mrs. Wheeler, she told me, had taken a sudden turn for the worse at about two o'clock that morning. Dr. Perry had been sent for immediately, of course, but he was out attending a maternity case, and in spite of all that Miss Dalrymple and the nurse could do, by the time that he arrived, which was not until nearly seven, all was over. The doctor had said that he could have done nothing had he been there in time, and I was glad to learn that the end had been altogether peaceful.

I dare say that I should not have been thinking of such things at such a moment, but, remembering our conversation of the evening before, I could not forbear saying,

"Then I suppose poor Mrs. Wheeler was never able to make a will after all?"

Then Miss Dalrymple told me her great news! It seemed that after the first seizure Mrs. Wheeler had rallied and remained quite conscious and sensible for several hours. And during that time, knowing that her last hour had come, she had been able to make her will. By that will, Miss Dalrymple told me, she had bequeathed one thousand pounds to her nephew, the vicar, and the whole of the rest of her fortune to Miss Dalrymple herself!

I could hardly believe my ears. It really seemed too good to be true, and I congratulated her most warmly, but, I hope, with the solemnity that the occasion required. Still I found it difficult to credit that the story should have had so happy an ending.

"Forgive me for asking you," I said, "but are you quite sure that this is really so? Have you seen the will yourself?"

"Indeed, I have," she told me. "We sent for the vicar, of course, as soon as we saw how gravely ill she was. The moment she recovered consciousness, she told him to write down what she wished. I saw her sign the paper, and then the vicar and I put our names underneath hers as witnesses."

When I had got as far as this in telling the story to my nephew John, he made a most peculiar noise, something between a snort and a laugh. Of course, with his knowledge, he saw at once what was wrong; but we are not all lawyers—thank goodness!—and neither Miss Dalrymple nor I had the least idea at the time that the will was anything but perfectly legal. Nor, I am sure, had poor Mrs. Wheeler, unless the knowledge was vouchsafed to her in Heaven, in which case it must have made her very unhappy, if such a thing is possible in Heaven. But it is the fact, cruel and unfair though it may seem, that the law does not allow a will to be legal unless it is witnessed by two persons, and that neither of those two persons is allowed to have any benefit from the will which they have witnessed. So that, as John put it, the only two people in the world who could not receive any of Mrs. Wheeler's money under her will were the vicar and Miss Dalrymple, the only two people whom she desired to give anything to! I said then, and I think still, that it is most unreasonable and a kind of trap for innocent people like companions and country clergy who could not be expected to know anything about the law, because, after all, who could be better suited to witness an old lady's will than her nephew and the woman who had looked after her for so many years? I think they should have thought of such things when the law was made, but I suppose it is too late to alter it now.

Of course, neither Miss Dalrymple nor I knew anything of this at the time, but we were speedily undeceived. The day after the funeral she came to see me in great distress and told me that she had been to consult a lawyer as to what was to be done about Mrs. Wheeler's estate, and he had told her that by witnessing the will she and the vicar had signed away all their inheritance. She told me also that the vicar had called upon her and expressed his sorrow that his ignorance had led to her losing the reward of her long years of service, not to mention his own thousand pounds, which he admitted was a serious matter for him, for the living was not a good one.

After that Miss Dalrymple left the village, and I understand she secured another post with a lady at Cheltenham, where she was not well paid, and where, I am afraid, she was anything but happy. Meanwhile we in the village awaited the dreadful moment when Mr. Charles Wheeler would descend upon us to take possession of the property

which had in this strange way become his after all. A
week or more went by, and then we heard the great and
unexpected news. I had it first from Mrs. Tomlin, at the
post office; and although I always suspect anything from
that source, it was soon afterwards confirmed by the
vicar himself. It appeared that as soon as it was established that the will was of no effect, the vicar had enquiries
made for the whereabouts of the son, and these enquiries
had met with a speedy and most unhoped result. Charles
Wheeler was no more! He had perished, very miserably,
I am sorry to say, in some foreign town, quite soon after
his last letter to his mother asking for assistance. The vicar
had been shown that letter at the time, and he told me
that in it he had stated that he was dangerously ill. It
was the vicar who had counselled Mrs. Wheeler not to
reply to it, thinking that the statement of his condition
was only a ruse to get more money from the mother who
had cast him off; and he said, very generously as I thought
at the time, that he now regretted that he had not allowed
his aunt to take measures which might have prolonged
the unfortunate man's life a little longer. But I told him
that although the sentiment did him credit, it was much
better as it was, and I remember that I went so far as to
say that the death of Charles Wheeler might be accounted
a providential event.

So after all the vicar, as the only living relative of his
aunt, came into all her possessions, and we were all so
pleased at this happy turn of events that I am afraid we
had very little thought to spare for poor Miss Dalrymple,
who, after all, was the person whom Mrs. Wheeler had
mainly had in mind. And the vicar was so popular in the
village—except, of course, with old Judd and people of
his stamp—that there was no one who did not rejoice in
his good fortune. Indeed, and this is my great difficulty

at the present moment, he is still just as popular as ever, simply because nobody, myself only excepted, knows the *truth*.

Just over a week ago I spent a night in London with my brother and sister-in-law, a thing I do very rarely, except when the summer sales are in progress. They took me to the theatre that evening, I remember—it was a most amusing piece, but I do not recollect the name— and invited to join the party a Mr. Woodhouse, whom I had never met before. During the interval, between the acts, he asked me where I lived and, when I told him, said, "Then I suppose you know Mr. ——" (mentioning the vicar by name).

"Indeed I do," I told him, and was about to go on to tell him something of the strange story of Mrs. Wheeler's will when he interrupted me.

"I was up with him at Oxford," he said. "A very clever fellow, I thought him."

"He is a very *good* man," I answered with some emphasis, "and I think that is more important." One does not somehow like to hear one's vicar described as "a very clever fellow", even if it is kindly meant.

"Oh, but he is clever too," Mr. Woodhouse persisted. "I remember he took a first-class honours degree in Law the year I graduated."

I was thunderstruck.

"In Law, Mr. Woodhouse?" I said. "Are you sure that you are not mistaken?"

"Quite sure," he said. "He was intended for the Bar, you know, but he changed his mind and went into the Church instead. Rather a waste of a good intellect, I thought."

Luckily the curtain rose for the next act before I could

ask him what he meant by his last very improper observation, and I took good care not to refer to the subject again.

All the way down in the train next day I could think of nothing but what Mr. Woodhouse had told me. If the vicar had really studied the law at Oxford how was it possible that he had made such a mistake as he had done about witnessing the will? I tried to comfort myself by reflecting that he might have forgotten this particular point, but it seemed hardly possible, and indeed John has told me since that it is one of the "first principles" of the Law of Wills—though why they should make a first principle of anything so unjust and cruel I do not in the least understand. But if he *knew* that by becoming a witness Miss Dalrymple was losing her right to Mrs. Wheeler's property, however hostile to her he may have felt, why had he been content to destroy his own chances of getting a thousand pounds also? It was all most puzzling and mysterious, and I made up my mind, come what might, to speak to him at the very first opportunity. And that opportunity came last Sunday, after matins.

I still blush when I think of it—not for myself, for I feel that I only obeyed my conscience in saying what I did, but for him. His effrontery was so astonishing. I can recall—I do not think I shall ever forget—exactly what passed between us.

I met him, as I said, just as he was coming out of the vestry door after the service. He said "Good morning" to me, and I responded as politely as I could.

Then I said, "I met an old acquaintance of yours in London, Vicar, a Mr. Woodhouse."

"Oh, yes, Woodhouse," he replied. "I haven't seen him for a very long time."

I resolved not to beat about the bush.

"He told me," I said, "that you had studied the law

41

at Oxford, and were awarded first-class honours for your proficiency."

He did not show the least confusion, but merely said, "It is pleasant to have one's little triumphs remembered."

"Then did you not know," I pressed him, "that Miss Dalrymple ought not to have witnessed that will?"

"Ought not, Miss Burnside?" he asked. "I should prefer to say that Mrs. Wheeler ought not to have tried to dispose of her property in the way that she did."

I could hardly speak for indignation.

"Then you deliberately so arranged matters that Miss Dalrymple should lose what Mrs. Wheeler wished her to have?" I said.

"I did."

"Even at the cost of losing your own legacy?"

"But you see, I have not lost it," he answered with a smile, and then I suddenly saw the light.

"Vicar!" I said. "You knew all the time that Charles Wheeler was dead!"

He nodded.

"I had a telegram from the British Consul informing me of his death some months ago," he said. "In view of my aunt's state of health I thought it wiser to keep the news from her. Do you blame me?"

I was so angry that I am afraid I lost all respect for his cloth.

"Blame you?" I said. "I think you have behaved like a common thief!"

And then he used those awful words that I have already mentioned: "Well, Miss Burnside, and what are you going to do about it?"

What indeed! Tomorrow it is Sunday again. I know that my absence from church would cause the most

undesirable talk in the place, but yet I feel as if, so long as
he is vicar, dear St. Etheldreda's can never be the same
place for me again. The Hall is up for sale and I hear
dreadful rumours that it is to be bought by a *builder*. All
our pleasant life in this village is at an end, so far as I
am concerned. I wish somebody would answer that
question for me: What am I going to do?

Name of Smith

On the death of Sir Charles Blenkinsop, some-time Judge of the High Court of Justice, the benchers of his Inn, as was only proper, arranged a memorial service for him. It was not so well attended as such functions usually are, for Sir Charles, in spite of his acknowledged competence as a lawyer, had never been popular. Moreover, there had been certain rumours concerning his private life of a type particularly detrimental to judges. Some of his colleagues had breathed a sigh of relief when Sir Charles, a few years before, had earned his pension and quitted the Bench without open scandal.

Francis Pettigrew, still "of counsel" but now in country retirement, was at the service. His friend MacWilliam, the Chief Constable of Markshire, had thought it his duty to attend, since the deceased had been a Markhampton man; and Pettigrew accompanied him, more on the chance of meeting old Temple acquaintances than as a tribute to Blenkinsop's memory. He was disappointed to see so sparse a congregation and was correspondingly pleased on leaving the church to find himself behind the familiar, square-built figure of his old friend Challoner, a well-known City solicitor.

He overtook Challoner at the door, introduced him to MacWilliam, and was standing with them in the porch when his eye was caught by a shabby man of about forty who smiled at him in a friendly but slightly embarrassed fashion and walked hastily away.

"Friend of yours?" asked Challoner, as they strolled down Fleet Street.

"Apparently," said Pettigrew. "He certainly seemed to know me, and I have an idea I've seen him before, but where, I haven't the remotest notion."

"Name of Smith."

"The name is certainly familiar."

"Charles Smith. Does a certain amount of reporting in the Courts. I dare say he was covering the service."

"Charles Smith," said Pettigrew meditatively. "Charles ——!" He stopped dead on the pavement. It may have been mere coincidence that it was at the door of a saloon bar. He took the solicitor by the arm and gently impelled him inside, leaving MacWilliam to follow. "Of course I know the chap. I defended him once—on a charge of murder."

"Really?" said Challoner with polite interest. "I don't read the Old Bailey reports."

"This wasn't at the Bailey. It was at Markhampton Assizes, six or seven years ago. And, what is more, old Blenkinsop, whose demise we have just been mourning, tried him. That would be before your time, MacWilliam."

"As a matter of fact——" said the Chief Constable. But Pettigrew's attention was devoted to ordering drinks, and he did not bother to complete the sentence.

"Odd running into Smith like that," Pettigrew went on a few minutes later. "I may forget faces, and cases too, as often as not, but that was a case I shall remember all my life. Cheers!"

"Your health, Pettigrew! Was it a difficult task to—ah— 'get him off' is the phrase, is it not?"

Pettigrew smiled grimly. "Very. Too difficult for me, at all events," he said. "On that evidence and before a local jury he never had an earthly. The case was as dead as mutton."

45

"That being so, I don't quite see why Smith isn't——"

"Isn't also as dead as mutton? Therein lies a mystery which will always puzzle me. Charles Smith escaped hanging solely and entirely through the positively goat-like conduct of Blenkinsop."

"As a matter of fact," said MacWilliam again, and this time he was allowed to go on. "As a matter of fact, I had occasion to read the summing-up in that case quite recently. It was remarkable."

"Remarkable? The Court of Criminal Appeal used stronger adjectives than that. I've never heard such a performance in my life. And from Blenkinsop, of all people! Now that we've done our duty by him in church we can speak the truth about him and we all know that by and large Charlie Blenkinsop was a pretty nasty piece of work, but, hang it all, the man was a lawyer. If anybody on the Bench knew his stuff, I should have said he did. But in this case the old boy went completely hay-wire. When I tell you that he actually directed the jury, as a matter of law . . ."

To detail all the iniquities of the summing-up took Pettigrew a full five minutes of blistering technicalities.

"Of course the thing was a push-over on appeal," he concluded. "The conviction was quashed with more rudery than I have ever heard applied to a Judge of Assize. That case should go down in history as Blenkinsop's biggest boner. But what will always puzzle me is—why on earth did he do it?"

"Had he—er—lunched very well on that day?" Challoner ventured.

"Not a bit of it. He was as sober as—as a judge, if you follow me."

"I have my own theory about the matter," MacWilliam put in. "I think the explanation is that all the parties

involved—including the judge—were Markhampton people.
You'll remember, Mr. Pettigrew, that your client came
from what was locally considered pretty poor stock. His
mother, Mary Smith—she's still alive, by the way—was
no better than she should be, and nobody ever knew who
his father was. The girl he was accused of killing, on the
other hand, belonged to one of the most respectable families
in the town. Her father was a pillar of the strictest sect
we have—and when Markhampton people are moral they
take their morality seriously. Smith had got her into
trouble, and she was desperate to be made an honest
woman of—which didn't suit Smith's book at all, as he
had engaged himself to a much wealthier woman. His
defence was that she had committed suicide rather than
face her family with the news of her downfall."

"Precisely," said Pettigrew. "Not the line of defence
to commend itself to a jury of townspeople inflamed with
piety and rectitude, even if the medical evidence hadn't
killed it stone dead."

"Very true. Local feeling was strong against Smith.
And my point is, that in this matter the judge was a
local man."

"He left the town quite young, did he not?"

"He did, sir, and according to my information he left it
under a cloud. Young Blenkinsop had not been one of the
respectables. My belief is that he took this opportunity
to put himself right with the town, by taking the part of
respectability, and ramming home every point against
the young sinner. Only, of course, he overdid it."

"It's an idea, certainly," said Pettigrew. "There must
have been some explanation for Blenkinsop's extraordinary
lapse. But why should you know so much about the case?
I should have thought there was enough current crime in
Markshire to occupy you without digging up the past."

"The past has a habit of digging itself up," said Mac-William. "The Smith case came alive again last week. That is why I turned up the records."

"Then you've been wasting your time. They can't try Smith again, you know."

"Unfortunately for Smith, they cannot. He was innocent."

"*What?*"

"The girl's father died a few days ago. He left a full confession. He killed her himself to punish her for her sins. He quoted a number of texts to justify his action. He was a religious maniac—poor fellow."

Nobody said anything for an appreciable time after that, and then Challoner remarked quietly, "I think this round is on me." When the drinks had been brought, he asked MacWilliam abruptly, "What is Mary Smith's address?"

"Whose?"

"Mary Smith's—Charles Smith's mother."

"Why, she lives where she always has lived—Lower River Lane. Why do you——?"

"Number Nine?"

"That's right. How did you know?"

Challoner pursed his lips.

"I was the late Sir Charles Blenkinsop's solicitor," he said. "By his will, he left a substantial sum of money in trust for this lady during her life. You can draw your own conclusions."

Pettigrew whistled.

"There is one obvious conclusion to draw," he said. "But beyond it, I see another. The judge was Charles Smith's father."

"It certainly seems probable."

"But this is outrageous!" cried MacWilliam. "He tries

48

his own son for murder and does his damnedest to send him to the gallows. What sort of a father do you call that?"

"I should describe him as somewhat unnatural, I admit. But there are the facts."

"The old devil!"

It was at this point that Pettigrew burst out laughing. MacWilliam looked at him in disapproving surprise.

"I don't see what there is funny about it," he said severely.

"Don't you?" spluttered Pettigrew. "I bet Blenkinsop does, if he can see anything now. He always had a low sense of humour. I've just seen the point of that famous summing-up of his. It explains everything. He made a muck of it *on purpose*! He knew that Smith hadn't a chance with the jury, so he did the next best thing, by giving him a cast-iron case on appeal. Unnatural father, my foot! He was a damned affectionate one, who was prepared to spoil his reputation and pervert justice to save his son's neck. I never thought the old ruffian had so much humanity in him."

He raised his tankard.

"Here's to you, Charlie Blenkinsop, wherever you are," he said. "When you misdirected a jury you knew what you were about—which is more than I can say of some of your learned brothers!"

"It is satisfactory to think," MacWilliam added, "that the misdirection prevented a grave miscarriage of justice."

"That, my dear Chief Constable," said Pettigrew loftily, "is a mere side issue. Your irrelevancy will cost you another round of drinks."

Murderer's Luck

Everybody who knows London knows the Progress Club. It is one of the most impressive buildings in Pall Mall, and every line of its architecture proclaims that for the best people Progress stopped in 1850 or thereabouts. I am not a member, but my friend Prothero is, and I was his guest there at dinner one evening recently. Prothero likes to call himself a "criminologist". Murder is his hobby, and I have long since lost count of the famous crimes which he has "written up". I was not surprised, therefore, that among the friends of his who joined us in the smoking-room after dinner was a rather exalted official at Scotland Yard by the name of Wrestall.

Over our coffee and liqueurs Wrestall happened to ask me whether I had been in the club before.

"Yes," I told him, "but not for several years. I remember that the last time I was here the member who entertained me was Sylvester Kemball."

It was not a very tactful remark, seeing that Kemball had quite recently been hanged for murdering his wife. But my companions took it in good part.

"I have always thought," said Prothero, rather pontifically, "that the Kemball case was one of the most successful examples of modern detective methods. It was a great triumph for our police organization—and for you personally, Wrestall," he added.

"If you say so," said Wrestall modestly. "But, as a

matter of fact, it was only by the merest stroke of luck that we obtained the evidence to bring it home to him."

"Luck!" said Prothero. "When you come to think of it, it is astonishing how often the most astute and careful criminal is defeated by some quite unforeseen accident— often by an extravagantly unlikely event which he could not possibly have guarded against. Take the Abertillery murder, for example. . . ."

But we never took the Abertillery murder. A man in the far corner of our group interrupted him without ceremony. "The unluckiest murderer within my recollection," he said, "was Anthony Edward Fitzpatrick Pugh."

Everybody turned to look at him. He was not much to look at—a small, insignificant fellow with a disagreeably complacent expression. I recollected that his name was Hobson and that like myself he was present as the guest of a member.

"Pugh?" repeated Prothero, and he contrived to make the name sound almost insulting. "Anthony Pugh, did you say?"

"Anthony Edward Fitzpatrick Pugh."

"You surprise me very much. I think I am tolerably well acquainted with every crime of any significance during the last century and a half, and I have never come across the name before. Wrestall, are you familiar with the case of the homicidal Mr. Pugh?"

Wrestall shook his head.

"You see, Mr. Hobson," Prothero went on, "you appear to be the possessor of knowledge quite unknown even to Scotland Yard. I hesitate to make the suggestion, but are you quite sure of your facts?"

"Perfectly. Would you care to hear them?"

"We are all ears." Prothero settled himself back in his chair with an indulgent smile.

# Murderer's Luck

"It's a very simple story, really," said Hobson, "and I only mentioned it because whenever the subject of bad luck comes up it always brings Pugh to my mind. Mind you, he deserved his luck, as people generally do. He was a disagreeable type, selfish and greedy as they make them. His bad luck began when he entrusted practically the whole of the fortune he had inherited from his parents to a get-rich-quick schemer in the City. He should have known better, of course, but there it was. He lost the lot. Then he brought an action at law to recover his money. He secured a judgment quite easily. Ten thousand pounds and costs. It must have sounded most impressive. But it's one thing to get a decision from the courts and quite another to make it effective, as Pugh found out. His lawyers went through the usual motions, of course, which added quite a tidy figure to the bill of costs which Pugh had to foot. It was no good. Their man went gracefully and artistically bankrupt. Pugh could whistle for his money—it simply wasn't there. What made things still more aggravating for him, destitution didn't seem to make the slightest difference to the debtor's style of living. He remained in residence on his comfortable estate in Sussex. He continued to travel up to London every day with a reserved seat in a first-class smoker, and the porters touched their caps to him. Poor Pugh lived in the same neighbourhood and caught the same train, travelled third-class non-smoker, because he grudged the cost of a packet of cigarettes, thinking about his ten thousand pounds every mile of the way.

"The secret of the happy bankrupt's prosperity, of course, was that he personally had never owned anything. Every stick and stone of the Sussex mansion, the pedigree Jerseys in the park, the racehorses in the stables, the money that paid the servants' wages and the butcher's

52

bills and the first-class fares to London—the whole boiling, in fact—was the sole, separate property of his wife—who was, incidentally, a very attractive, good-natured woman, and much too good for her scamp of a husband, who treated her extremely badly.

"That daily encounter on the railway station platform made Pugh feel positively murderous. One could hardly have blamed him if one fine morning he had slaughtered the man out of hand. But Pugh wasn't that sort. Money was what he cared about, not revenge, and killing his debtor wouldn't have got his ten thousand back. What he wanted was to find some means of putting money into his debtor's pocket, where his lawyers could get at it. He thought the matter over in his cold-blooded way, and hit upon a very simple, logical solution. The fellow had made his property over to his wife. Pugh proposed to reverse the process. He could be fairly certain that in such a set-up the lady would have made a will leaving everything to her husband. He had only to put her out of the way, and there would be more than enough money in the husband's hands to satisfy his little claim. That was his calculation and, as it turned out, he was dead right.

"Once having made up his mind to commit the murder, he carried it out with great simplicity and ease. He discovered by observation that his intended victim was in the habit of driving herself into Worthing every day. To get to the main road from the park she had to go through a gate across the drive which was kept shut on account of the Jersey cows. He concealed himself behind a hedge at that point, waited till she came along and then shot her through the head at close range as she got out of the car to open the gate. He used an old German pistol he had picked up years before. Then he walked quietly away, leaving the pistol in the hedge. He saw no reason why anyone should

53

connect him with a woman to whom he had never even spoken in his life. And, indeed, there was none."

"Then how was he convicted?" asked Prothero.

"He wasn't," Hobson replied. "I never said that he was. I merely said that he was the unluckiest murderer within my recollection, and that was strictly true. You see, although he had been absolutely right in his calculations and completely successful in his crime, he never got his ten thousand pounds.

"Pugh had been so careful to avoid being suspected himself that it had never occurred to him to wonder who would be likely to be accused of the crime in his place. But of course when a rich woman with a penniless husband is murdered there is one obvious person for the police to pick on, if you don't mind my putting it that way, Mr. Wrestall. If Pugh had thought the matter out a little more carefully he would have seen that he was also the one person he couldn't afford to have convicted.

"When the authorities began to look into the case against the husband Pugh's bad luck started to operate in real earnest. It turned out that the couple had had a flaming row that very morning and that the wife was actually on her way to see her lawyer about making a new will at the moment when she was killed. It turned out, further, that the cheap revolver Pugh had used was the dead spit of one owned by the accused and—so he said—lost by him only a week or two before. That made quite a sizeable case against him, but the crucial piece of evidence arose from the unlikeliest stroke of luck you could well imagine.

"A witness was found to prove that the husband was near the scene of the crime within ten minutes or so of the critical moment. He was the prisoner's gardener, and he had no business to be there at all at that hour. His presence was due solely to the fact that his wife had scalded herself by upsetting a kettle and he was on his way to telephone for the doctor. Result: The alibi which the defence tried to set up was blown to bits, and the husband was hanged. His conviction, of course, deprived him of all his rights in the deceased's estate and he died as penniless as he had lived. You may say, then, that Pugh lost ten thousand pounds just because somebody else's gardener's wife was a bit clumsy taking a kettle off the hob. Oh, he was unlucky all right! So, when you come to think of it, was the chap who was convicted."

There was a long pause, and then Hobson's host said, "By the way, what was the husband's name? I don't think you mentioned it."

Hobson didn't seem to have heard the question. He was looking at his watch. "Heavens! I'd no idea it was so late!" he exclaimed. "I've a train to catch at Victoria. Do you mind if I rush away now, old man?"

His departure broke up the party, and as I am not fond of late hours I took the opportunity to thank Prothero for a pleasant evening and made my way out. As I went, I caught sight of Wrestall, looking, it seemed to me, distinctly thoughtful. I found Hobson outside the club hunting for a taxi. As I may have indicated, I had not taken to the man very much, but I had my car round the corner and Victoria was on my way home, so it seemed only decent to offer him a lift.

"I suppose the husband in your story was Sylvester Kemball?" I asked, as we took the corner by Marlborough House.

"Oh yes," said Hobson complacently.

"And his execution was a complete miscarriage of justice! How horrible!"

"Oh, you needn't waste any pity on *him*. He deserved all he got. His treatment of his wife alone merited hanging."

"You seem to know a lot about him," I observed.

"Well, she was my aunt. The only relation I had in the world."

I said no more until we were passing Buckingham Palace.

"When did you come to learn the truth about your aunt's murderer?" I asked him.

"About halfway through Kemball's trial," said Hobson calmly. "I knew Pugh fairly well, and I used to discuss the evidence with him. One evening we were dining together and he got a bit tight. He slipped out something that he hadn't meant to say and I broke him down. He told me the whole story."

"What on earth did you do?"

"Nothing at all. I looked at it this way: Kemball was every bit as bad as a murderer. I think he would probably have killed my aunt anyway, if Pugh hadn't got in first. And hanging Pugh wouldn't have done her any good. Besides, I couldn't afford to see him hanged."

"What do you mean?" Thank heaven, Victoria was just ahead. I could hardly bear the man's presence any longer.

"Well, I was a poor man, and I was my aunt's next of kin. If Kemball was acquitted it meant that her will leaving everything to him was good. If he was convicted, I scooped the pool. I am sure my dear aunt would have preferred to have it that way."

I stopped the car with a quite unnecessary jerk. Hobson got out.

"Thanks for the lift," he said. "Perhaps I shall see you again some day. I'm putting up for election to the Progress, by the way."

I wondered, as I drove home, whether I ought to warn Prothero about this candidate for his club. I decided not to do so. After all, I am not a member.

The Tragedy of Young Macintyre

"My boy," Macintyre's rich uncle is reputed to have said to him, "if you go to the Bar you will make a name for yourself." There were sound reasons for the old gentleman's optimism, for Macintyre had many advantages. He had good looks, a pleasant manner and, above all, an unusual capacity for assimilating everything he learned. It was this last quality which, oddly enough, led to his failure at his profession, although, still more oddly, it helped him to make a name for himself more famous than the most optimistic of uncles could expect. For it cannot be denied that in a remarkably short space of time young Macintyre's name became famous in the courts and to the public outside them. It is indeed written large over many pages of many reports in several successive years. The only objection from his point of view was that it was written in the wrong place. It is the ambition of every young barrister to figure in the law reports, and Macintyre was no exception; but he had always seen himself in the role of "*Macintyre* (with him *Biggs*) for the plaintiffs" or even (in his higher flights of fancy) as "Mr. Justice Macintyre agreed". It was not to be. For him was reserved a fame of a different sort, less glorious but perhaps more lasting—the fame that attaches to the names of John Doe and Richard Roe. Lawyers will understand what I mean when I explain that the unfortunate subject of this tale was the hero of those famous actions, *Macintyre v. Speckles* and *Speckles v. Macintyre*, which in their turn produced the scarcely less celebrated cases of *Fandango v. the Agglomerated Press Ltd.* and *In re Beckwith, Simperton and Others.* Their legal aspects have been fully treated in the monumental fifty-fourth edition of Bloggs on Tort, and I can only refer my readers to those pages for consideration of the important problems involved. My purpose is to unfold something of the human interest which underlay them, and which at the time convulsed the whole nation, monopolised the picture papers and nearly caused a General Election.

Macintyre was duly called to the Bar, and duly had his first case. It was a defence at the Old Bailey, and his kindest friends could not have called it a very successful performance, for the jury did not even go through the formality of leaving the box before returning a verdict of guilty, and a sentence of three years' penal servitude followed as a matter of course. None the less, this was a quite inadequate reason for the deep depression into which he sank as a result of the trial. It was in vain that his friends pointed out to him that his client (a larcenous gentleman of some celebrity) was much too well known even to have had a chance of being acquitted; that his ill-considered action of picking the foreman's pocket while on bail and waiting for the case to come on had ruined all prospects of appealing to the sympathies of the jury; and finally that the letting loose of such an unpleasant specimen would have been a serious blow to the Brighter London movement. Macintyre refused to be comforted.

"If they had only listened to me," he said, "I shouldn't have minded so much."

"Of course they didn't listen to you. It was nearly one o'clock, and they wanted their lunch."

The Tragedy of Young Macintyre

"Still, out of mere decency they might . . . I think I know what it was. My manner didn't appeal to them. You know what I mean. Stance all wrong. Didn't keep my eye on the ball and forgot to follow through at the end of my sentences. And I don't think my voice carried, either. There was a man at the back who had his hand to his ear the whole time."

"You needn't worry about him. He was stone deaf, anyway. I heard him explaining afterwards that he thought they were trying a bigamist."

"Well, anyhow, it's not good enough. What's the good of being a barrister if you can't make the jury hear you?"

"You ought to take lessons," said someone, all unconscious of the fearful consequences that his words were to have.

"I've a jolly good mind to. If I can't do better than this I shall have to give it up. I shouldn't have minded so much if only——"

But by this time his friends had followed the example of the jury and gone to lunch.

The idea, once formed, that he was in need of training in the art of elocution rankled for the rest of the day in Macintyre's mind. It was still there when that evening, as he gloomily made his way home on the top of an omnibus, fate, in the shape of a prolonged traffic block, intervened. The block occurred in the Strand, just opposite one of those nondescript buildings which are always upon the verge of demolition in the sacred cause of street widening. He noted idly that on the ground floor a hopeful jeweller was for the second year running announcing stupendous reductions in all his stock in trade because another few days was the most that his shop could hope to live. Then, raising his eyes to the first-floor level, he became aware of two dingy windows on which faded gold lettering announced "T. SPECKLES, EXPERT ELOCUTIONIST".

The Tragedy of Young Macintyre

In a moment Macintyre, with grim determination in his eye, had leapt from the bus, and before the traffic block had resolved itself he was in T. Speckles's consulting-room.

Mr. Speckles seemed glad to see Macintyre. Indeed he was quite effusive in his welcome. From his appearance and his surroundings Macintyre judged that the aspirants to the art of elocution were few, for neither indicated much prosperity. He was a small, dark-haired, sallow man with a mournful black moustache and a black frock coat which had certainly known better days and probably a better owner. Altogether his looks did not inspire much confidence. But when he spoke it was at once obvious that he did not take the name of elocutionist in vain. His voice was something between a bark and a boom. The vowels were prolonged to twice their usual length, and every consonant made itself felt with a distinctness that was a little short of appalling. The unprejudiced would not have called the result beautiful, but it was music to Macintyre's ears. Here, he felt, was the fellow who could really deliver the goods, and when Mr. Speckles in ear-piercing tones assured him that he would be happy to accommodate him on the most generous terms for a full course of a dozen lessons, beginning the very next morning, he felt that the road to fortune was open before him.

Next day saw Macintyre in Mr. Speckles's office once more, eager to begin. But before the lesson commenced his teacher insisted on two things. One was payment in advance for half the course. That was perhaps only to be expected, and Macintyre submitted without a murmur. The other was more unusual. From the depths of a musty cupboard Mr. Speckles produced an aged dictaphone, and invited Macintyre to make use of it. "It will be an inter-r-resting compar-r-rison," he bellowed. "When your vocal qualities are matur-r-red, you will be able to estimate how much you have impr-r-roved." (But it is useless to trouble the printer in an attempt to reproduce Mr. Speckles's voice. It must be taken for granted, or half this tale would have to be printed in capitals.) Macintyre asked diffidently what he should say.

"Just what you like," said Mr. Speckles. "Imagine that you are addressing a jury."

He switched on the machine and signed to his pupil to speak.

"Er—members of the jury," began Macintyre in a gentle, deprecating voice, "I rise to address you on behalf of poor old—er—I mean the unfortunate Mr. Speckles. Really, you know, members of the jury, he's not such a blight—er—he is not so—I mean, things may look pretty black against him at present, but really, you know, taking everything into consideration and so forth, so to speak, I shouldn't wonder if you didn't find he was more sinned against than sinning. Really, you know, it is the Englishman's privilege to be found guilty until he is innocent—er —I should say—the other way round, if you follow me— and this poor man Speckles—that is, of course, if you can find it in your hearts to say he is a man——"

"I think that will do," said Mr. Speckles severely, cutting off the machine. "You have much to learn. I will have a gramophone record made of that for you. It may entertain you when you have progressed somewhat. Now we will begin Lesson 1: Exercises of the Vocal Chords."

They began. They exercised the Vocal Chords and on the next day the Labial Muscles. During succeeding weeks together they trod the difficult path of Voice Production, Expression, Breath Control (with Muscular Exercises), the mastery of the Epiglottis, and all the other mysteries of Mr. Speckles's craft. And Macintyre (who was, as I have said, a diligent young man) continued his exercises at

home. He practised them in his bath. He practised them
when he got up in the morning and when he went to bed
at night. No matron in the forties determined to recover
that schoolgirl figure exercised half so hard as he did.
For nearly a month his friends saw nothing of him, and
as he lived alone, with only a deaf old housekeeper for
company, nobody knew anything of the tremendous effects
of Mr. Speckles's teaching. Nobody, that is, except Mr.
Speckles himself. His pride in Macintyre's progress was
immense. He frequently declared that he was the best
pupil he had ever had. Once, indeed, towards the end of
the course, he even went so far as to say that he, Speckles,
could not have done so well.

It is a curious fact, but very few people are conscious
of the sound of their own voices. (Which is not to say that
they do not like the sound of their own voices, but that
is another matter.) They can tell you that So-and-so's
voice is hard or soft, and that someone else speaks through
his nose, but they have not the smallest idea as to what
their own is like. So it was in complete innocence that
Young Macintyre returned to his chambers when the
course was completed. He knew, of course, that his voice
had gained in resonance, and his manner in assurance as
the result of Mr. Speckles's ministrations—the occasion
when every passenger on the top of a bus passing down the
Strand looked up to the sky expecting a thunderstorm when
he fulminated in Mr. Speckles's room was still a precious
memory—but how much he had changed he did not realize.

He was not left very long in doubt as to the real state
of affairs. At his first tremendous bark of greeting his clerk,
a bald and blameless old man, leapt bodily a foot from
his seat before collapsing in a faint to the floor, two panes
of glass were shivered and a pigeon dropped dead in the
Temple Gardens. When he called a cheery "Good morning!"

to his friend Goodbody, who shared his room, the learned K.C. who lived on the floor below sent up to complain that the plaster of his ceiling was cracking. Shouting at the top of his voice to make himself heard, Goodbody besought him to moderate his tones.

"I'm sorry, old man," said Macintyre, in what seemed to him to be little more than a whisper, but still in a tone which bored through his hearer's ears like an auger. "I didn't mean to talk so loud, but I've been studying elocution. I told you I'd learn to deliver the goods, and by Jove I can make myself heard now, can't I?"

"You certainly can," assented Goodbody with conviction. "Heaven help any jury you get in front of now. But for goodness' sake drop it for a bit and talk normally for a change."

"Confound you," replied Macintyre, with a stridency that would have turned Mr. Speckles green with envy, "I *am* talking normally. What on earth are you driving at?"

Goodbody's face took on an expression of horror.

"Heaven and earth!" he murmured piously. "Do you really mean it's stuck like that for good?"

Our nurses told us that if we made ugly faces like that, and the wind changed, we should stay like that for always. What the wind had been doing while Macintyre was in Mr. Speckles's office I do not know, but there was no question that his voice was changed, and changed permanently. Gone were the gentle tones, the soft and hesitating utterance with which Nature had endowed him. Mr. Speckles had set his stamp upon him and it was not to be effaced. He could talk now with the utmost fluency on any subject under the sun; he could talk with perfect clarity and distinctness, giving its due value to every consonant and leaving his hearer in no possible doubt about the vowels; he could make himself heard first time at a public telephone call office; he could do anything, in fact, except talk like a normal human being. It took some time for the truth of the change that had taken place in him to sink in. In spite of the asseverations of Goodbody, of his clerk (who gave notice immediately afterwards), and of everybody else whom he consulted, for a long time Macintyre persisted that he was all right, a little improved and strengthened in voice production, but no more. At last he remembered Mr. Speckles's gramophone record.

"We'll try it out," he said to Goodbody, "and if there's been any change worth talking about I'll——"

Happily he did not promise to do anything particularly rash, for scarcely had the needle of Goodbody's gramophone touched the disc before the horrid truth dawned upon him. It was a dreadful moment. Dean Swift in his old age, reading one of the works of his youth, was heard to murmur sadly, "What a genius I had when I wrote that book!" but even his sorrow cannot have equalled Macintyre's as he listened to the dulcet voice that once was his and never could be again. As the gentle, wavering tones smote his ear his eyes filled with tears.

"Well?" said Goodbody when the record came to an end. "Do I win?"

"Win?" roared Macintyre with a bellow like a ship's siren. "That swine Speckles! 'More sinned against than sinning', indeed. Let me only get hold of the blighter who's done this!"

He snatched up the record and was about to fling it out of the window when Goodbody seized it from him.

"Don't smash this," he said. "You will want it."

"Want it? What on earth for?"

"For evidence, of course."

"What evidence?" asked Macintyre. "Where the—why the——"

The Tragedy of Young Macintyre

"Do you mean that you're not going to sue this fellow for the damage he's done to your voice?" said Goodbody. "You're not going to take this lying down, surely! Get hold of your solicitor and go for him."

Macintyre considered for a moment. "By gum," he said at last, "I will."

Such was the origin of the famous action of *Macintyre v. Speckles*. (*Speckles v. Macintyre*, of course, was Mr. Speckles's action for the balance of his fees for the lessons. The two were eventually consolidated, but not until, after the best legal fashion, some thousands of pounds had been wasted in trying to try them separately.) It was fully reported at the time, and I need not trouble with the legal details of it. It took about two years to decide whether or not Macintyre had any claim for damages at all. His counsel enjoyed themselves immensely over it. They claimed for Trespass, for Contract, for Tort and breach of Copyright. Speckles's men gave as good as they got, and said it was neither one thing nor the other. Eventually, after the case had been twice up to the House of Lords and down again on preliminaries, the case came on for hearing before Mr. Justice Snorebury and a special jury. Macintyre had briefed Sir Eliphaz Snarler, K.C., and Mr. Speckles had selected Mr. Snorter, K.C. (whose ceiling Macintyre had brought down, and who had hated him ever since). The court was crowded when Sir Eliphaz rose to open the case for the plaintiff. The crowd overflowed from the public galleries into the Strand and the mounted police had twice to charge to keep order.

Sir Eliphaz was at the top of his form, which considering he had a thousand guineas on his brief and a "refresher" of a hundred a day was not perhaps surprising. The conclusion of his speech was masterly.

"Members of the jury," he said. "Before my unhappy

client fell a victim to the blandishments of Mr. Speckles he was blessed with a diffident unassuming manner and a soft and charming voice. Those priceless attributes he has lost, and lost for ever. His manner is now blatant and assertive, his voice coarse and unattractive in the extreme. And this, members of the jury, I am in a position to prove. Before my client goes into the witness-box to demonstrate by every word and gesture 'the pernicious effects of Mr. Speckles's training I shall place before you unimpeachable evidence of what he was before the unhappy occurrences I have described. I have here a gramophone record which will be played to you by the instrument now on the table before me, and when you have heard it and compared it with the lamentable noises now produced by my client you will in my submission have no hesitation in finding a verdict in his favour, and that for the most substantial, nay exemplary, damages."

Mr. Snorter was on his feet immediately, objecting that the gramophone record could not be received in evidence. He had been speaking for over three-quarters of an hour when it was observed that the judge was asleep, and the court adjourned for the day.

The discussion as to the advisability of gramophone records lasted three days and cost the parties something over a thousand pounds apiece. (Perhaps I should explain at this point that the impecunious Mr. Speckles was supported in his action by the Amalgamated Society of Elocutionists and Voice Production Professors, and that Macintyre's wealthy uncle was blessed with a sense of humour.) Finally, the record was admitted in evidence and a hushed court heard the soft tones that had been Macintyre's lisping the defence of the man who was about to ruin them.

By the time the trial was nearly over, some highly profitable weeks for Sir Eliphaz and Mr. Snorter having

The Tragedy of Young Macintyre

elapsed, Macintyre felt fairly confident of the result. The judge had listened to his evidence with attention (he had been deaf for ten years, and Macintyre's was the only voice in all that time which had reached him), and there were four women on the jury whom he was sure he had impressed. But it was these very women who were to prove his undoing—they and the gramophone which Sir Eliphaz had fought for so strenuously. For when Mr. Justice Snorebury's long, learned and painfully boring summing-up came at last to an end, with "Kindly consider your verdict", the youngest and prettiest of the jurywomen leaned forward, smiled sweetly and said, "My lord, may the jury take the gramophone and record with them to help in considering the verdict?"

In spite of his age the judge was still susceptible to feminine charms. He was dimly conscious that a good-looking young woman was asking him something, and having disposed of a long and tiresome case he was feeling in a state of sleepy amiability.

"Certainly," he smiled kindly. "Oh yes, decidedly! Anything that you wish, my dear young lady."

And the gramophone was picked up and carried out in triumph by the foreman of the jury.

The case had come to an end at a quarter to four, and those experienced in the ways of juries have been heard to say that at that time of day they are never very long in coming to a decision. Human nature being what it is, they say, the claims of justice never very long resist the attractions of the train home to tea. But on this occasion the cynics were confuted. Half an hour, an hour went by, and still the jury came not. The crowd in court had begun to melt away. Macintyre and Mr. Speckles, at opposite ends of the same bench, having passed through all the stages from excitement to utter boredom, were dully

67

staring in front of themselves, long past caring what happened. Sir Eliphaz and Mr. Snorter had departed, leaving their unfortunate juniors to see the end of it. As for the judge, he was the only happy man in court, for he was sound asleep. At last, after the jury had been gone an hour and a half, something, perhaps the pangs of hunger, woke him. He yawned, stretched, and looked incredulously at the clock.

"Good gracious!" he said. "This jury is deliberating for an exceedingly long time. Usher, be good enough to enquire whether they are desirous of any further direction on points of law or fact, and if so I shall be glad to assist them."

The usher departed on his errand, and the court sank back into slumber. He was gone some time, and when he reappeared he was as pale and shaken as so dignified a person can ever be.

"Well?" asked his lordship. "Does the jury require any assistance."

Speechless, the usher shook his head.

"Then if they cannot agree upon a verdict they must be discharged. Do they say they cannot agree?"

The usher shook his head again.

"Then what in the name of Blackstone are they doing?" asked the judge.

"May it please you, my lord, they're dancing," quavered the usher.

His lordship could not believe his ears. Considering their quality, there was no reason why he should.

"They are what?" he cried. "Speak up, man, I can't hear you."

"D-d-dancing, my lord."

"I cannot hear a word you say. Here, Mr. Macintyre, I can always understand you. What is it this fellow here is trying to tell me?"

"My lord," answered Macintyre in a voice of thunder. "He says that the jury are DANCING!"

"Dancing!" ejaculated his lordship. "Most improper! Unheard-of behaviour! I've never known anyone dance in the courts of justice since I was called to the Bar. There must be some mistake about it. Usher, are you quite positive that you heard the sound of—of dancing proceeding from the jury-room?"

"Quite positive, my lord," answered that scandalized official. "And, what's more, I saw them ladies this morning when they went into the box with what looked like gramophone records under their coats. It's a put-up job, my lord, and that's the truth."

The truth was even worse than the gloomy usher imagined. For how could he tell, how could the judge tell, how could anyone have told that the jury-box had all this time been harbouring an angel unawares—in the far-corner seat of the back row to be precise—and that that angel was no other than the celebrated Mexican, Fandango? It was true, none the less, that for weeks the Royal Courts of Justice had been imprisoning in their gloomy walls the most famous ballroom dancer of the age. Fandango, the favourite teacher of half the crowned heads of Europe, the man who could make the fortune of any night-club by merely promising to look in for ten minutes during the evening. Fandango, the exquisite, the olive skinned, was on the jury; and pretty little Miss Beckwith, who sat next to him, was determined to make the most of it. So was plump, fair-haired Mrs. Simperton, when the great man had been induced to admit his identity one day at lunch. That thrilling but terribly difficult new dance, the Baltimore Squirm, had just been introduced; and the chance of a free lesson from the one man in all England who could dance it properly was not to be missed.

The Tragedy of Young Macintyre

It is not for me to say—because I do not know—by what means Miss Beckwith induced Fandango, who was notoriously averse from giving something for nothing, to lower himself so far as to give an exhibition of his art before an audience of eleven. One can only conclude that several weeks of the atmosphere of the courts had somewhat weakened his powers of resistance, and, after all, nobody can sit in such close proximity to a really charming girl, as Miss Beckwith was, without being affected in some degree. However it came about, there they were, at half-past five, turning the jury-room into as good an imitation of the Café de Paris as its limited accommodation allowed.

Meanwhile consternation reigned in court. Mr. Justice Snorebury was not a particularly quick thinker, and for the first time in his professional life he found himself confronted with something entirely without precedent.

"Most improper! Most improper!" he repeated again and again. "I—I really don't know what to do about this. Upon my soul I don't. I think I must consult my learned brethren about this. Meanwhile they can stay where they are. The court is adjourned."

And forthwith he left the bench, only to find that his learned brethren had long since gone home and that there was nobody left in the building to whom he could turn for guidance. "Most improper!" he murmured, as he took off his wig and gown in his room. "Most improper!" he repeated, as he put on his silk hat. His car was waiting patiently at the judges' entrance. Tired with his long day's work, he climbed wearily in. "Most imp——" His head sank forward, and the rest of the word was a snore. The wicked behaviour of the jury, the opinion of his learned brethren, were all forgotten. It was a Friday evening. And the Courts of Justice do not sit on Saturdays.

The Tragedy of Young Macintyre

It was the Sunday papers that started the agitation about the imprisoned jurors, but as Mr. Justice Snorebury never read the Sunday papers they did not worry him. The fact that his absent-mindedness had spread dismay into twelve blameless homes left him quite calm and unruffled. The existence of the dancing twelve had completely passed out of his mind, and unfortunately he was the only person who had power to release them. When on Monday morning he took his seat and somebody timidly ventured to remind him of their existence, he was as nearly startled as his great age and serenity ever allowed him to be.

"Dear me, yes!" he said mildly. "The jury? Of course, bring them in."

They were brought, or rather carried in. Sixty hours of incarceration, even with a gramophone and the world's best dancer for company, is a trifle trying. Pale, dishevelled and miserable, they were propped up before the bench.

"Let me see," asked the judge. "Have you agreed upon your verdict?"

It was the last straw. All four women fainted, and Fandango uttered remarks that were happily unintelligible.

"Apparently you haven't," said his lordship. "Ah, yes, I remember now. You were the people who spent your time dancing. Disgraceful! I have a good mind to commit you all for contempt of court! However, you can go now. Let us proceed with the next case." And with that the learned judge dismissed the jury from the court and the whole affair from his mind.

The great British public, however, and its mouthpiece, the great British press, did not treat the affair so easily. On the contrary, they took it to their hearts with gusto. Miss Beckwith had an uncle who was an O.B.E., and Mrs. Simperton was related to the Lord Mayor, so they were not people to be trifled with. Soon all England rang with

their grievances. They talked of Magna Charta and the
Bill of Rights, of Habeas Corpus and a variety of other
things which they did not understand. It so happened
that there was a lack of sensational murders and fashion-
able weddings at the time and the newspaper world was
overjoyed at the opportunity. "Should jurors dance?"
became the question of the hour, and the country was rent
in twain between those who answered "Yes, they should!"
and demanded poor Snorebury's blood, and the kill-joys
who said "No!" and were base enough to suggest that it
served them all right. But on the whole there could be
no doubt that the Ayes had it. The twelve jurors became
popular heroes. Their photographs were in every picture-
paper, the unmarried among them received a total of no
less than two hundred and fourteen proposals of marriage
(of which Miss Beckwith accounted for one hundred and
eighty-five), their views were invited by the Sunday news-
papers on every subject under the sun from shingling to
birth control, and the Baltimore Squirm was in their
honour renamed the "Jury-room Jeebies". Meanwhile
every effort was made to secure redress for the wrongs
they had suffered. Earnest M.P.s asked questions in
Parliament. Ministers were heckled in their constitu-
encies, actions were launched and struck out and recon-
structed and adjourned, and in the end I really believe
that the Government would have fallen if they had not
dealt with the matter boldly by passing a special Act of
Parliament, presenting the jurors with £100 apiece for
their trouble and promoting Mr. Justice Snorebury to the
Court of Appeal, where there would be no jurors to worry
him.

But the matter did not end there. As I have said, there
were kill-joys, who did not sympathise with the woes of
the jurors. Among them was the editor of the *Megaphone*

(which was owned by the Agglomerated Press, which is owned by Lord Baronscourt). It may or it may not be coincidence that that great journal was at the time conducting a campaign entitled "Keep the Alien Out of England", and that his lordship was largely interested in promoting the revival of Morris dancing on village greens; but the fact remains that it was bitterly hostile to the twelve all through their campaign, and after it was all over it rated them soundly in one of its most pompous leading articles. It was entitled "Aliens and the Law", and "the material parts", as they were afterwards described by learned counsel, were as follows:

"The disgraceful series of events which has recently been terminated by the intervention of the Government reveals a disquieting, not to say ominous, state of affairs. It is clear that the orgies by which British justice has been brought into contempt would never have occurred but for the presence upon the jury of a half-caste Mexican dancer to whose incitements the remainder of his colleagues succumbed. We have had occasion in the past to warn our readers of the presence of alien influence in the Army, the Church, the Post Office, the British Museum and the Commissioners of Woods and Forests, but this is the first time, we believe, that an alien hand has been permitted to pollute the fount of Justice."

The result of this effusion, as will be remembered, was the case of *Fandango v. The Agglomerated Press*, in which Fandango successfully proved that his name was William Griggs, that he was born in Peckham, and that he had never been nearer Mexico in his life than Bude. His counsel (need I say that it was Sir Eliphaz?) pointed out with irresistible logic to the jury that not only was it a horrid libel on an Englishman to call him an alien, but also that his client would suffer untold damages by being compelled to reveal that he was not a Mexican at all. "What attraction is there," asked Sir Eliphaz dramatically, "in dancing with a Mr. Griggs? What restaurant or cabaret will engage a mere Englishman for such a work? His livelihood is gone, and you must replace it." Profoundly moved, an English jury assessed the damages at £10,000 (a sum which Lord Baronscourt could well afford), and since, oddly enough, Fandango's popularity was not destroyed, as Sir Eliphaz had feared, but rather improved by the advertisement, he may be taken to have done well out of the affair.

As for Mr. Speckles, although he never attempted to have his action re-tried, and although the balance of Macintyre's fees are still due and owing, he is not to be pitied. Immediately after the action he was elected Perpetual President of the Amalgamated Society of Elocutionists and his name became known wherever the science of elocution is practised. He has offices now in the smart new building which has replaced the old one in the Strand, and when I last heard of him he was on his way to deliver a series of lectures in America.

And Macintyre—the innocent cause of all the trouble— what of him? I have called this truthful little history a tragedy, and so from the legal point of view it was, for the Temple lost a promising advocate and a charming fellow. But the ill wind that blew him out of the law blew him good after all, for it blew him to Hollywood, the one place in the world where expression counts for a great deal and voice production for nothing. He has, it appears, an ideal photographic face, and the only thing now that can prevent him making a fortune would be the universal introduction of Talking Films.

▶ P.S. I saw Sir Eliphaz going down Piccadilly yesterday in a new Rolls-Royce, so it seems that *he's* all right.

Weight and See

Detective-Inspector Mallett of the C.I.D. was a very large man. He was not only tall above the average, but also broad in more than just proportion to his height, while his weight was at least proportionate to his breadth. Whether, as his colleagues at New Scotland Yard used to assert, his bulk was due to the enormous meals which he habitually consumed, or whether, as the inspector maintained, the reason for his large appetite was that so big a frame needed more than a normal man's supply for its sustenance, was an open question. What was not open to doubt was Mallett's success in his calling. But if anybody was ever bold enough to suggest that his success might have been even greater but for the handicap of his size he would merely smile sweetly and remark that there had been occasions when on the contrary he had found it a positive advantage. Pressed for further and better particulars, he might, if in an expansive mood, go so far as to say that he could recall at least one case in which he had succeeded where a twelve-stone man would have failed.

This is the story of that case. It is not, strictly speaking, a case of detection at all, since the solution depended ultimately on the chance application of avoirdupois rather than the deliberate application of intelligence. None the less, it was a case which Mallett himself was fond of recollecting, if only because of the way in which that recollection

served to salve his conscience whenever thereafter he fell
to the temptation of a second helping of suet pudding.

The story begins, so far as the police are concerned, at
about seven o'clock on a fine morning in early summer,
when a milkman on his round came out of the entrance of
Clarence Mansions, S.W.11, just as a police constable
happened to be passing.

"Morning," said the constable.

"Morning," said the milkman.

The constable moved on. The milkman stood watching
him, two powerful questions conflicting in his breast. On
the one hand, it was an article of faith with him that one
whose work takes him to other people's houses at a time
when most of the world is only beginning to wake up
should never poke his nose into other people's business;
on the other, he felt just now a craving, new-born but
immensely powerful, not to be left out of the adventure
which some sixth sense told him was afoot. The constable was almost out of earshot before the issue was
decided.

"Oy!" shouted the milkman.

The officer turned round majestically.

"What is it?" he asked.

The milkman jerked his thumb in the direction of the
block of flats behind him.

"I don't know," he said, "but I think there's something
queer up there."

"Where?"

"Number 32, top floor."

"How d'you mean, queer?"

"The dog up there is carrying on something awful—
barking and scratching at the door."

"Well, what of it?"

"Oh, nothing, but it's a bit queer, that's all. It's a quiet dog as a rule."

"They've gone out and left him in, I suppose."

"Well, if they 'ave, they've left a light on as well."

The constable looked up at the windows of the top storey.

"There *is* a light on in one of the rooms," he observed. "Seems funny, a fine morning like this." He considered the matter slowly. "Might as well go up and see, I suppose. They'll be having the neighbours complaining about that dog. I can hear it from here."

With the milkman in attendance he tramped heavily up the stairs—Clarence Mansions boast no lift—to the top floor. Outside No. 32 stood the pint bottle of milk which had just been left there. He rang the bell. There was no reply, except a renewed outburst of barks from the dog within.

"Are they at home, d'you know?" he asked.

" 'S far as I know. I 'ad me orders to deliver, same as usual."

"Who are the people?"

"Wellman, the name is. A little fair chap with a squint. There's just the two of them and the dog."

"I know him," said the policeman. "Seen him about often. Passed the time of day with him. Didn't know he was married, though."

"She never goes- out," the milkman explained. "He told me about her once. Used to be a trapeze artist in a circus. 'Ad a fall, and crippled for good. Can't even get in or out of bed by 'erself, so he says."

"Oh?" said the constable. "Well, if that's so, per-haps——" He sucked his cheeks and frowned perplexedly. "All the same, you can't go and break into a place just because the dog's howling and someone's left the light on. I think I'd best go and report this before I do anything."

The milkman was looking down the staircase.

"Someone coming up," he announced. "It's Mr. Wellman all right," he added, as a rather flushed, unshaven face appeared on the landing below.

The constable put on his official manner at once.

"Mr. Wellman, sir?" he said. "There have been complaints of your dog creating a disturbance here this morning. Also I observe that there is a light on in one of your rooms. Would you be good enough to——"

"That's all right, officer," Wellman interrupted him. "I was kept out last night. Quite unexpected. Sorry about the dog and all that."

He fished a latchkey from his pocket, opened the door, and went in, shutting it behind him. The other two, left outside with the milk bottle for company, heard him speak softly to the dog, which immediately became quiet. In the silence they could hear his footsteps down the passage which evidently led away from the front door. They looked at each other blankly. The policeman said "Well!", the milkman was already preparing to go back to his round, when the steps were heard returning, there was the sound of the door of a room nearby being opened, and then Mr. Wellman was out of the flat, his face white, his eyes staring, crying, "Come here, quick! Something awful has happened!"

"But this," said Mallett, "is odd. Very odd indeed."

He sat in the office of the Divisional Detective-Inspector, meditatively turning over a sheaf of reports.

"Odd is the word for it," the D.D.I. replied. "You see, on the one hand there seems no doubt that the lady was alive at nine o'clock——"

Weight and See

"Let me see if I've got the story straight," said Mallett. "Mrs. Wellman is found dead in her bed at about seven o'clock in the morning by her husband, in the presence, very nearly, of a police officer and another man. She has been killed by a blow on the back of the head from a blunt instrument. The doctor thinks that death occurred about seven to eleven hours previously—say between eight o'clock and midnight the night before. He thinks also—in fact he's pretty sure—that the blow would produce instantaneous death, or at all events instantaneous unconsciousness. There are no signs of forcible entry into the flat, and Mrs. Wellman was a cripple, so the possibility of her getting out of bed to let anybody in is out of the question. Am I right so far?"

"Quite correct."

"In these circumstances the husband quite naturally falls under suspicion. He is asked to account for his movements over night, and up to a point he seems quite willing to do so. He says that he put his wife to bed at about a quarter to nine, took the dog out for a short run—— What sort of a dog is it, by the way?"

"An Alsatian. It seems to be a good-tempered, intelligent sort of beast."

"He takes the Alsatian out for a short run, returns it to the flat without going into his wife's room, and then goes out again. That's his story. He says most positively that he never came back to the place until next morning when the constable and the milkman saw him going in. Asked whether he has any witnesses to prove his story, he says that he spoke to the constable on night duty, whom he met just outside Clarence Mansions on his way out, and he further gives the names of two friends whom he met at the Green Dragon public-house, half a mile from Clarence Mansions——"

"Seven hundred and fifty yards from Clarence Mansions."

"I'm much obliged. He met his two pals there at about a quarter-past nine, and stayed there till closing time. He went from the public-house with one of them to the nearest tram stop, and took a No. 31 tram going east, or away from Clarence Mansions. His friend went with him on the tram as far as the next fare stage, where he got off, leaving Wellman on the tram, still going away from home. Is that all clear so far?"

"Quite."

"Further than that Wellman wouldn't help us. He said he'd spent the rest of the night in a little hotel somewhere down Hackney way. Why he should have done so he didn't explain, and when asked for the name of the place he couldn't give it. He thought it had a red and green carpet in the hall, but that's all he could remember about it. The suggestion was, I gather, that he was too drunk to notice things properly when he got to the hotel, and was suffering from a bit of a hang-over next morning."

"He certainly was when I saw him."

"Things begin to look rather bad for Master Wellman. They look even worse when we find out a few things about him. It seems that he hasn't a job, and hasn't had one for a very long time. He married his wife when she was travelling the country as a trapeze artist in a small circus, in which he was employed as electrician and odd-job man. When a rope broke and she was put out of the circus business for good, her employers paid her a lump sum in compensation. He has been living on that ever since. His accounts show that he has got through it pretty quickly, and it's odds on that she had been wanting to know where it had gone to. It's not very hard to see a motive for getting rid of her."

"The motive's there all right," said the divisional inspector, "but——"

"*But*," Mallett went on. "Here's where our troubles begin.—Wellman is detained for enquiries, and the enquiries show that his story, so far as it goes, is perfectly true. He did meet his pals at the Green Dragon. They and the publican are positive on that point, and they bear out his story in every particular. Therefore if he killed his wife it must have been before a quarter-past nine or after half-past ten, which was approximately the time when he was last seen on the No. 31 tram. But Mrs. Wellman was alive when he left Clarence Mansions, because——"

He pulled out one of the statements before him.

"Statement of Police Constable Denny," he read. "At approximately nine o'clock p.m. I was on duty in Imperial Avenue opposite Clarence Mansions when I saw Wellman. He had his dog with him. We had a short conversation. He said, 'I've just been giving my dog a run.' I said, 'It's a nice dog.' He said, 'I bought it for my wife's protection, but it's too good-natured for a watch-dog.' He went into Clarence Mansions and came out again almost at once. He had a small bag in his hand. I said, 'Going out again, Mr. Wellman?' He said, 'Yes. Have you seen my pals about anywhere?' I informed him that I did not know his pals, and he replied, 'I expect they're gone on ahead.' He then said, 'I'm waiting to see if the wife has turned in yet.' I looked up at the windows of Clarence Mansions, and there was a light in one of the windows on the top storey—the window to the left of the staircase as you look at it. I have since learned that that is the window of the bedroom of No. 32. As I was looking, the light was extinguished. Wellman said to me, 'That's all right, I can get along now.' We had a bit of a joke about it. He then went away, and I proceeded on my beat. At approximately

ten-thirty p.m. I had occasion to pass Clarence Mansions
again. There were then no lights visible in the top storey.
I did not pass the Mansions again until on my way back
from duty at approximately six-fifteen a.m. I then
observed that the same light was on, but I gave the matter
no thought at the time."

Mallett put down the statement with a sigh.

"What sort of a man is Denny?" he asked.

"Very intelligent and observant," was the reply. "One
of the best uniformed men I have. And not too blooming
educated, if you follow me."

"Very well. We have it then on his evidence that Mrs.
Wellman, or somebody else in the flat, extinguished the
light at a little after nine o'clock, and that somebody
turned it on again between ten-thirty and six-fifteen. I
suppose Mrs. Wellman could turn it off and on herself, by
the way?"

"Undoubtedly. It was a bedside lamp, and she had the
full use of her arms."

"Therefore," Mallett went on, "we are now driven to
this—that Wellman killed his wife—if he killed her—
after ten-thirty, when he was last seen on the tram, and
before midnight, which is the latest time which the doctor
thinks reasonably possible. Then comes the blow. To test
Wellman's story, for what it is worth, we have made enquiries in Hackney to see if we can find a hotel of the kind
that wouldn't mind taking in a gentleman the worse for
liquor, with a red and green carpet in the hall, and handy
to the No. 31 tram route. And the very first place we try,
we not only find that they remember Mr. Wellman there
but are extremely anxious to see him again. They tell
us that he came to their place about half-past eleven—
which is the time you would expect if he left the neighbourhood of the Green Dragon by tram an hour before—

persuaded whoever it was who was still up at that hour to give him a room, and next morning was seen going out at six o'clock remarking that he was going to get a shave. He never came back——"

"And he never got that shave," interjected the D.D.I.

"True enough. And when the hotel people opened his bag—which Police Constable Denny has identified, incidentally—it contained precisely nothing. So——"

"So we packed him off to the Hackney police to answer a charge of obtaining credit by fraud and asked the Yard to tell us what to do next."

"In other words, you want me to fix this crime on to somebody who has to all appearances a perfect alibi for it."

"That's just it," said the divisional inspector in all seriousness. "If only the blighter had had anything on him that could have been used as a weapon!"

" 'On Wellman'," said Mallett, reading from another sheet of the reports, " 'were found a pencil, a small piece of cork, a pocket-knife, two shillings silver and sixpence halfpenny bronze.' Why," he continued, "do we have to go on saying 'bronze' when all the rest of the world says 'copper', by the way? But the weapon—he could have taken that away in his bag and disposed of it anywhere between here and Hackney easily enough. We shall be lucky if we ever lay our hands on that. The alibi is our trouble. From nine o'clock onwards it seems unbeatable. Therefore he must have killed his wife before nine. But if he did, who was it that turned the light off in her room? I suppose the dog might have done it—knocked the lamp over, or something."

"There's no trace of the dog having been in the room all night," said the other. "His footprints are quite plain on the carpet in the corridor, and I've been over the bedroom carpet carefully without any result. Also, there

83

seems no doubt that the bedroom door was shut next morning. Wellman was heard to unlatch it. Besides, if the dog turned the light off, how did he turn it on again?"

Mallett considered.

"Have you tested the fuses!" he asked.

"Yes, and they are in perfect order. There's no chance of a temporary fault causing the light to go off and on again. And Wellman was waiting for the light to go off when he was talking to Denny."

"Then," said Mallett, "we've got to work on the assumption that someone else got into the flat that night."

"Without disturbing the dog?"

"A good-natured dog," Mallett pointed out.

"But there are no signs of any entry whatever. I've looked myself, and some of my best men have been on the job."

"But I haven't looked yet," said Mallett.

No. 32 Clarence Mansions was exactly like all the other flats in the block, and indeed in Imperial Avenue, so far as its internal arrangements were concerned. Three very small rooms, looking on to the Avenue, opened out of the corridor which ran from the front door. Three still smaller rooms opened out of another corridor at right angles to the first, and enjoyed a view of the back of the Mansions in the next block. At the junction of the two corridors the gloom of the interior was mitigated by a skylight, the one privilege possessed by the top-storey flats and denied to the rest of the block. The bedroom in which Mrs. Wellman had died was the room nearest the entrance.

Mallett did not go into this room until he had first carefully examined the door and the tiny hall immediately inside it.

Weight and See

"There are certainly no marks on the lock," he said at last. Then, looking at the floor, he asked, "What is this powdery stuff down here?"

"Dog biscuit," was the reply. "The animal seems to have had his supper here. There's his water-bowl in the corner, too, by the umbrella-stand."

"But he slept over *there*," said Mallett, nodding to the farther end of the corridor, where underneath the skylight was a large circular basket, lined with an old rug.

They went into the bedroom. The body had been removed, but otherwise nothing in it had been touched since the discovery of the tragedy. On its dingy walls hung photographs of acrobats, dancers and clowns, and the framed programme of a Command Variety performance— memorials of the trapeze artist's vanished career. The crumpled pillow bore a single shapeless stain of darkened blood. On a bedside table was a cheap electric lamp. Mallett snapped it on and off.

"That doesn't look as if it had been knocked over," he remarked. "Did you notice the scratches on the bottom panel of the door, by the way? It seems as though the dog had been trying to get in from the passage."

He went over to the sash window and subjected it to a prolonged scrutiny.

"No," he said. "Definitely, no. Now let's look at the rest of the place."

He walked down the corridor until he reached the skylight.

"I suppose somebody could have got through here," he observed.

"But he would have come down right on top of the dog," the D.D.I. objected.

"True. That would have been a bit of a strain for even the quietest animal. Still, there's no harm in looking."

85

He kicked aside the sleeping-basket and stood immediately beneath the skylight.

"The light's in my eyes, and I can't see the underside of the frame properly," he complained, standing on tiptoe and peering upwards. "Just turn on the electric light, will you? I said, turn on the light," he repeated in a louder tone.

"It is on," was the reply, "but nothing's happened. The bulb must have gone."

"Has it?" said Mallett, stepping across to the hanging light that swung within a foot of his head. As he did so, the lamp came on.

"Curiouser and curiouser! Switch it off again. Now come and stand where I was."

They changed places, and Mallett depressed the switch. The light was turned on at once.

"Are you sure you're standing in the same place?"

"Quite sure."

"Then jump!"

"What?"

"Jump. As high as you can, and come down as hard as you can."

The inspector sprang into the air, and his heels hit the floor with a crash. At that instant, the light flickered, went out and then came on once more.

"Splendid!" said Mallett. "Now look between your feet. Do you see anything?"

"There's a little round hole in the floorboard here. That's all."

"Does the board seem at all loose to you?"

"Yes, it does. Quite a bit. But that's not surprising after what I've done to it."

"Let me see it."

Mallett went down on hands and knees and found the

hole of which the other had spoken. It was quite small—hardly more than a fault in the wood, but its edges were sharp and clear. It was near to one end of the board. That end was completely unsecured, the other was lightly nailed down. He produced a knife and inserted the blade into the hole. Then, using his knife as a lever, he found that he could pull the board up on its end, as though upon a hinge.

"Look!" he said, and pointed down into the cavity beneath.

On the joist on which the loose end of the board had rested was a small, stiff coiled spring, just large enough to keep that end a fraction above the level of the surrounding floor. But what chiefly attracted the attention of the two men was not on the joist itself but a few inches to one side. It was an ordinary electric bell-push, such as might be seen on any front door in Imperial Avenue.

"Do you recollect what Wellman's job was, when he had a job?" asked Mallett.

"He worked in the circus as odd-job man, and—— Good Lord, yes!—electrician."

"Just so. Now watch!"

He put his finger on the bell push. The light above their heads went out. He released it, and the light came on again.

"Turn on another light," said Mallett. "Any light, I don't care which. In the sitting-room, if you like. Now . . ." He depressed the button once more. "Does it work?"

"Yes."

"Of course it does," he cried triumphantly, rising to his feet and dusting the knees of his trousers. "The whole thing's too simple for words. The main electric lead of the flat runs under this floor. All Wellman has done is to fit a simple attachment to it, so that when the bell-push is pressed down the circuit is broken and the current turned off. The dog's basket was on this board. That meant that when the dog lay down out went the light in the bedroom—and any other light that happened to be on, only he took care to see that there wasn't any other light on. When the dog begins to get restless in the morning and goes down the passage to see what's the matter—you said he was an intelligent dog, didn't you?—on comes the light again. And anybody in the street outside, seeing the lamp extinguished and lighted again, would be prepared to swear that there was somebody alive in the room to manipulate the lamp. Oh, it really is ingenious!"

"But——" the divisional inspector objected.

"Yes?"

"But the light didn't go off when I was standing there."

"How much do you weigh?"

"Eleven stone seven."

"And I'm—well, quite a bit more than that. That's why. You see, there's a fraction of space between the board and the bell-push, and you couldn't quite force the board far enough down to make it work, except when you jumped. I had the advantage over you there," he concluded modestly.

"But hang it all," protested the other, "I may not be a heavy-weight, but I do weigh more than a dog. If I couldn't do the trick, how on earth could he? It doesn't make sense."

"On Wellman," said Mallett reflectively, "were found a pencil, a small piece of cork, a pocket-knife, two shillings silver and sixpence halfpenny bronze. Have you observed that the little hole in the board is directly above the button of the bell-push?"

"Yes. I see now that it is."

"Very well. If the small piece of cork doesn't fit into

88

that hole, I'll eat your station sergeant's helmet. That's all."

"So that when the cork is in the hole——"

"When the hole is plugged the end of the cork is resting on the bull-push. It then needs only the weight of the basket, plus the weight of the dog, to depress the spring, which keeps the end of the board up, and the cork automatically works the bell-push. Now we can see what happened. Wellman rigged up this contraption in advance —an easy matter for an experienced electrician. Then, on the evening which he had chosen for the crime, he put his wife to bed, killed her, with the coal hammer most probably—if you search the flat I expect you will find it missing—and shut the door of the bedroom, leaving the bedside lamp alight. He next inserted the cork in the hole of the board and replaced the dog's basket on top. With a couple of dog biscuits in his pocket, he then took the dog out for a run. He kept it out until he saw Police Constable Denny outside the flats. Probably he had informed himself of the times when the officer on duty could be expected to appear there, and made his arrangements accordingly. Having had a word with Denny, he slipped upstairs and let the dog into the flat. But before he came downstairs again he took care to give the dog his biscuits in the hall. It would never have done if the light had been put out before he was out of the building, and he left the dog something to keep him the other end of the passage for a moment or two. He knew that the dog, as soon as he had eaten his supper and had a drink of water, would go and lie down in his basket. I expect he had been trained to do it. Alsatians are teachable animals, they tell me. Down in the street he waited until the dog had put the light out for him, and called Denny's attention to the fact. His alibi established, off he went. But he had to get

89

back next morning to remove that bit of cork. Otherwise the next person who trod on the board might give his secret away. So we find that when he came to the flat the first thing he did was to go down the corridor—before ever he went into the bedroom. That little bit of evidence always puzzled me. Now we know what he was doing. He was a fool not to throw the cork away, of course, but I suppose he thought that nobody would think of looking at that particular place. So far as he knew, nothing could work the lights if the cork wasn't in place. He thought he was safe."

"And," Mallett concluded, "he would have been safe too, if there hadn't been that little extra bit of weight put on the board. He couldn't be expected to foresee *me*."

Which explains, if it does not excuse, the slight but unmistakable touch of condescension with which Inspector Mallett thereafter used to treat his slimmer and slighter brethren.

"It Takes Two . . ."

I t takes two to make a murder. The psychology of the
murderer has been analysed often enough; what quali-
fies a man to be murdered is a subject less frequently discussed, though sometimes, perhaps, more interesting.

Derek Walton, who was killed by Ted Brackley on a
dark December evening in Boulter's Mews, Mayfair, was
uniquely fitted for his part in that rather sordid little
drama. He was a well-built young man, five feet eight
inches high, with dark hair and hazel eyes. He had a toothbrush moustache and walked with a slight limp. He was
employed by Mallard's, that small and thriving jewellers'
establishment just off Bond Street, and at the time of his
death had in his pocket a valuable parcel of diamonds
which Mallard had told him to take to Birmingham to be
reset. The diamonds, naturally enough, provided the
motive for the murder, but Walton would not have died
exactly when and how he did had he been fat, or blue-
eyed, or more than five feet nine, for Brackley was a
cautious man. There was one other fact in Walton's life
which finally loaded the scales against him—he was given
to gambling on the dogs, and fairly heavily in debt.

There was very little about Walton that Brackley did
not know, after a period of intense study which had extended now for a matter of months. Patiently and remorse-
lessly he had studied his quarry in every aspect. Every
detail in his physical appearance, down to the least trick

91

of gesture, gait or accent, had been noted with a more than lover-like devotion. A creature of habit, Walton was an easy subject for observation, and his goings-out and comings-in had long since been learned by heart. Brackley knew all about the lodgings in West London where he lived, the pubs he frequented, the bookies he patronized, his furtive and uninteresting love affairs. More than once he had followed him to Birmingham, where his parents lived, and to the very doors of Watkinshaws, the manufacturing jewellers there who carried out the exquisite designs on which old Nicholas Mallard's reputation had been built. In fact, Brackley reflected, as he waited in the shadows of Boulter's Mews, about the only thing he did not precisely know about Walton was what went on inside his head. But that was an irrelevant detail, as irrelevant as are the emotions of a grazing stag to the stalker the moment before he presses the trigger.

Walton was later than usual that evening. Brackley took a quick glance at his wrist-watch and frowned. In ten minutes' time the constable on his beat was due at the end of the Mews. He decided that he could allow himself another two minutes at the most. After that, the margin of safety would be too small, and the operation would have to be called off for the night. A later opportunity would offer itself no doubt, and he could afford to wait, but it would be a pity, for the conditions were otherwise ideal. The shops had closed and the sound of the last assistants and office workers hurrying home had long since died away. The tide of pleasure traffic to the West End had not yet set in. A faint mist, too thin to be called a fog, had begun to rise from the damp pavements. What on earth was keeping Walton back?

The two minutes had still thirty seconds to run when Brackley heard what he was waiting for. Fifty yards away, in Fentiman Street, he heard the back door of Mallard's close, and the rattle of the key in the lock as Walton secured the premises behind him. Evidently he was the last out of the shop as usual. There was a pause, long enough to make Brackley wonder whether his quarry had defeated him by deciding to walk out into Bond Street instead of taking his usual short cut through the Mews; and then he heard the unmistakable limping footsteps coming towards him. He realized, as he slid back into the open doorway behind him, that the steps were decidedly faster than usual. That was unfortunate, since everything depended on precise timing. Now, at the critical moment, so long prepared, so carefully rehearsed, there would have to be an element of improvisation, and improvisation meant risk. Brackley had been to endless pains to eliminate risk in this affair. He resented having any put upon him.

After all, he need not have worried. The business went perfectly according to plan. As Walton passed the doorway Brackley stepped out behind him. A quick glance to either side assured him that the Mews was deserted. He took two soundless paces in time with his victim. Then the rubber-handled cosh struck once, behind the right ear, precisely as he had intended, and Walton pitched forward without a groan.

The body never touched the ground. Even as he delivered the blow, Brackley had followed up and caught it round the waist with his left hand. For an instant he stood supporting it, and then with a quick heave lifted it on to his shoulder and carried it into the entry from which he had emerged. The whole incident had not taken more than ten seconds. There had been no sound, except the dull impact of the blow itself and the faint clatter made by the suitcase which Walton had been carrying as it fell to the ground. The case itself and Walton's hat, lying side by side in the gutter, were the only evidence of what had occurred. Within as short a space of time again Brackley had darted out once more and retrieved them. The door closed silently behind him. Boulter's Mews was as silent as a grave and as empty as a cenotaph.

Panting slightly from his exertions, but completely cool, Brackley went swiftly to work by the light of an electric torch. He was standing in a small garage of which he was the legitimate tenant, and he had laid the body upon a rug behind the tail-board of a small van of which he was the registered owner. The cosh was beside it. There had been little bleeding, and he had made sure that what there was had been absorbed by the rug. Quickly and methodically he went through Walton's pockets. The diamonds, as he expected, were in a small, sealed packet in an inside coat pocket. A brown leather wallet contained some of Walton's business cards, a few pound notes and some personal papers. Then came an agreeable surprise. In a hip pocket, along with a cheap cigarette case, was a thick bundle of pound notes. Brackley did not stop to count them, but he judged that there were a hundred of them, more or less. He grinned in the darkness. Other arrangements had compelled him to allow Walton to go to the dog races unattended during the last two weeks. Evidently his luck there had turned at last—and just in time. He stuffed the notes along with the rest into his own pockets and then minutely examined the appearance of the dead man from head to foot.

What he saw satisfied him completely. Walton, that creature of habit, had dressed for his work that day in exactly the same clothes as usual. The clothes that Brackley was now wearing were identically the same. Brackley's shoulders were not quite so broad as Walton's, but a little padding in the shoulders of the overcoat had eliminated that distinction. Brackley stood only five feet seven inches in his socks, but in the shoes he had prepared for the occasion he looked as tall as Walton had been. A touch of dye had corrected the slight difference between the colours of their hair. Brackley stroked the toothbrush moustache which he had been cultivating for the last month and decided that the resemblance would pass.

No casual observer would have doubted that the man who limped out of the southern end of the Mews carrying a small suitcase was other than the man who had entered its northern end a scant five minutes earlier. Certainly the newspaper seller in Bond Street did not. Automatically he extended Walton's usual paper, automatically he made the same trite observation he had made to Walton every evening, and heard without comment the reply which came to him in a very fair imitation of Walton's Midland accent. By a piece of good fortune, a policeman was passing at the time. He would remember the incident if the newspaperman did not. Walton's presence in Bond Street was now firmly established; it remained to lay a clear trail to Birmingham.

A taxi appeared at just the right moment. Brackley stopped it and in a voice pitched loud enough to reach the constable's ear told the man to drive to Euston. For good measure, he asked him if he thought he could catch the 6.55 train to Birmingham, and expressed exaggerated relief when the driver assured him that he had time to spare.

Walton always took the 6.55 to Birmingham, and travelled first class at his firm's expense. Brackley did the same. By a little touch of fussiness and a slightly exaggerated tip, he contrived to leave an impression on the porter who carried his bag to the train which he hoped would be remembered. Walton always dined in the restaurant car. Brackley was in two minds whether to carry his impersonation as far as that. The car was well lighted, and some of these waiters had long memories and sharp eyes. He decided to venture, and had no cause to regret it. The attendant asked him if he would have a Guinness as usual, and remarked that it was some time since he had seen him on that train and hadn't he grown a little thinner? Brackley, taking care not to show his teeth, which were more irregular than Walton's, agreed that he had, and drank off his Guinness in the rather noisy manner that Walton always affected. He left the dining-car just before the train ran into New Street, taking care not to overdo the limp.

As he made his way back to his compartment he reflected with the conscious pride of the artist that the campaign had been a complete success. What was left to be done was comparatively simple, and that had been prepared with the same methodical detail as the rest. At New Street station Walton would abruptly and finally disappear. His suitcase would go into the railway cloakroom, to be discovered, no doubt, in due course when the hue and cry for him had begun. Walking through carefully reconnoitred back streets, Brackley would make his way from the station to the furnished room where a change of clothes and identity awaited him. Next day, in London, the van in which Walton's body was now stiffening would drive quietly from Boulter's Mews to the garage in Kent, where a resting place was prepared for its burden beneath six inches of newly laid concrete. There would be nothing to connect that unobtrusive journey with a young man last seen a hundred miles the other side of London.

"It Takes Two . . ."

The trail would end at Birmingham, and there enquiries would begin—and end. Walton's parents, who were expecting him for the night, were unlikely to inform the police when he failed to arrive. The first alarm would probably be sounded by Watkinshaws, when the diamonds they were expecting were not delivered in the morning. Whether Walton's disappearance was held to be voluntary or not was an academic question which it would be interesting to follow in the newspaper reports. But he judged that when the state of Walton's finances was revealed the police would be cynical enough to write him off as yet another trusted employee who had yielded to temptation when his debts got out of hand. A hunt for a live Walton, fugitive from justice, would be an additional assurance that Walton dead would rest undisturbed.

As the lights of New Street showed through the carriage windows, Brackley tested in his mind the links of the chain he had forged. Were they adequate? The newspaper seller—the taxi-driver—the porter—the waiter—would they come forward when required? Would they remember him with certainty? Human testimony was fallible, after all, and the chain might snap somewhere. Yet short of proclaiming himself aloud as Walton on the station platform there was nothing further he could do.

He was gazing absently at the elderly lady who shared his compartment when it suddenly came to his mind that there was still something that might be done, a last artistic touch to put the issue beyond a doubt. Her suitcase was on the rack above her head, and his—Walton's—lay next to it. He noticed for the first time that they were remarkably alike. (It was a cheap line from Oxford Street, he knew. He had bought the twin of it himself, in case it was wanted for his impersonation but he had not needed it.) Seizing the chance which a kind fate provided, he rose

G   97

quickly when the train stopped, took her bag from its place and stepped out on to the platform.

It worked like a charm. Before he had limped half the length of the train his late companion had overtaken him, carrying his case and calling on him to stop.

"Excuse me," she piped, in a high, carrying voice, "but you've made a mistake. That's my bag you've got in your hand."

Brackley smiled tolerantly.

"I'm afraid you've made a mistake yourself, ma'am," he said. "You've got your own bag there. You see how alike they are."

"But I'm *positive!*" the old lady shrieked. She was doing her stuff magnificently, as if she had been coached for the part. "It was right above my head and you took it. That's my bag you've got. I'd know it anywhere."

Just as he had hoped, the form of a railway policeman loomed magnificently on to the scene.

"What's going on here?" he asked.

The lady drew breath to speak, but Brackley got in first. He was not going to lose the opportunity he had worked for.

"This lady seems to think I've stolen her bag, officer," he said. "I've done nothing of the sort. I'm a perfectly respectable person. My name is Walton, and I'm employed by Mallard's, the London jewellers. I've my business card here if you'd like to see it, and——"

"That'll do, sir, that'll do," said the constable good-humouredly. "Nobody's said anything about stealing yet."

"Of course not," the lady put in. "It's a mistake, that's what I keep telling him. But I want my bag, all the same."

"Quite so, madam." The officer was enjoying himself hugely. "Now let's have a look at them." He laid them side by side upon the platform. "They *are* alike, aren't they? No labels, no marks. You careless people! That's the way luggage gets lost, and then it's all blamed on to the railways. What do you say, Mister——"

"Walton is the name."

"Have you any objection to my opening one of these? That will settle it once for all."

"Not the smallest."

"And you, madam?"

"Not at all."

"Here goes, then."

He took Walton's suitcase, put it upon a bench and unfastened the catch. The lid opened and the pitiless glare of the station lights illuminated what it held. They shone down upon the myriad facets of a mass of jewellery, hastily crammed together, and on top of all a rubber-handled cosh, its tip hideous with a congealed mass of blood and hair— white hair, the hair of old Nicholas Mallard, who even now was lying huddled beneath his counter in Fentiman Street where Walton had left him.

Death of a Blackmailer

The detective-inspector and the county pathologist were at the mortuary.

"It's a rum business," said the inspector. "This fellow was a blackmailer all right. We'd suspected him for some time, but nobody would talk. It's the old story. He drives one of his victims a bit too hard, and this is the result. That's plain enough. What I can't understand . . ."

Sybil Mainwaring, verging on middle age, but still handsome in a rather hard style of good looks, held her head high in the society that centred round the county town of Markhampton. She was well off, well connected, married to a leader in local circles, herself prominent in the affairs of the neighbourhood, a pillar of respectability. Michael Jaye was employed in Mainwaring's office in Markhampton. He was at least fifteen years her junior, vulgar, uneducated and penniless. She had met him at a staff party and had fallen in love with him at first sight. She knew him to be in every respect hopelessly inferior to herself, but with her eyes wide open she had continued to love him, passionately and unreasonably, but—as she fondly imagined—secretly.

It was an incredible folly for a woman in her position to commit. Nobody who knew her would have believed that she would ever put herself in a position where she could be blackmailed. But anybody who knew her really well—and there were remarkably few who did—could have foretold that to hope to blackmail Sybil Mainwaring with impunity was an act of folly indeed.

The unsigned, typewritten letter was explicit in its terms. She was to leave fifty pounds in notes at a given spot by the roadside near her house between the hours of nine and ten o'clock that evening. The alternative was the exposure to her husband "and all others whom it might concern" of what the writer knew of her affair with Michael Jaye. Further details followed that proved beyond doubt that what the writer knew of that affair was both extensive and accurate.

Sybil burned the letter and ground the ashes to powder. Then she went out into the garden to think things over. At first she found it hard to believe that what had occurred was really true.

They had been so careful! Except for the half-witted old man who kept the garage where she left her car when she went to meet him, nobody had so much as seen them together. She went over in her mind all the precautions they had taken and could find no flaw. It was impossible that anything should have leaked out, and yet the impossible had happened. She, Sybil Mainwaring, was faced with a ruinous scandal unless she complied with a demand which, common sense told her, would only be met to be repeated again in due course. By turns, she felt frightened, humiliated and angry.

Anger was uppermost in her mind as she paced the lawn, but it was a cold, calculating anger. Now that the first shock was over, she took stock of the position with ruthless calm. Of one thing she was determined: that the unknown who had threatened her should pay for his presumption. She would not to go the police. A woman of her standing could not afford to do so. Nor would she consult Michael. Instinctively she felt that he would be useless in an affair of this sort. This was her business and she would deal with it herself—exactly how, she could not yet determine. A wasp settled on the grass in front of her and she crushed it under foot. If only she could destroy her unseen torturer as easily!

That evening she took an envelope containing fifty pounds and placed it between the roots of an oak tree that grew in the hedge bordering the lane outside her house. Having done so, she concealed herself in the entrance to the drive and set herself to watch. Her husband was away and she need account to no one for her movements. A few minutes after ten a motor-bicycle came down the lane and stopped opposite the oak. The tail light was too dim for her to read the number plate, and the rider was no more than a blurred shape in mackintosh and goggles. The rider dismounted, apparently to make some adjustment to his seat, and in doing so, looked cautiously in both directions. Then in a quick movement he scooped the envelope from its resting-place, remounted and rode rapidly off to the main road. Looking after it, she saw the headlight of the machine swing left-handed in the direction of the town.

So that's how it's done! she thought, as she went back into the house. So simple, and yet so efficient! She was fifty pounds poorer and no nearer to finding out who the blackmailer was and where he came from. And when the performance was repeated—as it surely would be—she would be no nearer still.

It was while she was undressing for bed that she remembered the wasp in the garden and an idea came to her. As a child she had been told by an old gardener how to find a wasps' nest. All you had to do, he said, was to watch a homing wasp as far as you could see it. Then

go to the place where it passed from your view and wait
for the next wasp flying in the same direction. Follow
that to the limits of your vision and wait for the next one.
Sooner or later, you will find yourself at the nest. What was
true of wasps should be true of larger, fouler pests. Sybil
went to sleep feeling that perhaps she had not wasted
fifty pounds after all.

The next demand arrived a fortnight later. Again it
was for fifty pounds. Again she placed the money in the
tree roots in the lane. But this time she waited in a car at
the junction of the lane with the main road. At five minutes
past ten a motor-cycle swung out of the lane and roared
off towards Markhampton. Following, she was able to
keep it in view right into the main street of the town. She
lost sight of it finally when it turned the corner past the
church. By the time she had reached that point it had
vanished into one of a number of side-streets which inter-
sected the main thoroughfare thereabouts.

So far, so good. She had had a good view of the cycle in
the street lights and would know it again. Next time—or
the time after, it mattered not—she would track the wasp
to its nest. The excitement of the chase strong upon her,
she waited with positive impatience for the next anony-
mous letter, and when it came she left the money in the
lane as cheerfully as an angler baiting a swim for fish. By
the time it had been taken from its hiding-place she was
already in position at the church corner. The hunter had
become the hunted.

It cost Mrs. Mainwaring in all five instalments of fifty
pounds each to establish exactly where her money was
being taken. The chase led her eventually to a small block
of buildings in the business quarter of the town. A little
simple research satisfied her that it consisted entirely of
offices which were normally deserted at night. When the

sixth summons came, she did not go to the expense of leaving money in the lane. Instead, she left an envelope stuffed with waste paper, and drove straight into the town.

As the climax approached, Sybil felt positively exhilarated. Michael had been moody and depressed that afternoon, but she had rallied him by the sheer force of her light-heartedness. She was about to put an end to the creature that menaced her existence and the thought gave her a savage joy. The fact that Michael would never even know the peril in which they had stood added a keen edge to her pleasure.

At half-past ten she parked her car in a side street near her destination and walked the rest of the way. Her bag was in her hand, and in the bag was the automatic pistol which she had taken from her husband's desk. In the yard of the office block she saw a familiar motor-cycle. One window, on an upper floor, was illuminated. The side entrance of the building was ajar. Quietly she pushed it open and tiptoed up the dark stairs. A faint bar of light shone beneath the door of a room near the second landing. She pulled the pistol from her bag and walked straight in.

It was a small room with a large desk in it. Seated at the further side of the desk was a man, his head bent low over a pile of papers. He looked up at the sound of her entrance. She found herself staring into the astonished face of Michael Jaye.

She had known it all along. At the back of her mind she had always been sure that only one person in the world could know the truth about her and Michael, and that was Michael himself. But she had not believed it. She had refused to believe that he could be so base as to take her favours and turn them into hard cash, because against all sense and reason she had loved him, worthless

104

though she knew him to be. Now with the proof before her eyes she did not hesitate. The bullet took Michael squarely in the heart, and he fell backwards in his chair without a cry, the look of astonishment still upon his handsome young face.

". . . What I can't understand," the detective-inspector was saying, "is *this*."

"This" was a body, neatly laid out upon the mortuary slab.

"I don't follow," said the pathologist. "Isn't this the blackmailer you were talking about?"

"Lord, no. This is a young chap called Jaye. His only trouble was that he was too fond of the women. Here's the blackmailer next to him. Old Wickfield. He kept a garage just outside the town as a blind, and passed for simple-minded—which he wasn't, by any manner of means. We found him in the back room of his office with his head stove in. Master Jaye had one of his demand notes in his pocket, so that seems easily explained. But if so, what was Jaye doing in the front room of the same office with a bullet through him? Can you answer that one, doctor?"

"You answer your own questions," said the pathologist. "I have troubles enough of my own. When I've finished with this pair I've got to go out to do the post mortem on Mrs. Mainwaring. They fished her car out of the river this morning with her inside it. Funny thing for a sensible woman like that to do, wasn't it? It just shows, you never can tell with women drivers."

The Old Flame

To commit a murder on a Bank Holiday at a popular seaside resort in broad daylight argues a good deal of courage, of a sort; but courage was the one good quality in which Jack Saunders was not deficient.

In fact, when he began to make his plans for the elimination of Maggie, he soon realized that, as so often happens, the boldest course was the safest.

In some ways he genuinely regretted the necessity of what he was about to do, but once he had recognized that Maggie was an insurmountable obstacle to his career, he firmly put any useless repining to one side.

A phrase from a bit of poetry learned by heart at school —that must have been in his last term before he was expelled—came faintly back to his memory. Something about rising on stepping stones of our dead selves to higher things. It seemed oddly appropriate—with this important difference, that it was on the stepping stone of Maggie's dead self that he proposed to rise.

As to the higher things—they, of course, were represented by Mary Rossiter—Mary and her money and her absurdly gullible family, who had taken him at his face value and accepted him as Mary's fiancé without making the smallest inquiry into his past. Saunders could not but grin when he thought of the Rossiters.

They would be sailing back to Australia once they had seen their daughter wedded to the gentlemanly Englishman who had been so kind and useful to them during their visit to the old country. They were in Paris now, buying Mary's trousseau, and he was to join them there for a little holiday—at their expense, of course.

Once the wedding was over they would not trouble him, but Maggie would—Maggie with her prison record as an expert sneak thief and pickpocket and, what was worse, her knowledge of his prison record.

It had been all that he could do to keep her in the background while he was cultivating the acquaintance of the Rossiters. Already she had tried a little gentle blackmail. Decidedly, there was not room in his life for Maggie and Mary.

And so to Bank Holiday, the day on which Saunders was to sail to meet the Rossiters in Paris, the day which he had decided on as Maggie's last.

To all appearances, nothing could have been more innocent than the little jaunt to the seaside that he proposed, and with which Maggie, who had been pestering him for his company for some time, fell in so readily.

Nothing more innocent than the elderly family saloon in which they pottered in an endless string of other elderly family saloons along the road to the coast that morning. (Somewhere a family was wondering what had become of their saloon, which they had incautiously left unattended in the West End overnight. It had fresh number plates now and a skilfully altered licence.)

Nothing more natural than that the drive should have ended on the downs overlooking the harbour where the Channel boat was making ready to sail. And if the couple in the car chose to recline on the back seat very close in each other's arms, well, could anything be more natural than that?

The Old Flame

There was a sharp breeze blowing in from the sea across the top of the hill, and the car was only one of dozens parked near by, occupied by other couples similarly employed.

A flight of jet aircraft screamed overhead. Under cover of the sound Saunders slipped out of the car.

By the time that the heads and eyes of the throng of holidaymakers had turned from following them, he was yards away from it, an inconspicuous unit in the mass, making his way down a cliff path towards the sea.

It had been extraordinarily easy, he told himself—so easy that he almost felt apologetic towards the girl who had allowed herself to be snuffed out with so little trouble.

She had guessed, as he had expected that she would, that this Bank Holiday outing was in the nature of a farewell; but, as he had not expected, she had not made a scene when she realized it.

It was the only respect in which things had not gone exactly according to plan.

He had braced himself for a quarrel, but there had been none. The foul-mouthed little thief had been sweet forgiveness itself.

She had only asked for a last kiss. And what a kiss! Saunders's lips still tingled with it as he strode nonchalantly along.

Which, of course, had made things childishly simple. A commando training in unarmed combat qualified a man to do harder things than squeezing the life out of a girl already limp and helpless in one's arms.

It was simply a matter of remembering one's instructions about pressure points . . .

All the same, it was a pity. Maggie must have loved him after all. Mary would never learn to kiss like that.

Perhaps he had been wrong and could have kept them both. For a moment Saunders wondered whether it had been right to murder Maggie.

Still keeping up his unhurried stroll, Saunders approached the harbour. He had worked to a careful time-table, and like everything else on this successful day, it fitted perfectly.

The boat-train was just coming in. A flood of chattering tourists surged towards the Customs sheds. Saunders allowed himself to be caught up in the crowd and waited patiently as it marshalled itself into the inevitable queue.

Slowly now, step by step, they moved forward, jostling, laughing, bumping one another with their suitcases and haversacks. Somewhere ahead a tired voice was chanting: "British passports this way! Have your passports ready, please!"

It was not until he had nearly reached the barrier that Saunders felt in his breast pocket—felt once, twice and yet again in desperate unbelief. Then he fell out of the queue and began to go through all the pockets in his suit, in vain.

He tore open the little handbag that he carried and found nothing there but his things for a night or two away from home.

"Have your passports ready, please!" the voice repeated just over his head. "British passports this way!"

A long time after, it seemed to Saunders, another voice close by said to him,

"Lost your passport, sir? That's a bit of bad luck. Perhaps you had your pocket picked? It happens here sometimes, you know."

Saunders nodded dumbly. He could still feel Maggie's arms as they went tenderly round him in that last, close embrace.

"Afraid you can't go on board without a passport," the voice went on. "Spoiled your holiday, I'm afraid. But I shouldn't worry too much, sir, just give the particulars in at the office. The police will find it all right."

And sure enough, they did.

"As the Inspector Said . . ."

It would be impossible to say precisely when Charles Darrell and Sonia French made up their minds to murder Sonia's husband, Robert. Engagements to commit a crime, like engagements to marry, are sometimes agreed upon by the parties concerned long before anything is put into words. In the situation in which they found themselves, for persons of their character, murder was the obvious solution, and now it was merely a question of finding a suitable opportunity to carry it out.

Sonia had been married to Robert for ten years. He was nearly twice her age, and for at least eight years out of the ten she had treated the weak little man with a bored contempt to which he—absorbed in his books and his collections of silver and porcelain—seemed completely impervious. She had known Charles for six months. They had been lovers for four. Things were fast moving towards a crisis. People were beginning to talk. It could only be a matter of time before Robert became aware of the position. She knew well enough that beneath his mild detachment lurked a rock-like obstinacy on certain matters, and that divorce was of them. More important, neither she nor Charles had a penny of their own. Robert was rich. The proceeds of his collections alone would provide enough for his widow and his successor.

Ironically enough, it was a policeman who presented them with the ideal method of attaining their object. The

111

local inspector called one evening at the Frenches' house, when Charles, as usual, had dropped in for a chat on his way home from work. The officer had come with a warning. There had been a number of burglaries in the district recently, he told them, and the perpetrator was still at large.

"We know who the man is," he said, "and it can't be long now before we catch up with him. But meanwhile, short-handed as we are, we're very worried. He carries a gun, and although we shall never prove it against him, we know he has a murder to his credit just over the border in the next county. Now this house, Mr. French, is in rather an isolated position. Except for Mr. Darrell here, you have no near neighbour. You have a quantity of valuables which make this place very attractive from our man's point of view, and you have no indoor staff. I suggest that it would be as well to take precautions."

Robert cleared his throat in the way that never failed to grate on Sonia's nerves.

"Er—what sort of precautions had you in mind?" he asked.

"Well—in your place, sir, I should certainly begin by buying a reliable house dog."

"I don't like dogs," said Robert flatly.

"Then I suggest that for the time being, while this man is at large, you should send your best things to the bank for safe custody. All this silver, for example——"

Robert looked round the room, crammed with the fruits of years of ardent collecting. His faded eyes seemed to brighten as they lit on one choice piece after another.

"Send them away! I shouldn't care to do that," he said.

"Well, sir," said the inspector rather tartly, "don't say I didn't warn you, that's all." And he took his departure.

After he had gone, Charles said in the deep, vibrant voice that contrasted so strongly with Robert's thin pipe, "Well, the inspector didn't bother to warn me, I noticed. He knows I've got nothing worth stealing. But if this gunman did visit me by mistake I fancy I should make him regret it. I've still got my revolver from the last war and I shouldn't think twice before I used it."

He rose and stretched himself, six feet two inches of magnificent masculinity. Sonia did not trouble to conceal the admiration in her face.

"I should be sorry for the burglar who tried conclusions with you, Charles," she said. "Robert, what would *you* do if I woke you up in the night and told you someone was making off with your precious silver? Put your head under the bedclothes and pretend you hadn't heard?"

"On the contrary, I should come straight downstairs."

"You'd be much too frightened to do anything of the sort."

"I should be frightened, certainly, but there is always a reasonable chance that the intruder would be equally frightened. House-breaking must be a nerve-racking business. Besides, he might be amenable to reason. If I could make him understand how small the value of this silver would be when melted down compared to——"

"Robert, you are ridiculous!"

"Perhaps I am, Sonia, but you asked me what I should do, and I gave you the best answer in my power. Now, if you will excuse me, I have some sale catalogues I want to look after before dinner. Give Charles a drink before he goes."

He shuffled off to his study, leaving the two together. Before the first cocktail had slipped down their throats the plan for his extinction had been perfected.

Three nights later Sonia lay awake in the room which, to her disgust, Robert still insisted on sharing with her.

The illuminated hands of her watch pointed to ten minutes to two. Ten minutes, that was, to wait before the time agreed upon for Charles to make his entry. She strained her ears in the darkness, none the less, every nerve in her body tense with excitement. Above the deep breathing of her husband in the twin bed beside her own she fancied that she could hear stealthy sounds—the creak of a door in a room downstairs, a light footfall on a loose board in the hall. But even as she heard them she knew that her imagination was playing her false. A bat flew past the window, echoing the noise of an unoiled hinge with its high-pitched squeak, and the antique tallboy at the end of the room cracked its joints in the dark as she had so often before heard it do in the long hours of sleepless nights. She set her teeth and composed herself to watch and wait while the hands of the watch crept slowly on.

Punctual to the minute, the sound she was awaiting reached her. This time there could be no mistake. There was the tinkle of breaking glass, followed by the groan of a window being pushed up. In the silence of the sleeping house it was as startling as a clap of thunder in her ears, but Robert slept on as peacefully as ever. She waited a little longer, listened for the thud of Charles's feet as he landed inside the window, and then leaped out of bed to play her part.

"Robert!" She shook him violently by the shoulder. "Robert! Wake up! There's somebody downstairs!"

Robert struggled reluctantly into wakefulness.

"What's that?" he murmured. "Someone downstairs? Nonsense, Sonia! You're imagining things! Just because that inspector fellow—— By Jove!" He sat up in bed. "There *is* someone, though! I'd better go down, I suppose."

Reluctantly, but without hesitation, he swung his thin legs to the floor, groped for his slippers, put on his shabby

114

grey dressing-gown and went out of the room. Alone in the dark, Sonia waited breathlessly for what she knew must follow. She waited for what seemed to her an unendurably long time, but was actually less than half a minute. Then, everything seemed to happen at once. There was the snap of a switch and a faint glow of electric light showed beneath the bedroom door. Almost at the same instant she heard a startled exclamation in her husband's voice, cut short by an explosion that echoed through the house. Then, so hard upon one another that one sound seemed to blend into the next, a heavy fall, a door being flung violently open and the patter of flying feet on the gravel path outside.

She let the footsteps die into the distance before she made the next move. Charles must have time to make his getaway before she called the police, but it would be unsafe to wait too long, in case any stray passer-by had heard the shot. Then she switched on her bedside lamp and got out of bed. Now that it was all over, she felt strangely calm, exhilarated even. As she crossed the room her thoughts raced ahead of her. She knew in advance just what she would say to the police, what her demeanour at the inquest would be. How soon could she marry Charles without exciting comment? Would six months be long enough? They would go to Venice for their honeymoon. She had always wanted to see Venice . . .

As she reached the door it opened in her face and Robert shuffled in.

"Robert!" For a long moment she could say nothing else. She could only stare at him in sickened apprehension. He looked back at her in silence—pale, dishevelled, but indubitably alive.

"What—what has happened?" she faltered.

Robert cleared his throat.

"Er—he got away," he said. "I'm afraid he's taken a lot of stuff with him—an awful lot of stuff. Some of my best pieces. I ought to have taken advice and sent it to the bank. It was foolish of me—very."

"But I heard a shot. I thought you—you're not hurt, Robert?"

"No, Sonia, I'm not hurt. But I'm afraid I must prepare you for some bad news. It is Charles. The dear, brave fellow must have been watching and followed the man in, to protect us. He—he's at the foot of the stairs. I fear there is nothing we can do for him. He——"

Sonia pitched forward in a dead faint.

With some difficulty Robert contrived to lift his wife from the floor and lay her on the bed. Then he made his way downstairs. As he reached the bottom step he had to walk over the body which lay huddled close against it on the floor. He did so without a tremor, glancing down only to avoid treading in the pool of blood which was spreading slowly over the hall carpet. But when he passed into the dining-room, and looked once more at the sideboard, swept bare of its treasures of silver plate, there were tears of emotion in his eyes.

He closed the door softly and went into his study. The telephone was there and he had to communicate with the police. But before doing so, he was careful to clean and oil the little pistol in his dressing-gown pocket and lock it away in his desk. Having eliminated one disturbance from his well-ordered life, he was naturally anxious to avoid further trouble for himself. As the inspector said, it was as well to take precautions.

Death Among Friends

"And now," said the chairman, "I should say a word in tribute to the management and staff of your company, to whose devoted efforts the success of the year's trading is so largely due. We at Wimblingham are, indeed, a band of brothers. I like to think that the heads of our various departments are not merely my loyal assistants but my personal friends. . . ."

Even for a speech at a company meeting, it was a grotesque untruth. To do him justice, however, Sir Charles Gilray was not conscious of deliberately lying. The truth or untruth of the words did not concern him. He said this sort of thing because it was the sort of thing to say. The shareholders expected it. A more sensitive man in his position would have been aware that he was cordially detested by most of his subordinates at the Wimblingham motor-works. On the other hand, a more sensitive man would not have been in his position, so the question did not arise.

But it would have taken an exceptionally sensitive man to realize that in the case of Powell, the chief designer at the works, he had aroused a feeling of loathing which could be assuaged by nothing short of murder. For Powell did not wear his heart, or his hatreds, on his sleeve. Small, dark and wiry, he was not unlike Sir Charles to look at, but in all other respects he was utterly different. He was intensely shy, and could no more have talked platitudes

117

to a public meeting than jumped over the moon. He could express himself only in his work, which approached genius, and on which the fortunes of the company were mainly based. What went on in Powell's mind when it was not occupied with problems of mechanics was something that nobody—least of all the chairman—ever knew or suspected.

This was the man whom Sir Charles had contrived, in a score of different ways, mortally to offend. Not once during the ten years of his service with the company had Powell by word or sign expressed resentment. He was not the man to dissipate his hatred in futile little explosions. Instead, he had treasured each petty slight and insult as a miser treasures coins, until, like a miser, he had become half crazy from counting over and over the hoard that had obsessed him.

For some time past all that had been needed to push Powell to the point of committing murder was one last provocation. Then Sir Charles provided it, and with a generosity foreign to his nature, gave for good measure an ideal opportunity to carry out his own destruction. Oddly enough, the provocation did not affect Powell personally. It struck at him through his friend—probably the only friend he had in the world.

Only the attraction of opposites could explain Powell's friendship for McDougall, the works manager at Wimblingham. McDougall was a giant of a man, red-headed and raw-boned, with a temper that was the terror and admiration of the men under him. He did not profess to understand Powell and tolerated his silent devotion without ever really returning it. All the affection of which his violent nature was capable—and that was great—was reserved for his wife, a woman of rare beauty, ten years younger than himself.

118

Death Among Friends

Powell was one of the first to discover that Sir Charles and Sylvia McDougall were lovers. He was certainly not the last, for in a small community like Wimblingham an affair of this kind cannot be kept secret for long—except, as sometimes happens, from the husband. But what for others was a subject of cynical amusement was for Powell, quite literally, a matter of life and death. Himself a profoundly unhappy man, he had found compensation in McDougall's happiness. That this should be menaced by his own hated enemy filled his cup of gall to overflowing. Rapidly and methodically, he made his plans to avenge them both at one blow.

He had little time to lose if he was to eliminate Sir Charles before some kind acquaintance destroyed Mc-Dougall's peace of mind for ever. But his victim made things easy for a murderer, who, by reason of his calling, naturally thought in terms of mechanics. Night shifts were being worked at Wimblingham just then, and Gilray took advantage of this to visit Sylvia on evenings when McDougall was taking a turn of night duty. Powell ascertained that on these occasions he left his car in a quiet lane within a stone's throw of McDougall's house. The lane ran steeply to the foot of the hill, where it turned to the right along the bank of the deep, sullen river Wimble. It was a sharp bend, and there had been a fatality a year or two before when a car had failed to take the corner and plunged through the fence into the stream below.

It was a very simple matter for Powell, that brilliant designer, to design just such another fatality. He found Gilray's car in the expected place one dark winter's evening and ran it silently down the hill. There he started the engine and drove quickly to his private office on the outskirts of the factory buildings. The chairman's big car

119

was a familiar sight in the neighbourhood at all hours and nobody questioned its presence there. In a dark overcoat and wide-brimmed hat drawn over his eyes, Powell looked sufficiently like Sir Charles to deceive any casual passer-by who saw him alight.

In the deserted office he picked up the tools he required. Then he returned by a roundabout route to a point in the lane a few yards above where the car had formerly stood and out of sight of McDougall's house.

Powell could have dismantled and reassembled one of his own machines blindfold and he scarcely needed the assistance of his pocket torch to do what was necessary. Ten minutes later he allowed the car to roll very slowly down the slope and brought it to a halt with the hand-brake. It was now in the same position as before, and to all appearance in the same condition. The only difference was that now the steering wheel could not travel more than five degrees to the right and the foot-brake was useless.

The trap was set. With a warm feeling of confidence Powell opened the car door and stepped out. As he did so, a tremendous blow struck him on the nape of the neck and he pitched forward on to his face.

McDougall, a blood-stained tyre-lever in his vast hand, glowered down at the sprawled body at his feet.

"So it was true, after all, what they were saying!" he muttered. "You thieving bastard!"

He did not trouble to turn the body over. Contemptuously he picked it up by the coat collar and hurled it into the back of the car.

"Lie you there, till I can dispose of you and your damned car too!" he said.

Then, jumping into the driver's seat, he started the engine and drove down the lane.

Death Among Friends

"I must here mention," the chairman went on, "the loss through a tragic mishap of two of our most valued servants. We may say of them, indeed, that they were lovely and pleasant in their lives and in their death they were not divided. I would ask you to stand for a few moments in tribute to their memory. . . ."

The Story of Hermione

When Richard Armstrong, explorer and mountaineer, disappeared in a blizzard in the Karakoram, his only daughter Hermione was just turned twenty. He bequeathed her a good deal of unusual experience gathered in remote parts of the world, but very little else. For more tangible aids to living she had to look to her uncle Paul, who was in a position to supply them on a very lavish scale. Paul Armstrong had confined his explorations to the square mile of the earth's surface lying east of Temple Bar and found them extremely fruitful.

Hermione was a slender, fragile creature, with observant blue eyes, a determined chin and a small mouth that remained closed unless speech was absolutely necessary. She gave her uncle and aunt no sort of trouble, submitted quietly to the horse-play which passed for humour with her tall, athletic cousins Johnny and Susan, and kept her own counsel. In that cheerful, noisy household she passed almost unobserved.

In the following winter Susan Armstrong was killed by a fall in the hunting field. Six months later, Johnny, playing a ridiculous game of leap-frog with Hermione on the spring-board of his parents' swimming-bath, slipped, crashed into the side of the bath and broke his neck. Paul and his wife had worshipped their children with uncritical adoration. The double blow deprived them of all motive for living, and when shortly afterwards they fell victims to

an influenza epidemic they made not the slightest resistance.

Even with death duties at their present level, Hermione
was a considerable heiress. With the calm deliberation
that had always characterised her she set out to look
for a husband suitable to her station in life. After carefully
considering the many applicants for the post, she finally
selected Freddy Fitzhugh. It was an altogether admirable
choice. Freddy was well-to-do, well connected, good-
looking and no fool. Their courtship was unexciting but
satisfactory, the engagement was announced and on a
fine spring morning they went together to Bond Street
to choose a ring.

Freddy took her to Garland's, those aristocrats among
jewellers, and the great Mr. Garland himself received them
in his private room behind the shop. Hermione examined
the gems which he showed her with dispassionate care
and discussed them with an expertise that astonished
Freddy as much as it delighted Mr. Garland. She ended
by choosing a diamond as superior to the rest as Freddy
had been to his rival suitors, and they took their leave.

Meanwhile, the shop outside had not been idle. Shortly
after the door of Mr. Garland's room closed on Freddy
and his beloved two thick-set men entered and asked the
assistant at the counter to show them some diamond
bracelets. They proved to be almost as difficult to please
as Hermione, without displaying her knowledge of precious
stones, and before long there were some thousands of
pounds worth of brilliants on the counter for their inspection.

To the bored assistant it began to seem as though they
would never come to a decision. Then, just as Mr. Garland was bowing Freddy and Hermione out of the shop,
everything began to happen at once. A large saloon car

slowed down in the street outside, and paused with its engine running. At the same moment one of the men with lightning speed scooped up half a dozen bracelets and made for the door, while his companion sent the door-keeper flying with a vicious blow to the stomach.

Freddy, who had stopped to exchange a few words with Mr. Garland, looked round and saw to his horror that Hermione was standing alone in front of the doorway, directly in the path of the man. She made no attempt to avoid him as he bore down upon her. It flashed across Freddy's mind that she was too paralysed by fear to move. Hopelessly, he started to run forward as the man crashed an enormous fist into Hermione's face.

The blow never reached its mark. With a faintly superior smile, Hermione shifted her position slightly at the last moment. An instant later the raider was flying through the air to land with a splintering of glass head first against the show case. The whole affair had only occupied a few seconds of time.

"You never told me you could do Ju-Jutsu, Hermione," said Freddy, when they eventually left the shop.

"Judo," Hermione corrected him. "My father had me taught by an expert. It comes in handy sometimes. Of course, I'm rather out of practice."

"I see," said Freddy. "You know, Hermione, there are quite a few things about you I didn't know."

They parted. Hermione had an appointment with her hairdresser. Freddy went for a quiet stroll in the park. Then he took a taxi to Fleet Street, where he spent most of the afternoon browsing in the files of various news-papers.

They met again at dinner that evening. Freddy came straight to the point.

"I've been looking at the reports of the inquest on your cousin Johnny," he said.

"Yes?" said Hermione with polite interest.

"It was very odd the way that he shot off the spring-board on to the edge of the bath. How exactly did it happen?"

"I explained it all to the coroner. I just happened to move at the critical moment and he cannoned off me."

"Hard luck on Johnny."

"Very."

"Hard luck on that chap this morning that you just happened to move at the critical moment. I don't think you told the coroner that you could do this Judo stuff?"

"Of course not."

"Hard luck on Susan, too, taking that fall out hunting."

"*That*," said Hermione flatly, "was pure accident. I told her she couldn't hold the horse."

Freddy sighed.

"I'll have to give you the benefit of the doubt over that one," he said. "But I'm afraid the engagement's off."

Hermione looked at the diamond on her finger and screwed her hand into a tight little fist.

"I can't stop you breaking it off, Freddy," she said. "But you'll find it very expensive."

He did. Very expensive indeed. But he thought it well worth the money. As has been said, Freddy was no fool.

A Surprise for Christmas

They had had their Christmas dinner in the middle of the day because this year there were children in the house. Turkey and plum pudding and all the drinks that rightfully go with them had reduced Jimmy Blenkiron to a pleasant state of somnolence. Lying back in an armchair in front of the library fire, he could just discern the red glow of the logs through his half-shut eyes. His hands still caressed the glass that had held his liqueur brandy. It was half-past three and he was at peace with the world.

Anne Blenkiron came into the room and dropped thankfully on to a sofa beside her husband's chair.

"Thank goodness, there's the washing-up done at last," she said.

"Good for you," said Jimmy approvingly. Always a pattern of consideration where his wife was concerned, he shifted his legs slightly to allow some of the warmth from the fire to reach in her direction.

"Why didn't you get the children to help you?" he asked.

"Oh, they're much too busy on their own affairs. They are preparing a surprise for you at tea-time."

"Wonderful they've got the energy to do anything after what they put away at dinner," said Jimmy with a yawn. "What sort of a surprise?"

"That you're not to know. I'm in the secret, of course. But I think you'll like it. It's their own idea entirely."

"Nice kids," commented Jimmy tolerantly.

A Surprise for Christmas

"You're sure you don't mind having them?"

"Not a bit—so long as they don't bother me, they're welcome. After all, they'd nowhere else to go, poor little devils. It was rotten luck their mother dying just before Christmas. I felt very sorry for them."

Jimmy set down his glass and stretched his legs once more to the blaze.

"Do you know," said Anne after a pause, "I think that Derek has a great look of his father."

"God forbid!" said Jimmy. Then, seeing the look on his wife's face, he added, "After all, Anne, even if he was your brother, you must admit that Billy was no sort of good."

Anne was staring into the fire, and her eyes were moist.

"Poor old Billy," she said. "Always hard up, always in trouble. The black sheep of the family, even when he was a little boy. I was very fond of him, all the same. And when he died——"

"Now, Anne, you're just being maudlin!"

Anne dabbed at her eyes with a handkerchief.

"I'm sorry," she said with a gulp. "I know it's silly of me, but I feel in a way we were responsible."

"Responsible? For a bomb hitting Eastbury Station? That's a new one on me. I'd always thought it was Hitler who was responsible."

"I know, but it was our fault that Billy was there, waiting for his train. He wanted to spend the night, and if we'd only let him——"

"Now look here, Anne," said Jimmy reasonably, "it's no manner of good getting morbid over what's past and done with. We were neither of us responsible. You were in bed with 'flu—don't you remember? I had to go out on Civil Defence duty—why, I was at Eastbury just after the incident and a nice shambles it was. Billy couldn't have stayed the night, even if I'd have had him—which I wouldn't."

127

"I know," said Anne, miserably, "I know . . ."

"Well, let's just forget it, shall we?"

"If only you could forget things by just wanting to——"
She pulled herself together. "Look at the time! I must go
and see about getting tea."

It was with an agreeable feeling of superiority that Jimmy
watched her go before he turned back to the fire again.
What bundles of nerves women were! Brooding over
things that had happened—ten, was it?—no, by jove,
twelve years ago! And all this nonsense about forgetting
—you could forget anything if you gave your mind to it,
with enough time, and a good digestion and a sensible
outlook on life. Anything.

It was a remarkable thing, Jimmy reflected, that until
his wife's ill-timed reminiscences had brought it back to
his mind he had genuinely forgotten that he had killed
his brother-in-law on the night of the raid on Eastbury.
And it wasn't just a figure of speech, either. Even with the
fellow's son and daughter staying in the house, he had
really and truly forgotten what he had done to their
father. (Not that it would have made any difference to
his treatment of them if he had remembered. It was not
their fault, and he bore them no malice.)

He grinned to himself. It *was* pretty extraordinary being
able to forget a thing like that. Nobody would believe it
if you told them—if you could tell anybody. A pity in a
way that you couldn't. It would show some people who
always pretended to know everything just how little they
knew about human nature. What they didn't understand
was that if you had no regrets there was no reason why
you should have inconvenient memories. Anne, in her
silly fashion, regretted her poor Billy, and that was why
she still let her conscience torment her over his death.

He had no regrets for that sneaking, blackmailing swine,
and consequently no conscience. It was as simple as that.

All the same thought Jimmy, indulging in the unusual
luxury of reminiscence, he had been pretty frightened at
the time. But for a marvellous stroke of luck he would
never have got away with it. If Jerry hadn't chosen to
come over that evening Billy's disappearance would have
taken a bit of explaining, and the newly dug patch in the
garden looked obvious enough next morning to anyone
who cared to make enquiries. But it had all ended happily.
Good old Civil Defence! No tiresome inquests in those days.
Billy's cigarette case shoved into the pocket of a coat
covering a fragment of somebody's carcass had been
evidence enough of identity.

As for the other matter, a man could do a lot to a garden
in twelve years, with Nature to help him.

In spite of the warmth of the fire, Jimmy found himself shivering. That was what came of remembering things.
Now he felt thoroughly upset, all thanks to Anne's
stupidity. He picked up his liqueur glass. Empty, of course.
Well, there was still time for another drink to set himself
up before tea. He made his way to the dining-room.

"Oh, Uncle Jimmy, you oughtn't to have come in!" His
niece Tessa looked up at him reproachfully from the floor.

Looking down, Jimmy saw the carpet covered with a
mass of shiny objects—silver tinsel, coloured glass balls
and miniature wax candles among them.

"What on earth are you up to?" he asked.

"It's your surprise, and now you've spoilt it because
it won't be a surprise any more."

"That's all right," said Jimmy kindly. "I'll look the other
way, and forget all about it in no time. I'm awfully good at
forgetting."

I   129

He turned to the sideboard and filled his glass. The warm spirit made him feel better again at once. He toasted himself in the looking-glass. "Here's to forgetting!" he murmured.

He put the glass down, and went through into the kitchen. Anne was buttering slices of bread for tea.

"You oughtn't to have gone in there," she said.

"So Tessa told me. What is it all about?"

"The children wanted to give you a Christmas tree, to thank you for having them to stay. Isn't it sweet of them? Tessa has been getting all the old decorations out of the attic."

"Really? That's jolly decent of them. It shows they appreciate things, doesn't it? They've kept it very dark. Where did they hide the tree? I haven't seen it anywhere."

"I told Derek he could get it out of the garden. You know, that little spruce at the end of the vegetable patch. It's just the right size. You don't mind, do you?"

"D'you mean to say he's cut down the little spruce——?"
It was all Jimmy could do not to laugh outright. After what he had been thinking of that afternoon the coincidence seemed irresistibly comic.

"No, dear, not cut down. I knew you wouldn't like that. I told him to dig it up very carefully by the roots, so that we could plant it again. That was all right, wasn't it?"

Jimmy turned and walked out of the room. It was a difficult thing to manage, but he walked. Once out of the house door he ran as he had not run for years. But even as he ran, he knew that it was too late. Fifty yards away he could see the top of the little spruce tremble and sink over to one side, and as he arrived breathless at the spot he saw his nephew standing there, staring incredulously down into the hole where its roots had been.

The Heel

The police car, summoned from County Headquarters
at Markhampton, skirted the aerodrome and drove
quickly on up the village street. It was half-past eight on a
fine spring morning, and the road was empty except for
a string of the American army trucks that now seemed a
permanent feature of the country roads in that particular
part of England. Sergeant Place, of the Markshire County
Constabulary, sitting beside the young detective who was
driving him, eyed them with disfavour. He had no objection to Americans as such. By and large, they were no
worse behaved than the natives. But their pattern of
misbehaviour was different, and to a man nurtured in
routine that was in itself an offence. This job at Hawthorn Cottage, now—ten to one there was an American
at the back of it, and that would mean trouble.

Hawthorn Cottage was an ancient, rather depressed
little house standing isolated on the farther side of the
village. It was typical of the small residences in the locality
whose owners had cashed in on the invasion by letting
them furnished to visiting officers at exorbitant rates. A
car containing the police surgeon drew up behind the
police car as it reached the entrance, and the three men
went into the house together.

It was something of a relief to the sergeant to find the
door opened by an obvious Englishman—a sallow, middle-
aged man in the discreet garb of a manservant.

The Heel

"Will you come this way, please?" he said in the accepted phrase of his profession, and led them upstairs to the best bedroom. He opened the door and stood aside for them to enter.

The man in the bed had apparently been dead some hours, for his body was already cold. He was in his middle forties, Sergeant Place judged. His features were round and indeterminate. He was dressed in expensive and rather garish silk pyjamas, which looked out of place in the shabbily furnished room. On the bedside table there were a half-empty bottle of whisky, an entirely empty glass, and a round cardboard box of the type used by chemists for dispensing pills, also empty. On the floor beside it was a letter with an envelope addressed simply, "Mr. William Harris." It had not come through the post.

Place gave some instructions to his assistant and left the room. He found the servant standing in the corridor just outside the door.

"Let's go downstairs, shall we?" he suggested. "We can talk better there."

The man preceded him down the narrow stairway into the sitting-room. Place eyed him narrowly as he stood, deferential and nervous, in front of the empty grate.

"You haven't been here long, have you?" he began.

"I—no, sir, only three days. We were in London before that. But how——"

"Easy," said Place with a grin. "You forgot to duck your head for the beam on the landing. This place was let furnished, I suppose. To an American?"

"Not American, actually, sir. Mr. Harris is—was—English. But he had lived in the States some years, I understood—and picked up some American habits, I may say, sir."

132

He was talking more easily now. Place's grin had an infectious quality about it.

"And what is your name?"

"Wilson, sir. Thomas Wilson."

"Well, Wilson, tell me: when did you find that your master was dead?"

"When I went in this morning to give him his cup of tea, sir. I didn't touch anything, but rang the police-station right away. I hope I did right."

"Quite right. And when had you last seen him before that?"

"Last night, sir, about 10.30. He'd given me the evening off and he was just getting into bed when I came in."

"And what can you tell me about Mr. Harris?"

"There's very little I can tell you, sir. I had only been with him two weeks altogether. He engaged me through Chiltern's—the domestic agency. You'll have heard of them, no doubt, sir. He was a little—well, strange in his ways, I can tell you that, sir."

"Strange? Well, naturally. You've just told me, he had American habits."

"Not in that way, I don't mean, sir. He was frightened."

"What of?"

"Oh—of people, sir. And of Americans, especially. That was why he took this house. He wanted to get right away from London, he told me—there were too many Americans there."

The idea of coming to Markshire to get away from that particular danger provoked Sergeant Place to laugh out-right.

"He chose the wrong spot to come to, then," he said. "Didn't he know about the air base in the village?"

"Apparently not, sir. I think it came as a great shock to him when he found out. Only yesterday he said to me——"

That was the worst of these nervous witnesses, Place reflected. Once help them to get over their fright and they'd ramble on for ever. It was time to get back to the matter in hand. He interrupted Wilson without ceremony.

"Do you know anything about this?" he said, producing the envelope which he had taken from the bedroom.

"That, sir? Oh yes. I gave it to Mr. Harris last night when I came in."

"Where did it come from?"

"The staff sergeant gave it to me to give him."

"I don't understand. What staff sergeant?"

"I was going to tell you, sir, when you interrupted me," the man said patiently. "It happened yesterday morning. Mr. Harris drove me down to the village to do some shopping. We were held up in the village street where they are doing road repairs. Only single-line traffic, you know, sir. There was an American army truck coming the other way. This staff sergeant was sitting beside the driver —left hand drive, of course, sir, so he came past next to Mr. Harris. He seemed to recognize him, sir."

"How did you know that?"

"He spoke to him, sir. Just one word. It sounded like —Blimey!"

"Not a very American word, Wilson. Are you sure it wasn't—Limey?"

"It could have been that, sir. What would that mean, if I might ask?"

"It's a slang word for an Englishman. Go on."

"Whatever it was, it seemed to upset Mr. Harris a lot, sir. He drove on as soon as the truck had passed, and never stopped in the village at all. We did our shopping in Markhampton. Then last night I saw the staff sergeant again."

"Where?"

"At the Spotted Dog, sir. I was spending my evening out there. The place was full of American soldiers, and he was with them. He recognized me at once, and spoke to me. He stood me a drink or two and then he—well, I suppose you might say he pumped me, sir."

"Found out who you were and where you were living and so on?"

"Just so, sir. Then just before closing time he asked the barman for a bit of paper and an envelope and wrote something and told me to give it to Mr. Harris. So I did, sir."

"And you don't know what the letter said?"

"Naturally not, sir." There was a world of reproach in the man's civil tones. Sergeant Place acknowledged the reproof with a wry smile.

"You might be interested to know. Here it is." The sergeant read:

"*Well, Limey, this is quite a surprise. I'll be looking in on your hidey-hole around noon tomorrow, so you'd best open up.*"

"Is that all, sir?"

"That's all. And it's signed—Joe."

"That would be the staff sergeant, no doubt, sir."

"Would you know him again if you saw him?"

"These Americans all look very much alike to me, sir, but I dare say I should."

"Well," said Place, putting the letter away, "that appears to be that. You gave him that letter, and he is dead. Dead from—from what, exactly, doctor?" he asked, as the police surgeon came into the room.

"One of the barbiturates, undoubtedly. I can't say more until we've had an analysis. Death took place about eight to ten hours ago, I should think. No sign of violence that I can see. If you don't want me further I shall be going now. Shall I make arrangements to have him moved?"

"Not just yet, thank you, Doctor. I'd rather not have any coming and going here till the afternoon. Perhaps we shall have a visitor about midday."

After seeing the doctor out, Place called upstairs.

"Percy?"

"Yes, Sarge?"

"Take the car round to the back of the house, will you? Somewhere where it won't be seen from the road."

Percy came downstairs.

"I've had a good look round his room," he observed. "Lovely clothes he's got. Yank stuff—very flash. I found this in a drawer; I thought it might interest you."

He handed the sergeant a slim bundle of press cuttings and went out to the car.

Place glanced at the papers in his hand. They were all from American newspapers and were arranged in reverse order of date. The top one on the bundle caught his eye. "*This morning John Benjamin Spencer went to the electric chair for the slaying of janitor Edward Hart*," it began. He delved a little further down, and found a familiar name. "*English-born William S. Harris, one-time associate of accused John B. Spencer; took the stand today as State witness . . .*"

"Will you be requiring me any more, sir?"

"No," said Place, intent on his reading. "Yes," he added immediately. "What did Mr. Harris do when you gave him the note?"

"He read it, sir."

"Anything else?"

"Then he sent me downstairs for the whisky and two glasses."

"Two glasses?"

The Heel

"Mr. Harris was like that," the man explained. "Very free and easy. Quite the American in his ways, for all he was as English as you or I. He asked me to have a drink with him. Not at all like any other gentleman I've been with."

Place looked at his unhealthy face, his unsteady, tobacco-stained fingers. "You drink quite a bit, don't you, Wilson?" he said.

"A trifle, sir, I must admit—on occasion."

"Was that how you came to lose your last post?"

"No, sir!" He was all virtuous indignation. "I've been in first-class service all my life, and always had a good character. My last position was with Lord Gaveston—five years in his lordship's service, and only lost that when the household broke up after the divorce. This place was beneath me altogether. I only took it because it was all Chiltern's had to offer at the time, and the money was good. Chiltern's will answer for me, sir—they know me there, and always pleased to recommend me to the best houses. Ask them now, if you don't believe me. Belgrave 8290, the number is. You can ring them on long-distance right away, if you like."

"That will do, Wilson. There's nothing to get excited about," said Place soothingly.

"I'm sorry, sir, but a man in my position has nothing but his character to depend on. I've had rather a shock, and—and I've had no breakfast this morning, yet."

"Just finish your story and take it quietly. You brought Mr. Harris the whisky, you were saying. . . ."

"That's right, sir. When I brought it up he was sitting on the side of his bed. He poured out two glasses, and we each had one. Then he told me to leave the bottle and his glass with him and said Goodnight. That's the last I saw of him till I found him this morning."

"Thank you, Wilson; you've been most helpful. Now go to your kitchen, and get yourself something to eat."

Place looked at his watch. It was just nine o'clock. That meant three hours to wait, if Staff Sergeant Joe was punctual. And if he chose not to keep his appointment—how many staff sergeants, he wearily wondered, would there be at the swarming air base who answered to the name of Joe? And how long would it take him to sort them out? It could have been worse, of course. The letter might have been signed Butch or Red. To judge from the delinquents who passed through his hands fifty per cent of the United States forces bore those outlandish names. But Joe was bad enough. Meanwhile, he must wait.

Waiting is part of police routine, and Place found it no great hardship. He had, for once, a comfortable chair to wait in and a bunch of press cuttings to while away the time. These he found to be the record of a very commonplace murder—the killing of a hapless employee in the course of a raid on a bank. And John B. Spencer, to judge from his photograph, had been a very commonplace young man—as murderers, in the sergeant's experience, were apt to be. As for Mr. Harris, it seemed that he had been lucky to have figured in the trial as a witness and not with Spencer in the dock. Or had he been so lucky? Thinking of the man who had been frightened of Americans, and was now lying in the bed upstairs, Sergeant Place was not so sure.

He read and re-read, savouring with delicate contempt each item where American judicial procedure differed from the familiar perfection of the Markhampton Assize Court. Finally, some sixth sense told him to raise his head and look out of the window just as Percy called from the hall, "Here he comes, Sarge!"

The Heel

Place opened the door to a thickset young man in khaki, who looked at him in surprise.

"Have I come right?" he asked. "They told me it was Mr. Harris's place."

"They told you quite correctly. Come in."

Hesitantly, the visitor entered. He looked hard at Place, and then at his subordinate.

"You're dicks, aren't you?" he said. "What's happened?"

"Did you write a letter to Mr. Harris last night?"

"I did."

"He was found dead in bed this morning."

The newcomer took a little time to digest this information. His fresh young face seemed deliberately drained of expression. To Place, watching him, there seemed something familiar in the set of the jaw.

"Well . . ." he said at last. "That kinda saves a lot of trouble, doesn't it?"

"Does it?" Place echoed. "That rather depends on what you wanted to see Mr. Harris for."

"Perhaps we don't need to go into that right now. I'm grateful to you gentlemen for giving me the news, that's all. I'd best be getting along."

"Just a minute. Before you go, there are two questions I'd like to ask you. What sort of a man was the late Mr. Harris?"

"He was a heel," said the staff sergeant shortly. "What's the other question?"

"Is your name Spencer, by any chance?"

"Joseph Wilbur Spencer, that's me."

"And John Benjamin Spencer?"

"Was my brother."

"Thank you, Spencer. I think you have told me all I want to know. Now would you care to identify the body?"

"Sir," said Spencer with dignity, "during my residence in this country I have learned to have a great respect for your police—a very great respect. If you tell me that Harris is dead, I don't ask for any ocular demonstration. No, sir! The word of the British police is good enough for me. All I've got to say is this: you've given me a piece of news that's going to spread joy in a lot of hearts where I come from when it gets around, as it certainly will. And I wish you a very good day."

"Percy, ask Wilson to come in here for a minute," said Place, after the visitor had gone.

Percy went out to the kitchen, and returned with a grin on his face.

"I think Wilson has breakfasted on whisky," he said. "I can't get him to stir."

"Well—he's had a shock, as he said himself. Perhaps I can do without him. We'll ask the Yard to send a man round to Chiltern's. They may give us a line on the late Mr. Harris. The coroner will want to know something about him beyond the fact that he was a heel."

He picked up the telephone.

"Get me Trunks, will you, Miss? I——"

He put the instrument down with a crash.

"Percy?" he barked. "Get the car out, quick, and go after that staff sergeant. Bring him back at once—by force, if need be."

To a puzzled and rather resentful Spencer Sergeant Place said, "I'm sorry, but I find that I shall have to ask you to identify Harris after all."

"If you say so, Sergeant. I've no objection in principle to stiffs, but I should have thought——"

The Heel

He broke off abruptly as Place threw open the door of the kitchen.

"Limey!" he exclaimed. He bent over the semi-conscious, stertorously breathing figure sprawled in a chair. "They said you were dead!"

"Not yet," said Place cheerfully. "But he soon will be. Our criminal procedure is rather quicker than yours, I fancy. Now, if you don't mind, we'll go upstairs and you can identify the body of Thomas Wilson—the poor innocent servant Harris poisoned last night, when he got your note. He reckoned that when you spread the news of his death he wouldn't be bothered by John Spencer's friends and relations again. It was a neat plan—and it might have come off, if he hadn't forgotten himself and talked about long-distance telephones instead of trunks. As he told me himself, he'd picked up a lot of American habits while he'd been away. I expect he came down here for the express purpose of running into you and staging this suicide. Quite a clever ruffian, Mr. Harris."

"Didn't I say he was a heel?" said Staff Sergeant Spencer.

The Rivals

The detective-sergeant's report was as follows:

To the Chief Constable.

Sir,

On the night of the 10th inst., at 7.31 p.m., a telephone
message was received at this station to the effect that a
girl had been stabbed in Vicarage Lane, Didford Parva.
The caller gave his name as John Dennison, already known
to me as a youth living in Council Cottages, Yewbury,
and the subject of proceedings in the Juvenile Court at
Markhampton for assault and larceny (File 892 of 1954
refers).

I proceeded to the scene, arriving at 8.37 p.m., where
I found the body of Christine Barking, aged 18, of Jubilee
Terrace, Didford Parva. The Medical Report (herewith)
shows that she had been killed by a stab wound between
the shoulders, consistent with the use of a long-bladed
knife.

I was immediately joined by John Dennison, who
approached from the direction of the telephone kiosk,
distant approximately 150 yards. He was in a highly
emotional state. He informed me that he had met the
deceased by appointment that evening with the intention
of accompanying her to an old-tyme dance at the Town
Hall, Markhampton. They were proceeding to the bus
stop at the end of Vicarage Lane with the intention of

taking the 7.40 p.m. bus to the city, when a man, whom he could not distinguish in the darkness, sprang out from behind the bushes bordering the lane, struck the deceased from behind and immediately ran away.

Questioned further, Dennison volunteered the information that he believed the assailant to be Charles Packer, already known to me as a youth, living at Riverside Lane, Didford Magna, and the subject of proceedings at the last Assizes for malicious wounding (File 493 of 1954 refers). He stated that Packer had twice threatened him with bodily violence on account of his association with the deceased, who, I have reason to think, was a girl of bad character and flighty disposition.

After making the necessary arrangements for the removal of the body, I invited Dennison to accompany me to the police station. Here I found Charles Packer, who was just completing a statement taken down by Detective Constable Kimber.

On seeing one another, the two men assumed a fighting attitude, and it became necessary for their own protection to lock them in separate cells.

From D.-C. Kimber's report (herewith) it will be seen that Packer arrived at the police station at 7.40 p.m. (From experiment, I have established that it is just possible to run from the scene of the crime to the station in 10 minutes 12 seconds.) Packer's statement is to the following effect: He had met the deceased by appointment that evening with the intention of accompanying her to the Cairo Cinema, Markhampton. They were proceeding to the bus stop at the end of Vicarage Lane . . . but I need not continue, sir. As will be seen from a comparison of the two statements, they are to all intents identical.

Packer expressed to D.-C. Kimber his firm belief that

Dennison, who, he stated, had actually assaulted him on three occasions, was responsible for the murder.

In these circumstances, I had both men carefully searched.

On Dennison I found a handkerchief (soiled), a copy of the Markhampton *Evening Record*, a packet of cigarettes, a box of matches, a wallet containing four pound notes, 3s. 6½d. in cash, a pocket comb, and a sheath-knife. He informed me that he carried the knife for protection, with particular reference to Packer. It bore the appearance of having been recently cleaned. His suit was of the "Teddy boy" variety, and on the cuff of the right sleeve I discovered a smear of blood. He readily admitted that this in all probability came from the deceased, whom, he said, he had supported as she fell after the assault.

On Packer I found a handkerchief (soiled), a lighter, three indecent photographs (herewith), a wallet containing £2 10s., sixpence-halfpenny in cash, a pocket comb and a belt with an empty sheath. Examination of his cell revealed a knife, similar to that found on Dennison, hidden in a ventilator. After some difficulty, I induced him to agree that it was his property. He stated that he carried it for protection, with particular reference to Dennison.

It also showed signs of having been cleaned, but further inspection revealed traces of blood. Bloodstains were also discovered on his handkerchief. Packer explained these by saying that he was subject to nose bleeding. So far as the blood on the knife was concerned, he said that he had cut his hand while cleaning it. There was in fact a recently healed cut on his right thumb. No blood was found on his clothing, which was of similar type to Dennison's.

Analysis in the police laboratory (report herewith) established that all the blood found was of Group O, which is the blood group to which the deceased belonged.

It is also, unfortunately, the fact that Packer's blood is of the same group. Dennison, on examination, proved to be Group AB.

On the morning of the 11th inst. I returned to Vicarage Lane and examined the ground. The Lane being muddy, it was possible to distinguish the footprints of a man and a woman leading towards the scene of the crime. I also found the footprints of a man leading from the opposite end of the lane to a group of bushes at the same point (photos herewith). Here they became confused with those of the first pair and with those of myself and other police officers.

I secured the shoes worn by the deceased and was satisfied that these fitted the female footprints referred to. I then obtained the shoes worn by each of the two men, and was immediately struck by the fact that they were in every respect similar, being new, yellow-brown leather brogues with crêpe rubber soles, size 10. Enquiries revealed that they had been bought within a few days of each other at the same firm of outfitters in High Street, Markhampton. Both pairs were somewhat muddy, and, needless to say, each fitted perfectly both sets of footprints.

Pursuing my investigations, I interviewed the mother and sister of the deceased. The former was unable to throw any light on her daughter's movements, but the latter told me that the deceased had been in the habit of going out with both young men indiscriminately, and that she had been threatened by each of them on account of her partiality for the other. She was unable to say with which of them her sister intended to pass the evening in question, but she stated that she was deeply addicted to dancing, and regularly attended dances at the Town Hall. She added that she was a fan of Dwight Bibble, whose new film, *Passion in Paris*, opened at the Cairo Cinema on that day (advert. from the *Evening Record*, herewith, refers).

The enquiry now appears to be at a standstill. Both young men continue to assert the truth of their respective stories, and I am totally unable to determine which of them is lying. The possibility of further evidence coming to light seems to be remote, and, while it is quite certain that one of the two is guilty of wilful murder, I must regretfully conclude that there is no prospect of making an arrest in this case.

(J. B. PORTEOUS, Detective-Sergt.)

The Chief Constable read the report through twice. Then he wrote in the margin: "*Arrest Dennison immediately. He is a bold liar, but he made one mistake. If he was taking Christine to an old-tyme dance,* what was he doing in crêpe rubber soles?"

The Ruling Passion

"Really!" said Eleanor Pettigrew to her husband. "It's almost too picturesque to be true."

From where they stood they looked down over the full extent of Valley Farm. With its whitewashed walls, sagging thatched roof, mellow brick chimneys, it might have been a picture postcard of the English countryside.

"Too picturesque to be profitable, I should think," remarked Pettigrew. "These fields look to me decidedly neglected. I wonder the local Agricultural Committee——"

"Don't be so prosaic, Frank. I want to see more of this lovely place. Do you think they would give us tea if we asked very nicely?"

Any doubts on that score were resolved before they reached the door of the farm. A large sign read: "Mrs. Broadman: Farmhouse Teas with Genuine Devonshire Cream." They had some difficulty in finding space to put their car among those that were already established in the car park picturesquely concealed behind the barn.

The tea-room was a large room that had evidently been hastily tacked on to the house in an approximation to the original Tudor style. It was crowded, and Frank and Eleanor had to share their table with two men. One of them, an elderly man with a strained expression and bright, hard eyes, Pettigrew was sure he had seen before; where, he could not remember. The other was a complete stranger. The room was plentifully decorated with rustic objects in pottery and beaten metal work.

The whole place struck Pettigrew as thoroughly bogus; but his wife was in a mood to be pleased. She remained serene even when after a loud crash behind the kitchen door a harassed waitress appeared to say that there had been an accident with the tray and their tea would be delayed.

"Do you think any of those pottery figures are for sale?" she asked.

"All of them, I'm sure," said Pettigrew. "This place is very efficiently run, while the farm is scandalously neglected. I'd like to have a word with the farmer."

"Much good that would do you," said the man whom Pettigrew had not seen before. He tapped his forehead with his forefinger and went on:

"Harry Broadman don't talk to anyone but his missus. Not since he cracked his head motor-racing thirty years ago. I've seen him moving about the farm or sitting in his back room, but he won't speak. Just so long as everything's the same, day after day, he's as quiet as a lamb, she tells me. If anything's changed, he gets wild. She never lets him know what she does at this end of the house, and she keeps him and pays the rent out of it."

"I see," said Pettigrew. "I owe them both an apology. Mrs. Broadman must be a very brave woman."

"You must buy me one of her china dogs," said Eleanor. "Just to make amends."

"You'll be throwing your money away," said the man with the familiar face. "They're all supplied by the junk shops in the local town and sold on commission. There are no genuine farmhouse antiques left in the county. I ought to know. I've been through 'em with a fine tooth-comb. It's heartbreaking."

"When I was an undergraduate," said Pettigrew, "I stayed at a farm near here. The farmer told me that a gentleman from Barnstaple had given him £17 for a bit of old wood off the wall. It's in the South Kensington Museum now—a unique piece of sixteenth-century panelling."

"Seventeen pounds!" said Eleanor. "For something that must have been worth hundreds. What a miserable swindle!"

"Not at all," said the stranger. "The man from Barnstaple simply applied his superior knowledge. As he was entitled to do. As any collector is entitled to do. It's his only asset."

He spoke with the violence of a fanatic, and in that moment Pettigrew remembered all about him.

"Your name is Shaw, isn't it?" he said. "I saw you giving evidence in a case about antiques once. Let me see, your speciality was——"

"Early saltglaze ware and——"

He was interrupted by the reappearance of the waitress, who staggered up to the table and dumped a tray in front of Eleanor.

"I'm sorry about the teapot," she said. "We're that short with breakages, I had to give you this. It does dribble a bit, I'm afraid."

She flounced off, breathing heavily.

Twenty minutes later the Pettigrews were finishing their tea. Shaw, who had paid his bill some time before, was still lingering at the table, smoking a succession of cigarettes. Mrs. Broadman, a thin harassed woman, came up to them.

"Would you care to buy a little souvenir?" she asked. "A china dog, perhaps?"

Pettigrew obediently bought a china dog, and then Shaw remarked casually, "I rather like that teapot. It's different from the others."

"Oh dear!" The woman was evidently upset. "Mary had no call to take that out of the cupboard. It's the master's, and he'll be expecting to have his tea out of it directly. Do you mind if I take it now?" she added to Eleanor.

"Not at all," said Eleanor. "We've quite finished."

Shaw followed the teapot with his eyes and there was a look of sheer animal hunger in his face. He sat silent for a moment, and then muttering, "This is ridiculous," went hastily from the room.

"I am no expert," said Pettigrew. "But there was a photograph in the papers the other day of a teapot that fetched a record price for salt glaze ware at Christie's, and this one looks the dead spit of it. I wonder what happens next."

What happened next was that an empty-handed Mr. Shaw got into his old-fashioned green saloon just in front of the Pettigrews' car and drove away faster than was safe in the narrow Devon lanes.

"I feel that Mrs. Broadman should be warned," said Pettigrew to his wife next morning.

"But why? She doesn't want to sell the teapot, and that means that he'll have to offer her a good price if he wants it."

"I'm not so much troubled by the question of price, though of course Shaw will cheat her if he can. I'm more anxious about what will happen if she refuses to sell at all. You see, Shaw isn't quite sane where his speciality is concerned, and to get a really fine specimen he'd do anything. I mean, *anything*."

Eleanor needed the car for a shopping expedition that morning, so Pettigrew took a leisurely bus which deposited him half a mile from Valley Farm. He had reached the last bend in the lane on his way when he had to flatten himself against the hedge to avoid being run down by an old green saloon travelling much too fast. With a sense of foreboding he quickened his pace. The farmhouse door stood open, and there was no answer to his urgent ringing at the bell.

The hall was silent except for the ticking of a long case clock. The door into the kitchen was ajar and something dark was spreading slowly beneath it over the clean flagged floor. Pettigrew avoided it carefully as he pushed the door open and looked in.

Mrs. Broadman was lying on her kitchen floor face downwards. The back of her head had been battered in with appalling violence. A glass-fronted cupboard at the end of the room was open. It was crowded with crockery of all sorts, and there was a rather conspicuous gap in the middle of the bottom shelf. One other thing Pettigrew noticed before he turned to go for help, and that was a small folded piece of paper on the floor. It proved to be a five-pound note with the name of a local hotel stamped on the back.

It did not take Pettigrew very long to establish that he was the only living person in the place and that the house was not on the telephone. It took him considerably longer to make contact with the outside world. Eventually he was able to stop a passing motorist, who took him to the local police headquarters. There he was thankful to hand matters over to an alert young detective sergeant, to whom he gave the five-pound note together with all the information in his possession.

The sergeant promised to keep him informed of the investigation and he was as good as his word. Late that evening Pettigrew was called to the telephone at the inn where he and Eleanor were staying.

"That was Shaw's fiver all right," he was told. "He cashed a cheque at his hotel last night. He had not been seen there since ten o'clock this morning. We've got the number of his car from them and it's being circulated. That's all we can do at present."

"It's a bad business," said Pettigrew.

"It is." The sergeant rang off.

The next evening Pettigrew was summoned again from the parlour, but this time the sergeant called in person.

"There are one or two points in your statement I'd like to clear up," he said.

Pettigrew dealt with them, and the sergeant thanked him politely.

"I don't expect we'll be troubling you again," he said. "The case is cleared up. We've found Shaw. And his car. And the teapot," he added.

"Thank heaven for that," Pettigrew said. "It gave me the cold shivers to think of that man being at large. But of course he was mad."

"Quite mad, sir."

"I wonder, though, whether he was mad for the purposes of the criminal law?"

"I'm not a lawyer, sir, but no jury in these parts would say he was anything but mad."

"You surprise me, Sergeant. Was Shaw a local man?"

"I'm not talking of Shaw, sir. He's dead. We found him in his car in the old quarry pit near the farm, under ten feet of water. That's where Harry Broadman put them. Harry can't stand any changes, you see, large or small, and he just went off the handle when he found his wife selling his precious teapot to Shaw for a couple of fivers. (We found the other one underneath her body, by the way.) He's the simple type that doesn't know his own

152

strength. Doesn't know anything else much, either, the doctor says. It'll be unfit to plead and Her Majesty's pleasure for him, poor chap. I only hope it won't be the Lord's pleasure that keeps him long in this world."

"Amen to that," said Pettigrew.

The Death of Amy Robsart

Gus Constantinovitch was an Englishman. His passport said as much when he went abroad. His name, indeed, hinted at Russia or Greece, his complexion suggested the Levant, his nose proclaimed Judea. As for his figure, it was as cosmopolitan as the restaurant meals that were responsible for it. But nobody who had seen him standing by the door of the music-room of his house at Ascot, rolling a cigar from one corner of his mouth to the other, or heard the crisp monosyllables in which he took leave of his guests, would have been excused for thinking him American. For this his profession was responsible. As Chairman and Managing Director of Cyclops Films Ltd., the organization which was (in his own words) to beat Hollywood at its own game, he had adopted, quite naturally, the badges of his tribe.

The party in honour of the trade showing of "Amy Robsart—the film magnificent" was slowly petering out. Gus from his station at the door surveyed his few remaining guests with lack-lustre eyes. It was impossible to tell from his expression whether either party or film had proved to his liking. The long room was almost empty, its windows open to the sultry July night. A Strauss waltz was being played on the gramophone, but only one couple still gyrated in the middle of the polished floor—a slim young man in evening clothes and a fair, white-faced girl with

154

tired eyes who wore Amy Robsart's flowing Tudor dress. In a corner a lank young woman with a predatory face was sitting talking to a superbly handsome giant of a man.

"She's a pretty little thing, isn't she?" she said, indicating the dancer.

"Who do you mean—Camilla?" he asked. "Why, Lady Portia, she's lovely."

Lady Portia Fanning's mouth gaped in a tigerish smile.

"Yes, Mr. Brancaster, I had noticed during the evening that you thought as much. What does your wife think about it?"

Teddy Brancaster looked across the room to the bar, where his wife and one or two men were standing.

"We can leave Geneviève out of it," he said, reddening.

"Of course. Besides, she's French, and they look at these things differently from you Americans, don't they? Otherwise I should have expected her to look for consolation to that young man with her now. What is his name —Bartram, isn't it?"

"Dick Bartram's all right."

"I'm sure he is. But we were talking about Camilla Freyne—have you seen her film?"

"No. I was on the set this morning, and this afternoon I was practising dives in the swimming-pool here."

"Has Gus got his own swimming-pool?"

"Sure. In the garden. A very good one, too."

"How sweet! Too, too Hollywood! But does a champion like you need to practise?"

"Every day, Lady Portia, if I'm not to lose my form."

"How wonderful of you! Well, you didn't miss much— the film, I mean. Your Camilla may be all you think her, but as an actress she's the world's worst."

"Maybe."

155

She looked at her watch.

"I must go. Can't I give you a lift home, Mr. Brancaster?"

"No, thank you. I am staying here, you know."

"Of course, I forgot. Perhaps I shall see you in London some time, if Mrs. Brancaster will allow?"

She went up to her host.

"Good night, Mr. Constantinovitch. It's been such a delightful party, and I'm sure the picture will be a great success."

"Good night, Lady Portia. Happy to have you at my house."

The waltz came to an end. Camilla's partner bowed his thanks and took his leave. No sooner had he gone than in a flutter of long skirts she was across the room to where Teddy Brancaster was standing.

"Now I'm going to dance with you, Teddy," she said. "Put on another record, just for you and me—please." She looked up to his face like a small girl at the window of a sweetshop.

As if by magic, Geneviève, who had been standing contentedly during the dance among the group at the bar, materialized at her husband's side.

"She should not dance any more, Teddee," she declared. "But see how tired she is!"

"Sure," said Teddy equably. "Time little girls were in bed, Camilla." His voice, as he turned to her, took on an altogether new quality of warmth and tenderness.

"Oh, what's the use of going to bed when you can't sleep?" Camilla pouted. "I haven't slept properly for ages." She passed the back of her hand across her eyes with a gesture simple as a child's. "Not since I started work on the picture."

Gus Constantinovitch had joined the group.

"And the picture's finished now," he said. "You'll sleep sound tonight, Camilla. That's what you're in my home for, to sleep sound."

"But I want to dance, Gus. Just one more little dance with Teddy."

Teddy shook his head.

"It's too late for dancing," he said. "I guess I'll have a dip in the swimming-pool before I turn in."

"I too," broke in Geneviève. "I will come with you swimming, Teddee."

"Sure you will," said Teddy sardonically. "You'll fol-me round anywhere, won't you, Geneviève? Well, let's go get our bathing things."

"I'll come too," Camilla declared. "Bathing by moon-light—lovely!"

"You're going to bed," said Teddy firmly. "Besides, there's no moon tonight, no stars neither. It's as dark as pitch."

"Ah, but that makes it better still! To dive into the dark, when you can see nothing! That's what Amy Rob-sart did, wasn't it? Just fell in the dark, and it was all over." Her voice trailed away uncertainly.

"Camilla!" Gus spoke sharply. "Here, Mrs. Brancaster, take her upstairs to her room. You know where it is, don't you? Next door to yours. And see that she doesn't come down again."

Geneviève took her by the arm. For a moment it seemed as if she would try to resist, but the Frenchwoman had a grip of iron, and she gave way meekly enough.

"That's a good girl," said Gus paternally. "Go to bed now, and your Uncle Gus will come and tuck you up."

They made an odd couple as they moved together to the door—the fragile girl, wilting under her Tudor mag-nificence and the active, muscular young woman beside her. Teddy Brancaster seemed to feel the contrast as he stared after them.

"I'll go change," he said abruptly.

Among the group at the cocktail bar Dick Bartram was watching them too.

"She's very handsome," someone said.

"Pity she can't act."

"Act? Why, I bet she could if she ever tried."

"I like that! Hasn't she been trying hard enough these last six months?"

Dick blushed painfully.

"Oh—you mean Camilla! I—I thought you were talking about——"

There was a chorus of laughter, which made his cheeks redder than ever.

"My poor chap!" said the man who had spoken first. "Don't waste your young love in that quarter. Geneviève's a one-man's woman. Haven't you noticed that?"

"Pity her husband's not one woman's man," said another.

"Oh, I shouldn't worry. The fair Geneviève can be relied on to protect herself. A stiletto in her garter for any rivals —that's her type."

Without a word Dick left them and walked out of the room.

"And there goes the best cameraman in England," was the comment from the bar. "Well, if Gus goes on turning out tripe like his last opus, he'll soon be out of a job."

"Will America look at it, do you think?"

"Not a hope. I saw Souderberg after the show today, and he told me——"

"Gus was looking pretty green tonight, I thought."

"That doesn't prove anything. He always does. It's his British blood boiling in his veins."

"I hear there's been some trouble down at the studio. They've had a Scotland Yard man in."

"Oh, that's nothing. Some bright cashier been embezzling while the going's good."

"Where's Gus got to? He was here just now."

"Counting his losses, I expect. Well, here's luck."

Teddy Brancaster strode in, his magnificent brown body clad only in a pair of bathing trunks, a towel over his arm.

"Is Geneviève down yet?" he asked.

"My dear Apollo, was ever a woman ready when you expected her? Of course not."

Teddy went into the hall and called up the stairs.

"Hi, Geneviève! Are you coming?"

Geneviève appeared on the landing.

"Coming soon, Teddee!" she cried.

A bedroom door opened just behind her, and Camilla's white face appeared.

"Please, may I come too? Please, Teddy, just this once!"

Teddy smiled and shook his head.

"You shall not come!" said Geneviève with decision, and the door closed.

"I'm going down now," said Teddy. "See you at the pool, then. So long!"

From a chair in an alcove in the hall Dick Bartram, sick with envy, saw him go. Then he moved to the foot of the staircase.

"Geneviève!" he called softly.

II

Some twenty minutes later the last guests reluctantly decided that it was time to be going. They had damned *Amy Robsart* in general and Camilla's performance in particular, down to the last detail. They had cheerfully canvassed the prospects of a similar fiasco for the film which Teddy Brancaster was rehearsing, and they had almost exhausted their host's abundant supplies of drinks. At this point Gus again entered the room.

"Gus, old man, it's time I was going. It's been a great party."

"Glad you enjoyed it, Tom."

"Good night, Gus. That little Freyne girl is a real find. You'll make a big hit with *Amy Robsart*. All the boys think the same."

"Sure I hope so, Mike, I hope so."

"Good night, old boy. We've overstayed our welcome, I'm afraid."

"Not a bit, Jimmy. Always happy to see you."

"Good night . . . Good night . . ."

"Hey, you fellows! Anybody seen my wife about?"

Teddy Brancaster came in by the french window, his skin glistening with water drops, his bare feet leaving damp marks on the parquet floor.

"Hullo! It's Apollo back again! Didn't she keep her date with you, Teddy?"

"Nope. I've been swimming around the last quarter of an hour and she never came along."

"Too bad, Teddy. Quite a new experience for you to be jilted, isn't it? Sorry we can't stay for the end of the drama, but we're just off. Good night."

Teddy grinned cheerfully.

"Good night, you fellows. Guess I'll go look for her."

"Hope there's no bloodshed when you find her, anyway."

The guests took their noisy departure. Teddy followed them into the hall and went upstairs. A moment or two later he was down again. Gus was standing in the hall and Teddy looked down at him with troubled eyes.

"Gus, she isn't in her room. What's happened to her, d'you think?"

"I shouldn't worry, Teddy. Maybe she stayed in Camilla's room to help her sleep. I'll go and see, if you like."

"But she said she was coming swimming," Teddy objected.

"I'll go and look, all the same," said Gus, and mounted the stairs.

Teddy remained for a moment irresolute.

"Were you looking for me, Teddee?" said a voice behind him.

He spun round as if he had been shot. Geneviève and Dick Bartram had just emerged from a little sitting-room on the further side of the hall.

"I'm sorry I didn't come with you, Teddee," she began, but he cut her short. He had gone deathly pale, his eyes blazed.

"You . . . !" he exclaimed. "You . . . !" He seemed incapable of saying more.

"But what is the matter, Teddee?"

"What's the matter? Weren't you coming swimming with me? Where have you been? What have you been doing? And who—oh, my God!"

But Geneviève had found her tongue.

"Ah, so it is like that, is it?" she exclaimed. "So the great Teddy is become jealous all at once, is it not? And all because I did not come the moment I was wanted, eh? Is it so often you want me, then? Have I ever complained to you about your Rosa, your Kitty, and now your Camilla? You know now what it is to feel what I have felt, then? That is good!"

"You little bitch!"

"Look here, Brancaster," began Bartram, "you're not

to speak to your wife in that way. And if you suggest that she and I——"

"Be quiet, Dickee. This is my affaire."

"Hold your tongue, both of you. I——"

A fresh voice cut in above the noise of the dispute. Gus's voice, urgent with alarm.

"Stop that noise, for God's sake! Something is wrong here!"

All three were suddenly silent.

"Camilla's not in her room," said Gus. "And—and her window's wide open!"

It was an appreciable time before anyone spoke again. Gus came slowly down the stairs. His sallow face was as expressionless as ever, but his fingers twitched incessantly as they grasped the banister rail and his feet stumbled uneasily at every step. When he reached the foot of the stairs, it was as if a spell had been broken, and everyone began to talk at once.

"Camilla!" groaned Teddy. "No, it's not possible!"

"*Ah, la pauvre fille!*" exclaimed Geneviève. "*Elle est somnambule sans doute. C'est ce que j'ai toujours cru!*"

Dick said simply:

"Did you look in her bathroom, Gus?"

"I looked," Gus answered. "It was empty. Her clothes were all over the room and her bed hadn't been slept in."

Once more silence fell on the little group—an oppressive silence in which each looked at the others in growing perplexity and fear.

"But what do we wait for?" said Geneviève suddenly. "We must search—the house, garden, everywhere!"

"The garden!" said Dick. "Have you got a torch anywhere, Gus? Come on, quickly, for God's sake!"

But it was Teddy who led the blind rush through the garden door behind the staircase to the back of the house.

The Death of Amy Robsart

To eyes coming direct from the brilliantly lighted hall the garden was in utter darkness, and the party halted in momentary uncertainty on the threshold. From the open door behind them a broad shaft of light illuminated a section of the terrace which ran the length of the house, and a little of the lawn beyond. Their shadows wavered against the background of white stone and vivid green.

"To the right," said Dick. "That's where her window is, isn't it? Hurry up with that torch, Gus!"

But before the torch could be found, and while their eyes were still straining to accustom themselves to the dark, Teddy had seen something showing dully white against the surrounding blackness.

"There! There!" he cried, and ran in its direction.

The others heard the patter of his bare feet as he went towards it, heard the sharp intake of his breath as he reached it. Then Gus's fumbling fingers found the switch of the electric torch and the whole scene was revealed.

Teddy was kneeling beside the body of Camilla Freyne, a pitiful crumpled heap upon the wide stone terrace. Her bare arms and legs gleamed alabaster white in contrast to the dark-blue bathing dress which was her only covering. Her face was so hideously mutilated as to be scarcely recognisable. From a dreadful wound in the head the blood had soaked through the towel on which it lay, staining the stone a dull red.

Teddy was weeping unashamedly.

"Camilla! Camilla, darling!" he sobbed. "Why did you do it? I loved you! I loved you! I'd have given my life for you—Camilla!"

"Teddee!" Geneviève's voice was shrill. "Teddee, get up! There is nothing you can do."

The Death of Amy Robsart

Teddy rose to his feet. His grief-distorted face disappeared from the circle of light. In the darkness his voice sounded hollow.

"Sure, there's nothing we can do—nothing at all! Amy Robsart fell in the dark, that's all—and now I suppose you're happy!"

"How dare you!" cried Dick.

"Be silent, all of you!" Gus commanded. "Have you no reverence? Dick, you will please go and telephone for a doctor and the police."

"A doctor and a policeman!" echoed Teddy bitterly. "They'll be mighty useful! Will they give me Camilla back again? Ask them that! Ask them——" He sobbed afresh.

"Teddy," said Gus, with an air of authority, "you will go indoors. In my study there is brandy. Drink some. And do not come out again. Geneviève, you will stay here with me till help comes. It is not good for the dead to be alone."

III

It was a brilliantly fine morning. The sun, flaming out of a cloudless sky, penetrated into the room where Gus lay, sleepless. He rose from his bed and went to the window. The room occupied a wing built on to one end of the house, and from where he stood he could look along the whole length of the terrace. It was a placid, smiling scene, with nothing at first sight to remind him of the events of the night before. Only at one point on the terrace a single flagstone was covered with a rough piece of sacking. Gus averted his eyes from it hastily. The poor broken body of Camilla had been taken away overnight under the orders of a doctor who had murmured remarks about multiple head injuries and shock, and a police sergeant who had been a miracle of sympathy and calm.

164

About the house in which she had been the guest of honour a few hours before nothing of her remained except an ugly red stain, protected from the elements by an old half sack.

As Gus watched, two men came into his view round the further end of the house. One of them was the kindly sergeant of the night before. The other was a tall, broad-shouldered man in grey tweeds, with a fierce military moustache. As they walked round the corner they appeared to be deep in conversation.

". . . Danish bacon!" the one in tweeds was saying. "It's all very well, Parkinson, but when I come into the country I don't expect to be given Danish bacon!"

"I know, sir," said the sergeant sympathetically, "but it's like that everywhere nowadays. When I was a boy——er—here we are, sir!"

They had arrived at the piece of sacking. The sergeant pulled it away and together they looked at what lay beneath. Then he replaced it.

"You see where it lies, sir," he demonstrated. "Now, if anyone was to fall, or dive from that window above us, this is just where you would expect them to pitch."

"So I see," replied the other. "But, strictly speaking, you couldn't fall from the window. You would have to get on to the balustrade outside it."

"Exactly. But that's easy done."

"No doubt."

"You've seen the body, I suppose, sir?"

"Yes, I called at the mortuary on the way here."

"Well, sir, it certainly looks a simple enough case to me. This young lady, according to all accounts, was in a bad state of nerves. They often are, them actresses, you know. She takes it into her head that she wants to bathe last night—to dive into the dark, as he puts it. She's told she's not to, and put to bed. Then she gets up, sleep-walking like, if you follow me, pops on her bathing dress, and dives out of window."

"It seems simple, certainly."

"Why, sir, it's plumb natural, if you ask me. And I'll tell you another thing. This girl's been acting a part called Amy Robsart. Now Amy Robsart, so far as I can make out, is killed much the same way, only it wasn't a window she fell out of——"

"I know. I've read the book."

"It isn't a book, it's a film. But I daresay it's much the same thing. What I'm getting at is that with her in a bad state of nerves and all, she'd be quite likely not to know whether she was herself or whether she was Amy Robsart, and behave accordingly, if you follow me?"

"Amy Robsart didn't wear a bathing dress, did she?"

"That's true, sir, she didn't. But I reckon the young lady got into a proper muddle about things and forgot that."

"Very likely."

A door in the house opened, and Teddy Brancaster, dressed—or rather undressed—for swimming, came out on to the terrace. He stopped when he saw the two men.

"Good morning," said Sergeant Parkinson. "You're up early."

"I'm always up for a dip before breakfast when your English climate allows it," said Teddy. He looked hard at the man in tweeds. "Haven't I seen you before?" he asked.

"This is Inspector Mallett of Scotland Yard," the sergeant explained. "He has been doing some investigation at the Cyclops Studios, and he was good enough to come along this morning and help us."

"Pleased to meet you," said Teddy. "Well, if you gentlemen will excuse me, I'll be going."

"Perhaps you will give me a moment or two later, when you have had your breakfast," said Mallett.

"Surely."

The giant strode away across the lawn. He struck a narrow stone path that ran in the direction of a little shrubbery, and, following it, disappeared from view. A moment later the detectives heard the thud of a springboard, followed by a splash.

"A fine figure of a man, that," was Parkinson's comment. "It's easy to see that he keeps himself in 'good condition'. Makes men like us look quite flabby, doesn't it, sir?"

"At all events, I haven't got black circles under my eyes at this time of day," said Mallett in an aggrieved tone.

"Well, sir, we must make allowances for that. I don't expect he had much sleep last night. He was in a terrible state when I came in—crying and howling fit to burst himself, he was."

"Really? Suppose we go indoors now?"

They passed into the house. A scared housemaid fled at their approach.

"That reminds me," said Mallett. "What about the servants last night? Did they hear anything?"

"They had all gone to bed," Parkinson explained. "They sleep in a wing on the other side of the house. The guests at the party were looking after themselves. It was what they call a Bohemian party, I'm told—meaning that they could all drink as much as they liked without any servants to tell tales on them."

"I see. Now which way do we go?"

The sergeant led the way upstairs. He stopped before a door on the first-floor landing and unlocked it with a key which he took from his pocket.

"This is her room," he said. "Nothing has been touched."

It was a room of medium size, lit by one large sash window giving on to the garden. The bed was made, but had not been slept in. On it, and on the armchair at its foot, was distributed Camilla's finery of the night before— the heavy, embroidered Elizabethan gown and the stomacher stiffened with whale-bone contrasting strongly with the gossamer silk underwear of the twentieth century. The built-in wardrobe hung open. On the dressing-table a pearl necklace and some rings lay scattered. From an open powder bowl a faint scent permeated the room. To the right an open door led into the bathroom. Here, in contrast to the disorder of the bedroom, all was neatly arranged. The towels were folded; the sponges, hard and dry, in orderly array; and the bath mat, neatly centred, showed no sign of having been disturbed since the servant had laid it down. The window, a small one, was closed.

Mallett took in everything with a few quick glances. Then, returning from the bathroom to the bedroom, he went to the window. It was open at the bottom, and, leaning through, he looked out for a few moments. Outside the window was a balustrade, some two feet high, which ran the entire length of the house. Between this and the window was a small space, just sufficient for a man to stand in.

His survey completed, Mallett withdrew his head.

"Have you looked out of here?" he asked Parkinson.

"No, sir. It was dark when I was here last night, of course."

"Have a look now."

The sergeant did so.

"Well?" Mallett said. "Did you notice anything?"

"I did, sir."

"Yes?"

"The place where the body was found is not under this window, sir. It is farther along to the right."

"What does that convey to you?"

"Why, sir, it looks as if the young lady had walked along the balustrade that way before she fell off."

"Why should she?"

"Isn't that just the kind of thing a sleep-walker would do, sir? Walk along a dangerous place until she lost her footing? I'm sure I've heard of that sort of thing happening more than once."

"Sleep-walking . . . H'm . . . And where did she sleep, Sergeant?"

Parkinson looked at the bed, and flushed a little.

"She fell asleep in the chair, very likely," he suggested.

"On top of her undies? Well, that's always possible, though one would expect them to be more crumpled. But there's one thing you haven't accounted for."

"Indeed, sir?"

"If she went sleep-walking, as you suggest, why was her head wrapped in a towel when she was found?"

"Good Lord, sir! Why didn't I think of that at once? Of course, that explains it. It wasn't sleep-walking at all, but just plain suicide!"

"I don't quite follow."

"Why, sir, don't you see the pea sigh cology of the thing."

"The what?"

"The pea sigh cology, sir."

"Oh, the pea . . . No, I'm not sure that I do."

"Why, it's quite plain to me. Look here, sir. The young lady wants to kill herself. She makes up her mind to throw herself out of window. Then when it comes to the point she finds that she hasn't the nerve. So what does she do? She blindfolds herself with the towel, so that she can't see what's coming to her, if you follow me——"

"I do, Sergeant, I do."

"And just walks along the edge till she falls off, so taking herself by surprise in a manner of speaking. Am I right?"

"You may be, Sergeant. By the way, which window was it that she was found under?"

"Mr. and Mrs. Brancaster's bedroom, sir. That's next door to this, with just the bathroom in between."

"I see. Well, there doesn't appear to be anything further that we can do up here. We had better go downstairs now and see what the people in the house can tell us."

IV

In the dining-room the detectives found Teddy Brancaster finishing his breakfast. He had changed into a grey-flannel suit which set off his magnificent proportions to advantage.

"You are all alone, I see," said Mallett.

"As you see," assented the American gravely.

"Is Mrs. Brancaster breakfasting in bed?"

"I expect so. I haven't seen her this morning."

"How is that?"

"Well, if it interests you, I slept in my dressing-room last night—if you can call it sleeping," he added bitterly.

"When were you last in her bedroom?"

Teddy looked surprised at the question, and reflected a little before answering.

"Why, I guess it must have been before dinner last night," he said slowly.

"But didn't you go up there to look for her when you came in from bathing?"

"Sure, I did. I forgot that. She wasn't there."

170

"Can you tell me," the inspector pursued, "whether the window was open or shut when you went in?"

"Shut."

"Are you sure of that?"

"Positive."

"Do you know that it was under that window that Miss Freyne's body was found?"

"Is that so?" said Teddy slowly. "No, I did not know it."

"It occurred to me that she might perhaps have fallen from that window last night, but if you are right in your recollection that the window was shut it doesn't seem possible, does it?"

"It certainly does not."

"And you still say the window was shut?"

"I do, sir."

"When you went up to change last night, you didn't hear anything suspicious?"

"I did not go up to change last night. Gus lets me use the cloakroom down here as a changing room. It's more convenient for the pool, as I'm in and out all day."

"Thank you. That may be important. Now I must ask you about another thing altogether: was there something of a quarrel between you and your wife last night?"

Teddy's face darkened.

"There was," he admitted.

"Things were not altogether happy between the two of you?"

"Well—you've heard of film-stars' marriages not turning out well before now, I suppose?"

"Film stars' marriages don't often last as long as yours, Mr. Brancaster. Let me see, six years, isn't it?"

"You seem to know a lot about me, Inspector."

"You must remember that I have been carrying out a fairly thorough investigation at the studios, and I have found it necessary to examine the lives of pretty well everyone connected with it."

"You British are certainly thorough," said Teddy with a faint smile.

"We try to be. And your American police are not very far behind when we ask them for assistance. Now I find that since your marriage your name has been—connected, shall we say——"

"Connected will do very well."

"—with a number of women. There was Rosa Layton, for example. She was killed in an accident, wasn't she, Mr. Brancaster?"

"She was drowned in a boating accident—yes."

"Then there was Kitty Cardew."

"Sure. Poor Kitty, she died from an overdose of veronal."

"Was your wife jealous of these women?"

"Of them—and others. Yes."

"Was she jealous of Miss Freyne?"

"She most certainly was."

"Has it ever occurred to you, sir, that there might be some connection between these various accidents?"

Teddy Brancaster sat silent for a moment, staring at his plate. Then he said between clenched teeth, "Never—until now."

Dick Bartram came into the room. Teddy gave him a curt "Good morning!" and rose to his feet.

"I must be getting along to the set," he announced. "If you gentlemen want me again you know where to find me."

Bartram meanwhile had sat down at the table and was attacking a grapefruit with a gloomy air. He paid no attention to the other two men until Mallett addressed him.

"You know who I am, I think?" he began.

"Certainly. You're the Scotland Yard man, aren't you? How is your work at the studios going?"

"Pretty well. But that isn't what I'm here for today."

"No?"

"I am looking into the circumstances of the death of Camilla Freyne."

Dick pushed away his plate and looked up with interest.

"Do you really think," he asked, "that there may be something to—to look into, as you put it?"

"Every case of sudden death has to be investigated, naturally."

"But do you think that this case is—is something that needs special investigation?"

"I think it possible."

"Then I shall give you all the assistance in my power, of course. That is," he added, "if you don't mind my going on with my breakfast while I do it."

"Please do. . . . Your coffee smells remarkably good, if I may say so."

"Gus has it specially imported from Costa Rica. Would you care for a cup?"

"Well, since you press me. . . . Thank you. . . . Yes, that is certainly excellent coffee. Costa Rica, you say? I'll make a note of it."

"Would you care for some, Sergeant?"

"I thank you, no, sir," said Parkinson virtuously. "I drink tea myself."

"Now, sir," said Mallett, putting down his cup with an air of satisfaction. "I just want to put a few questions to you about your movements last night."

"They were very restricted movements, Inspector."

"After Miss Freyne had gone upstairs what did you do?"

"I stayed at the bar in the music room for a short time and then went into the hall."

"Yes?"

"I remained there till after Brancaster had gone out to the swimming-pool——"

"While you were in the hall, did you hear Mr. Brancaster speaking to his wife?"

"Yes, and I heard her speak to him and to Miss Freyne."

"You heard Miss Freyne's voice too?"

"Yes."

"No doubt about it?"

"None at all. I have had the job of photographing Miss Freyne every day for the last two or three months, and I'm not likely to be mistaken about her face or her voice or her scent or anything that is hers."

"Quite. Then what did you do?"

"As soon as Brancaster was out of the house I called upstairs to Geneviève. She came down immediately. I took her into the smoking-room next door to the hall and there we stayed till Brancaster came back."

"You did not leave the room during that time?"

"No."

"From where you were could you have heard anybody going up or down the stairs?"

"I think not. We heard Teddy's voice when he came in, but he was talking pretty loud."

"What were you and Mrs. Brancaster doing in the smoking-room?" asked the inspector suddenly.

Bartram answered without a tremor.

"I was trying to persuade Geneviève to come away with me."

Parkinson blew out his cheeks and looked shocked, but Mallett pursued, unruffled, "Did you succeed?"

"No," said Dick bitterly. "Nothing that I could say would induce her to leave that hulking brute of a husband of hers. I don't know what women can be made of. He has treated her disgracefully—neglected her for a simpering little doll who thinks she's an actress because she's got a pretty face——"

He stopped abruptly.

"Sorry," he murmured. "I forgot—she's dead. I shouldn't have spoken of her in that way. I daresay she didn't know what she was doing. She was very young, and infatuated with him. But she was breaking the heart of a woman worth ten of her, and I couldn't forgive her."

There was a pause, and then the inspector said in a matter-of-fact way:

"It comes to this, then, Mr. Bartram. You and Mrs. Brancaster were alone together from the time that Miss Freyne, so far as we know, was last seen alive to the time when she was found to be missing?"

"Yes."

"And there is nobody, apart from Mrs. Brancaster, who can verify—— Oh, good morning, Mr. Constantinovitch."

Gus's sallow face had appeared in the doorway.

"Good morning," he said. "You wished to see me, Inspector?"

"If you please. But it will keep till after you have breakfasted."

"I do not breakfast," said Gus, rubbing his great paunch reflectively. "Once, perhaps, but for many years—no, I do not breakfast."

"You have my sympathy. Then in that case——"

"Come this way, please."

The two men followed him into his study, a tiny room almost entirely filled by an enormous Louis XV desk, littered with papers. Gus sat down before it and sighed heavily.

"And what have you to tell me, Inspector?" he asked.

"The position is serious," answered Mallett. "The defalcations are on an even larger scale than was thought at first. They have been cleverly made, and very cleverly concealed."

"Ah . . .! It is that fellow Sneyd, I suppose?"

"It would appear so."

"We must prosecute, of course. But what good will that do us? All this is most unfortunate, Inspector, especially coming at this time. It puts the Cyclops set in a very difficult position. I say it within these four walls, but the position is difficult."

"Your organisation suffered a loss of a different kind last night," Mallett observed.

"The poor Camilla! Indeed, yes! An artist," said Gus sententiously, "whom the British film industry could ill afford to lose."

"Did your company insure her life?" Mallett asked abruptly.

"Certainly. We insure all our stars while they are under contract to us."

"What was Miss Freyne's contract?"

"For three years, at three hundred pounds a week. She was only beginning, you know," he added, as if in apology for the beggarly figure.

"And the insurance?"

"Twenty thousand pounds."

"So her death was not entirely a loss from the point of view of your company," suggested Mallett.

"One must look on the bright side, even of the greatest tragedy," Gus agreed.

"What were you doing last night," was the inspector's next question, "between the time when Miss Freyne went to bed and the time when you went to her room and found it empty?"

"After she had gone to bed," was the reply, "I stayed a little in the music room and looked at my guests—those who remained. They all seemed to be enjoying themselves without me, so I left them and came in here, where I remained until just before Mr. Brancaster came back from his swim. There were some figures and reports that I wanted to look at."

"Figures and reports relating to *Amy Robsart*?"

"Yes. My secretary had left them during the evening."

"They were not very satisfactory, were they?"

Gus made a deprecatory gesture.

"The preliminary bookings were disappointing," he admitted.

"Miss Freyne's tragic death will, however, give the film some assistance, I suppose?"

"We shall have some very useful publicity from it, I have no doubt."

"Thank you, Mr. Constantinovitch. I think that is all I want to know."

Mallett and Parkinson left the room.

"You certainly do know how to make them talk, sir," said Parkinson admiringly. "Now I suppose it's Mrs. Brancaster's turn to be put through it?"

"Mrs. Brancaster? No, I hardly think I need trouble her yet. I think I shall go for a walk in the garden. I've hardly seen it so far."

"The garden, sir? Oh yes, just so—the garden. Can I assist you in any way?"

"I don't think I need trouble you. I am sure you have plenty to do elsewhere."

"Since you mention it, sir, I have. Good day, sir!"

The sergeant left the house, and Mallett stepped out alone into the sunshine.

The garden was not a horticulturist's paradise. Its

principal attraction was the well-kept lawn which stretched broad and green for some eighty yards from the terrace. This was flanked on either side by some tasteless beds of antirrhinums and fuchsias, and at the further end by leaden statuettes intended to give an olde worlde atmosphere, and succeeding only too well. Beyond it, to the right, a rustic sundial formed the focal point of an unenthusiastic rose-garden, which was separated from the lawn by the path which led to the swimming-pool.

This path Mallett followed. It took him to the little shrubbery behind which he had seen Teddy Brancaster disappear that morning. Here it sloped steeply downwards, serpentined aimlessly left and right, and ended abruptly at the edge of the pool.

The pool was not large—some fifty feet long by twenty broad, its length running in the same direction as the path, but it was well equipped, with a high diving-board, water-climb and spring-board, all at the deep end of the pool where Mallett now found himself. He stopped, one foot on the spring-board, and gazed meditatively into the clear water, through which the pattern of the blue-and-white-tiled bottom wavered and sparkled. Lifting his eyes he saw at the other end of the pool another man, apparently similarly engaged. From his clothes it could be guessed that he was a gardener, and from his expression that he did not care much for his job. Mallett walked over towards him.

"Good morning," he said.

The man acknowledged his presence by a stare and a sniff.

"This is a pretty place you've got down here," the inspector went on genially.

"So 't oughter be with all the money it cost," was the answer.

178

"Ah! Expensive, was it?"

"Cost a packet to make and costs a packet to run. Money no objeck! And can I git any money for my 'ouses? Can I get s'much as a bundle of pea-sticks without there's Gawd Almighty's row first? No, it's always the same thing. 'Jenkins, I can't afford it!' 'Jenkins, the garden costs too much money!' But 'is lordship's loverly swimming-bath—that's quite another pair o' shoes!"

He spat disgustedly into the water. Mallett's face must have shown what he felt, for he added:

"Oh, you needn't worry! I'm going to clean her out now."

"It doesn't look as if it needed it."

"Needed it? Of course it doesn't need it. But that makes no difference. Twice a week it 'as to be done, while 'is mightiness is in residence. That's nice work for an Englishman, ain't it? Swilling out a bath for a pack of foreignborn film actors. Company's water, mind you! Waste of money, waste of time, I calls it."

"How long does it take?"

"Two hours to empty, four hours to fill. And the time spent in the scrubbing of it out."

"How is it emptied?"

"I'll show you. It's just over where you're standing. See? There's a cock 'ere. You turn it *that* way, and she starts to empty. Then when you want to fill 'er, you turn that cock there. That's all."

"Thanks very much. Now I wonder if you could do something for me. Perhaps I had better tell you who I am . . ."

Mallett continued to talk to the man for a full quarter of an hour, and then left him gloomily regarding the receding waters with the evident intention of doing no further work until the pool was empty.

The Death of Amy Robsart

On returning to the house, Mallett went straight to the little study. Gus was busy on the telephone. As he put down the receiver and turned to the inspector he displayed a countenance decidedly more cheerful than it had been an hour previously.

"You were quite right, Inspector," he said. "The publicity value of this business—this sad tragedy, I should say, is going to be very great. Greater than I had imagined, and I think that I should know something about publicity. Already I have given three interviews by telephone to press representatives, and now I think that the trade will begin to find that there is more in *Amy Robsart* than they had bargained for." He rubbed his hands. "Was I not right when I said that one must always look on the bright side?" he added.

"You were," the inspector admitted. "Now, Mr. Constantinovitch, there is only one more thing I should like you to do for me. I am going now, and shall not return until this evening. Can you arrange for all the people who slept in the house last night to be here then?"

"That can be done, Inspector. What time will you wish to see them?"

"I will be here at ten o'clock."

"Very good. Hullo? Yes? Mr. Constantinovitch speaking . . . Certainly I will give a message to your readers. 'The tragic death of the glamorous young star at the very moment of attaining the pinnacle of fame in a performance which experts acclaim as . . .' "

Mallett left Gus to the telephone and made his way to the police-station. Sergeant Parkinson greeted him eagerly.

"Can I help you in any way, sir?" he asked.

"Yes," said Mallett. "You can tell me where the offices of the local water company are."

Parkinson looked somewhat disappointed.

"I'll take you round myself," he said. "But I meant— that is, I hoped—well, I thought there would be something you wanted *done,* if you follow me."

"I'm afraid not—at the present, at any rate. But I'd like you to meet me outside Mr. Constantinovitch's house at ten o'clock this evening. Perhaps there will be something to be 'done' then."

Mallett would vouchsafe no more, and he parted from Parkinson at the offices of the water company. Here he interviewed an intelligent young engineer, who from being bored and suspicious became as the interview went on more and more interested, and finally very busy indeed.

v

It was an uneasy party that awaited Mallett's visit in the music-room that evening, after a dinner that had been eaten for the most part in silence. Gus, who was by a good deal the most self-possessed of the four, proposed a game of poker. He was a good player at all times, and on this occasion the others were no match for him. Geneviève seemed listless and preoccupied, Dick was nervous, Teddy out of temper with his cards, his companions and himself. It was a positive relief to all of them, except Gus, who had pocketed a good deal of his guests' money, when on the stroke of ten Inspector Mallett was announced.

"I think you know everyone here," said Gus, "except Mrs. Brancaster."

Mallett bowed to her. She inclined her head languidly and then looked away. Mallett stood in the middle of the room and cleared his throat.

"As you all know," he said, "I am enquiring into the circumstances of the death of Miss Camilla Freyne. There will have to be an inquest, of course, and you, who were the only persons in or about the place at the time, will all be essential witnesses. There are reasons, which I cannot go into now, why it is important that I should know exactly what were the movements of each of you between the time when Miss Freyne left this room and the moment when she was found outside the house."

"But we've told you all that already," Dick objected.

"I agree. But at the same time there are some points which I should like cleared up, and I think they can best be cleared up by your helping me, so far as possible, to reconstruct the events of last night—in so far as you were respectively concerned in them. I want everyone to go through the same actions in the same order and in the same place as they did last night. Is that agreed?"

There was a murmur of assent.

"Very good, then. We start from the moment when Mr. Constantinovitch asked Mrs. Brancaster to take Miss Freyne to bed. Where were you standing?"

"Here," said Gus.

"Very good. Mrs. Brancaster, go and stand there too, please. Were you with them, Mr. Brancaster? Then stand with them also. Where were, you, Mr. Bartram?"

"By the bar, at the other end of the room."

"Then go there, please. Now, Mrs. Brancaster, what did you do?"

"I left the room with Camilla, *so*."

"Did you follow, Mr. Brancaster?"

"Not at once."

Mallett followed Geneviève to the door. She walked up the stairs and stopped at the door of Camilla's room.

"I went in for a moment or two to talk to her," she explained.

"Go in there, then," said Mallett from the hall.

182

"Go in? In there? I cannot—I will not. It is not good in there."

Mallett shrugged his shoulders.

"Very well," he said. "Then stand at the door till it is time to come out. Now, Mr. Brancaster?"

Teddy came out of the music-room.

"This was where I went to the cloak-room and got into my bathing-kit," he said.

"Then go there now," said the inspector.

"And change my clothes?"

"Certainly. I want to see how long it takes you."

"Will any old bathing trunks do, or must it be the same ones?" asked Teddy sarcastically.

"That is of no importance. Who moves next?"

"I came out of the room just after Brancaster," said Dick, moving accordingly, "and sat in the hall, *here*."

From above, Geneviève's voice was heard.

"I leave this room now, and go to my own."

"Very good, Mrs. Brancaster."

Gus walked across the hall.

"I am going to my study to look at papers," he said.

A pause ensued, during which nobody moved. Mallett ran quickly up the stairs, surveyed the hall from the landing and came down again. Then Teddy came in, wearing his bathing trunks.

"Here I am, Sherlock," he announced. "Where do I go from here?"

"Wherever you went last night."

Teddy took a few steps into the music-room and back again.

"I'm looking for my wife," he explained.

"He call me, and I come out here," said Geneviève from above. "Then Camilla open her door, and I shut her back, so."

183

"And I go off for my swim," said Teddy, walking into the music-room again.

"Stay there a moment, Mr. Brancaster. What do you do, Mr. Bartram?"

"Call for Mrs. Brancaster."

"Without going upstairs?"

"Yes."

"Then come down, Mrs. Brancaster."

Geneviève came down.

"Now we go to the smoking-room," she said.

Mallett saw them go and then went into the music-room where Teddy was waiting.

"What next?" asked Teddy.

"Which way did you go?"

"Through here," he said, indicating the french windows.

"Then let's go."

Mallett walked with him out into the garden. The moon was up and they could see their surroundings clearly.

"It was pitch dark last night, of course," Teddy explained.

"But you knew your way well enough?"

"Sure. You just follow the path. It runs straight from here."

"We'll follow it, then."

Teddy shrugged his shoulders and they walked on together. When they reached the clump of bushes he stopped.

"That's all there is to it," he said. "I just run down here and dive in."

"We'll run, then," said the inspector amiably.

They reached the edge of the pool together.

"Dive in," said Mallett.

"Here, what's the great idea?" said Teddy violently.

Before them in the moonlight, the pool gleamed bare, polished, empty.

The Death of Amy Robsart

"Did you dive in last night?" Mallett asked in a new and terrible voice. "Or did somebody else—somebody who didn't know, who couldn't see, that she was diving into an empty pool?"

From the shadows behind them Sergeant Parkinson silently approached and stood at Brancaster's shoulder.

"You knew that it was empty," Mallett continued. "You had emptied it yourself. You arranged for your wife to come here last night, so that she might kill herself in the dark. You waited here, and saw her, as you thought, plunge to her death down there. You climbed down into the pool, wrapped her head in your towel, so that the blood drops might not betray you and carried the body back to beneath your wife's window, turning on the water to fill the pool again before you left. Then you went into the house and began asking where your wife was. It wasn't till you found her that you knew the truth—that it was not your wife but Camilla Freyne who had followed you—that you had killed the woman for whose sake you wanted to murder your wife. Is that not true?"

Teddy was shuddering convulsively, and his breath came in quick gasps.

"Sure, it's true," he muttered over and over again. "Sure, it's true—true. I killed her—I killed her! The only girl I ever loved—I killed her! Leave me go!"

As Mallett's hand closed upon his shoulder, he swung round, drove him off with a tremendous blow in the face, knocked Parkinson fairly over and made a rush for the spring-board. He leapt in the air, came down with all his weight upon its end and soared into the sky. In the moonlight his brown body gleamed for an instant as it turned in a perfect jack-knife dive, to crash head first on to the tiled floor below.

I Never Forget a Face

I'll tell you an odd thing about me—I never forget a face. The only trouble is that nine times out of ten I'm hanged if I can fit a name to it. I know what you're going to say: you suffer from the same thing yourself. Lots of people do to some extent, more people than not, I dare say. But I'm not like that. When I say I never forget a face, I mean it. I can pass a chap in the street one day and recognize him again months after, though we've never so much as spoken to each other. It's a gift. My wife says sometimes that I ought to be one of those press reporter fellows who hang about at dress shows and film premières spotting the celebrities. But, as I tell her. I should fall down pretty badly on a job like that if, when I'd spotted my celebrity, I couldn't say which one it was. That's my trouble, as I say—names.

Mind you, this matter of names has landed me in difficulties as it is, from time to time. But with a spot of ingenuity one can usually manage to get by one way or another. In my job, running round the City doing odd bits of business on commission, one has to be pretty fly not to let on that you can't for the life of you remember whether the blighter you're dealing with is called Smith or Moses. I've offended people that way and lost a good contract more than once. But on the whole, I reckon to gain more than I lose by this queer memory of mine. Many's the time I've gone up to a man in a bar who didn't know me from Adam. I've said "I think we've met before", and, what's more, I've been able to give him a hint where it was. I can always connect a face with a background, you see. Well, as I was saying, I can go up to this chap and remind him of the Candlestick Makers' dinner or the last big match at Highbury or whatever it was that his face puts me in mind of, and ten to one inside five minutes we're talking business. I can always get a line on his name later on. You'd be surprised how many good clients I've made that way, all for the price of a drink and a good memory for faces.

You can guess there's not a man, woman or child here in Bardfield that I don't know by sight. I've lived in Bardfield ever since the war. What I like about the place is that it's still quite countrified for all it's only forty minutes from Waterloo. It's a nuisance having the village the best part of a mile from the station, the other side of Bardfield Heath, but, after all, that keeps us nice and secluded. There's quite a pleasant crowd who travel up and down to the City from there most days; and I needn't tell you, I don't know the names of above half of them, though we pass the time of day cheerily enough. My wife complains that I don't know the names of our next-door neighbours, and that's true. All the same, when we got into a tangle with the car in Dover last summer I was able to pacify a very angry bobby simply because I recognized him from Bardfield, though it turned out he'd left the place two years before. He'd served behind the counter in the grocery shop, he told me, and I don't do the shopping once in a blue moon. See what I mean?

Well, on this particular evening I'd been kept a bit late at the office and it was quite a scramble to get to Waterloo in time to catch the 7.7. There was quite a crowd in the train at first, but they thinned out at the inner suburbs, and by the time we got to Ellingham—that's two stops before mine—there were only the two of us left in the carriage, myself and this fellow I was telling you about. He wasn't one of our regulars—they mostly keep directors' hours—but he was a Bardfield man all right. I knew that as soon as I set eyes on him, of course. I'd nodded and smiled to him when I saw him get in at Waterloo, naturally, and got a nod and smile back, but that didn't take me any further.

The annoying thing was that I couldn't *place* the fellow, if you know what I mean. His face said Bardfield to me, as plain as print, but that was all it did say. I couldn't bang it on to any particular thing in Bardfield—not the golf course, nor the Red Lion, nor any of my usual haunts. I guessed he must be one of those fellows who've moved in lately to the council houses by the bus-stop, though I couldn't be sure. Some of us old-timers are inclined to be stand-offish with the newcomers, but that's not my way— never has been. What I always say is, you never know where the next bit of business is going to come from in my line, and you just can't afford to neglect chances.

So when the two of us found ourselves alone in the carriage, with room to stretch our legs and be a bit comfortable, I started to talk, just as if we were old acquaintances, which, in a way, we were—on my side, at least. But I can't say I got very much out of him. He was a well-spoken young chap, I will say that for him, with a quiet, friendly manner, but he didn't open up a bit. I can generally reckon on finding out what a man's line of country is in ten and a half minutes—that's what it takes from Ellingham to Bardfield by train—and know whether he's a contact worth following up or not, but this one beat me. He looked a bit tired and peaky, I remember, as though he'd been overworking lately, and I thought maybe that made his reactions a bit slow.

I Never Forget a Face

"D'you generally travel down on this train?" I asked him. That's usually a pretty safe gambit, because either they do or they don't, and nine times out of ten they'll tell you why and what hours they work and what at. It's only human nature. But he just smiled and shook his head and said, "Not generally", which wasn't much help.

Of course I went on to talk about the train-service in general, comparing this train with that, but still he wasn't to be drawn. He just agreed with all I said, but he didn't seem to have an opinion of his own. I told him I sometimes went up to the City by road, but that didn't fetch him either. For that matter, I didn't think it would, because you don't expect a fellow living in a council house to run a car, though there are two or three of them who can afford television sets, and why we should be expected to subsidise their rents out of our rates I for one don't know.

Well, to cut a long story short, I had to give him up. I'd told him quite a bit about myself, of course, by way of making things pleasant. I'd even boasted a little about a rather nice little deal I'd pulled off that morning—a perfectly legal transaction, you'll understand, but not the kind that goes through one's firm's books, if you follow me. After all, if one couldn't do ready-money business from time to time we'd all be paying sur-tax and where should we be then? I've always found there's nothing like a little bragging to make a fellow open up. Sort of puts him on his mettle, you know. I'm bound to say he seemed interested in a quiet sort of way, but it was no good. He just wouldn't open up about himself. So, as I say, I gave it up and started to read my paper. And bless me, if the next time I looked at him he hadn't put his head back and gone off sound asleep!

We were just running into the station, and though the
train pulled up with a fair jerk it didn't seem to wake
him. Well, I'm a kind-hearted soul, and I wasn't going
to let a fellow Bardfield man be carried on all the way to
Dorbury if I could help it. So I tapped him pretty sharply
on the knee.

"Hey, wake up, old chap! We're there!" I said.

He came awake all at once and smiled at me.

"By jove, so we are!" he said and scrambled out after
me.

You know what the weather was like just then. When
we came out of the station together it was pitch dark and
raining cats and dogs. There was a wind blowing strong
enough to knock you over, and it was as cold as charity.
Filthy!

Well, what would you have done? The same as me, I
bet. I turned round and said to him.

"Look here, old man, the bus isn't due for a quarter of
an hour. I've my car in the station-yard and if you're in
one of the council houses, I can run you up there. It's all
on my way."

"Thanks very much," he said, and we splashed across
the puddles together to where my old bus was standing,
and off we went.

"This is awfully kind of you," he said as we started,
and that was the last thing he did say until we were half-
way across the heath.

Then he suddenly turned round and said, "You can
put me down here."

"What, *here*?" I asked him. It seemed crazy, because
there wasn't a house within five hundred yards and, as
I say, it was raining and blowing like the end of the
world. But all the same, I slowed down automatically as
anyone would.

I Never Forget a Face

The next thing that happened was that something hit me the most tremendous whack on the back of the head. I pitched forward over the steering-wheel and then everything went black. I can vaguely remember being tumbled out of the car, and when I came to I was lying in the ditch with the rain pouring down on me, with a splitting head, no car in sight and my pockets—as I found out later —as empty as a bank on Boxing Day.

I pulled myself up eventually and somehow managed to foot it into Bardfield. I made for the police station straight away, of course. It's the first building you come to from that side, anyway. So here I am, Sergeant, come to report the theft of a Riley 14 car, a new umbrella, a gold watch, and a wallet containing a hundred and fifty-two pound ten in notes.

Of course, the minute I got here I remembered who the blighter was. You've got his picture up outside now. I've seen it every day for the last week. That's why his face said Bardfield to me. "Wanted for Robbery with Violence and Attempted Murder—John——" Dash it! I've forgotten the name again. I just can't keep names in my head. But that's the man, Sergeant, you can bet your bottom dollar on that. I tell you—I never forget a face.

A Life for a Life

I forget exactly how the conversation in the smoking-room of the Fisherman's Rest got on to the subject of capital punishment. Probably it started with Colonel Hertford's making some such observation as that the fellow who used a wet fly on dry-fly water ought to be hanged, and with little Polkington, always deadly serious where his pet beliefs and causes were concerned, protesting against the expression, even as a joke. However it began, the discussion, once under way, seemed to show no signs of ever coming to an end. It is a subject which has the merit of being one on which everybody knows his own mind, and is quite intolerant of everyone else's opinion. Soon half a dozen of us were joining in. Instances, statistics and contradictions were flying across the room. Dry-fly men are a conservative breed, and the current of opinion flowed strongly against Polkington, who still, however, kept up his end quite unperturbed, and seemed to have an answer for everybody.

I remember Branshawe looking up from the mess of feathers and silk which he was hoping to transform into a fair imitation of a watery blue dun and saying in that gruff voice of his, "It's no good, Polkington, pretending that you can treat murder like any other crime. When a man has been killed there's no going back on it. The murderer alone of criminals can never make restitution. A burglar or a forger can. But a dead man's dead for good. There's the difference."

"Precisely," answered Polkington. "That is exactly my

argument against hanging. When you have killed your murderer—or rather the man you believe to be your murderer—for it never amounts to more than that—you've finished with him, for good or ill. Don't you see that you are cutting off also his opportunity of perhaps making some amends to the society which he has wronged? He has at least a right to be given a chance to redeem himself. When you hang him his chance goes for good."

"Now I wonder whether that's quite accurate," said a mild voice which had not yet spoken. It came from somewhere in the corner, and we all looked round a bit surprised. The smoking-room was a public room, of course, but the landlord generally managed to keep it pretty well private for us when we were down for the fishing. Then I remembered that he had mentioned to me that there was a commercial gentleman staying for the night. This was evidently the man—a small, thin fellow in the late forties, apparently, rather unhealthy-looking, I thought, but with an agreeable expression in his bright little eyes.

There was quite a long pause after he had spoken, and I'm afraid we all stared at him rather rudely. He did not seem to worry though, but sat quite still and simply stared back, not at any one of us in particular, but as if he was trying to make out something rather dim in the middle of the smoky room, invisible to everyone else. Finally Polkington, who seemed to be the person addressed —at least he had spoken the last—broke the silence.

"Whether what is accurate?" he asked in that rather sharp, testy manner which he affects in argument.

The stranger turned his head quickly, as if he had been suddenly recalled from his abstraction. He made as if to speak, and then hesitated. Finally he murmured apologetically, "Oh . . . I don't know. What you and the other gentleman were saying just now. About the finality of killing anyone, and redeeming one's faults and all that. I just wondered, that's all."

"Well, if you kill anyone, that's final enough, I should imagine," said Hertford rather contemptuously.

The little man rubbed his chin and seemed to consider the proposition thoughtfully.

"Yes, I suppose so," he said at last. "You kill and you're killed and there's an end of it. One life cancels out the other and all's square—or ought to be. But is it as simple as that, always? Suppose lives don't cancel out like sums on a black-board? Suppose there's something left over— even after a hanging?"

I began to think that we had got hold of a lunatic, or at least a crank of the worst type, and almost wished that we had snubbed him out of hand; but Polkington, who is a bit of an oddity himself and has a weakness for his fellow oddities, took him quite seriously.

"All this sounds very interesting," he said. "Can't you be a little more definite?"

The commercial smiled. (He had, incidentally, one of the most attractive smiles I have ever seen.)

"That's just the trouble," he said. "You can't be definite unless you've got something to go on. And I don't know that I have. Only I've been sitting here listening to you gentlemen all the evening, and I began to wonder what bearing it all had on something that happened to me a few years ago. But it doesn't help your argument much one way or the other, I'm afraid, gentlemen. That's a bit out of my line, and I hope I shall be excused from taking sides. I was thinking out loud just now, and I hope you'll pardon my interruption."

Naturally Polkington wasn't to be put off in this way. He liked queer fish as much as he did trout, and that was saying a good deal.

"You mentioned an experience of your own just now," he said. "Won't you do us the favour of letting us know what it was?"

The man hesitated for a bit, and then said, "If the other gentlemen wouldn't mind. It would be a relief in a way to talk about it."

None of us minded at all. We were fairly tired of arguing capital punishment by then, and at the worst this would be some sort of variation. Someone ordered him a whisky, we found him a chair in the middle of the ring round the fire, and in a quiet, unemphatic voice he began.

I travel in soap, gentlemen (he said), Mellon's Medicated Soap. When I first joined the firm, just after the war, they gave me the London area, but after one winter at it I found my health wouldn't stand it, and I asked to be transferred to the north. I soon found out my mistake. My trouble was lungs, you see—still is, for the matter of that, though it's better than it was. I don't know whether any of you gentlemen was ever gassed in France? Well, I got my packet in March '18, and I don't suppose I've been properly the same man ever since. I'd got it well into my system, the doctors said, and the first year or so afterwards I was only kept alive by injections. A semi-permanent condition of something or other, they said it was. I forget the name they gave it—it was nothing to what I called it, I can tell you. They pulled me through all right, and I was able to get about again, but still from time to time I'd have a relapse. Winters were the worst, of course, and foggy weather worst of all. A real London particular would knock me right out, and then there was nothing to be done but send for the doctor to jab me, and lie up till the weather cleared. Not much good for a man

on the road, you can imagine. That was why I asked to
be transferred. I'd got it into my head that you didn't
get fogs up in the north. Well, I was wrong, but how
wrong I never knew till I got to Gorblington.

I dare say none of you have ever been to Gorblington,
except perhaps to pass through it in the Scotch express.
I don't recommend a visit there—not on pleasure, anyway. It's a dirty, straggling town in the very nastiest part
of the industrial district of Yorkshire, and it manufactures
chemicals. Perhaps I'm a bit prejudiced against it, for I
certainly didn't see it at its best, the only time I went
there. It was the middle of February, and a beastly
February at that. I had had a hard day at Leeds, and was
feeling pretty down in the mouth by the time the train
put me down about seven o'clock of a dark, dreary evening.
The best hotel in Gorblington—and that's not saying
much, I give you my word—is the Greyhound, the opposite
end of the town from the station, and the first thing I
found when I came out was that the trams were on strike.
There were a few dilapidated-looking cabs about in the
station yard, but my firm was pretty close about travelling
expenses, and I was a newly married man, and had to
look twice at every shilling. So I made up my mind to
walk. I told myself that the exercise would be good for me,
though I knew quite well in my heart of hearts that it
wouldn't, asked the way from the porter, humped my bags
and set off.

I had my case of samples in one hand and my suitcase
in the other, and though I dare say any one of you gentlemen would think them no great load, the weight of them
was just about as much as I could manage. I hadn't gone
very far before I was cursing myself for a fool and simply
praying for the sight of a taxi. And, of course, as always
happens at such times, there wasn't one to be seen. There

wasn't much else to be seen, either. Gorblington station is some way from the centre of the town, and my way was through mean streets, with only an occasional lamp at the corners making a pool of yellow light on the slimy pavement. The place seemed almost deserted, for all it was so early, and there was hardly a sound except the *slap, slap* of my own feet to keep me company.

Presently I noticed that it was getting even darker. When I set out I could see half a dozen lamps ahead of me, then only three or four, then two, till finally it was all I could do standing under one light to make out the one next ahead. At first I thought that the gas-works had followed the tramwaymen out on strike, but before long I knew that my luck was dead out, and that I was in for a fog. It was swirling up in little wisps from the direction in which I was going, about the height of the first-storey windows, turning the yellow lights to orange, and from time to time blowing down close over my head. Once I got a mouthful of it and nearly choked, then an upward draught blew it away again, and I was able to go on. But it was getting thicker and I didn't like the look of things. I reckoned that I was about half-way by then and I put on pace to try to get in before it reached its worst. In my hurry I must have missed the turning which would have taken me into the High Street, for the next thing I knew I was in a little square, with iron railings surrounding a grassy enclosure and decent-looking old-fashioned houses on either side. That was all I had time to see, for the next minute the fog came right down on me, and everything was blotted out.

Fog! I assure you gentlemen I never knew what the word meant before. A London particular was nothing to it. That can be bad enough, the yellow sort especially, but this was green. It was like being at the bottom of a well, and not a well full of honest water, but of some horrible liquid mud. That's the nearest I can get to describing what it looked like, but what it felt like is beyond my telling. I took one gulp, and then it was simply the trenches in France over again. In less than no time I was gasping and choking like a drowning man, with my eyes streaming till I could hardly see and every vein in my body boiling fit to burst. Don't make any mistake about it, gentlemen, I wasn't simply feeling uncomfortable and unwell as anybody else might in a fog like that. I really was a drowning man at that moment. There was a whiff of something devilish in that greenish vapour—I suppose it came from the chemical works nearby, although I was too far gone to think of that then—and it had reproduced exactly all the symptoms of gas-poisoning. I was just as near to dying then as at any time since '18.

For a minute or two—it can't have been longer—I almost gave up hope. I remember I leant against the railings fighting for breath and simply waited, knowing though I did that there was nothing to wait for except death or a miracle. Then it seemed that the miracle had happened. An eddy of wind just lifted the fog for a moment and I saw on the outside of a house opposite something that glittered faintly in the light of a lamp. I had barely time to recognize it for a doctor's brass plate before the fog came down again. Then I knew that I had still a chance. A pretty slim chance, mind you, I realized that. Not every medico by a long way would have the right stuff handy for my trouble; and if he had, his surgery might be closed, or he himself on his rounds somewhere, lost in the fog like myself. But reach that brass plate I must; and head bent, staggering and swaying, still gripping those infernal bags, which for some reason or other I never dreamt of letting go, I fought my way towards it, inch by inch. I must have been a queer sight, shuffling those few yards with such awful toil, for all the world as though I had to push my way through some solid obstacle instead of mere vapour. Indeed it felt just as if I were struggling to push open an impossibly heavy door, with an enemy on the other side who had sworn to stop me. Only the enemy was inside me, you'll understand, choking the life out of my poor lungs and heart, till every fibre in me was crying out against the will that told it to go on. On I went, though, with my ears drumming madly and my smarting eyes half closed, till at last I lurched up to the brass plate. I got my head up to look at it, and my heart missed a beat. It wasn't a doctor's house at all.

"Atkinson, Trollope and Barr, Solicitors and Commissioners for Oaths." I read the words over again and again in a kind of stupid trance. Then I started to laugh, and that hurt more than anything that had happened yet. Finally I squared my shoulders, said out loud—I can hear my own voice saying it still—"Well, I'd better be getting on, I suppose," and actually began to walk away, though why or where to I had not the least idea.

Oddly enough, walking seemed suddenly to have become much easier now. I felt no better in myself—on the contrary, the pain in my chest and head seemed if possible worse than ever—but my legs now seemed to act as though independent of the rest of me. There was hardly any sensation in them, and I seemed to glide over the pavement without touching it. I remember wondering how long that would last, but mercifully I didn't have to put it to the test. I had hardly taken a dozen paces before I was aware of a light just in front of me and on my right-hand side. I knew at once that it was no street lamp. It was on the wrong side of me for one thing, and, besides, this was a diffused radiance that could only come from

an open window. Two steps more and I knew something
else about it. It had a pinkish glow that could mean only one
thing—the light was being projected through one of those
glass containers which you see in old-fashioned chemists'
shops. What happened next I hardly know. There were
steps up to the shop door, but I haven't the least idea
how I scaled them. I can only say that somehow I found
myself inside the place, half lying, half sitting on a chair
that was providentially near the entrance, asking myself
whether I was dead already or merely dying.

The chemist was standing behind his counter facing
me, pouring something out of a bottle into a glass beaker
which he held in his left hand. He was a big, pale-faced
man, with very dark hair and a long, heavy moustache.
He seemed to take my appearance surprisingly calmly.
He simply looked at me, and then put the bottle and
beaker down on the counter so quietly that I hardly
heard a sound. Then he slipped round from behind the
counter with astonishing quickness, and stood looking
at me for a second or two. He must have summed me up
at once, for he only uttered one word, and that in a tone-
less voice which was hardly above a whisper.

"Gassed?" he asked.

I nodded.

Still moving at the same extraordinary pace, but remarkably silently for a man of his size, he darted behind
the counter again and began mixing some ingredients
together. In a moment or two he was out once more
with a hypodermic syringe in his hand.

"Injection," he murmured, and my sleeve was turned
up before I knew what had happened. I felt the needle
go in—oh, there's no doubt about it, gentlemen, I felt
the needle go in.

I'm used to feeling a bit queer after an injection, but

this time it was worse than usual. Everything went black for the moment, and I suppose I lost consciousness. But somehow or other I must have staggered out of the shop, for when I came to I was on the pavement again, breathing almost without difficulty, and staring joyfully at the lights of a taxi which was bearing down upon me.

I croaked, "Greyhound Hotel", flung myself inside, and went to sleep straight away. I was as tired as though I had been walking all night, though from the time I left the station hardly half an hour could have passed. I was in bed within a few minutes of reaching the hotel, and slept like the dead till late next morning.

It was a fine day, thank heavens, and no trace of that damnable fog. The injection had done its work, and I was able to get about and pay a few calls. Only one thing bothered me. I had never paid the chemist. As he had certainly saved my life overnight, he was entitled to the price of his dope, at any rate. And I hadn't a notion where he lived. It wasn't till I was in the middle of my lunch that I suddenly remembered the brass plate of Atkinson, Trollope and Barr. I looked in the directory and found their address. It was Falke Square, and to Falke Square I went as soon as I had finished my chop.

The place looked pleasant enough under the wintry sun, and I could hardly believe that it was the scene of my agony of the night before. I walked all round it, admiring the old Georgian houses. It was really a charming little square, easily the best thing in Gorblington. In fact it had only one thing wrong with it. There was no chemist's shop to be seen in the length and breadth of it. I went round the square again, unable to believe my eyes, but there could be no doubt about it. Two doors from the solicitors' was a tailor's, and beyond him a bookshop, but they were the only two shops in the whole place.

As I finished my second round I saw someone approaching Atkinson's office. He was a florid, complacent-looking fellow, apparently just back from a better lunch than mine had been, and I put him down as a partner. I caught him as he reached the entrance.

"Excuse me," I said, "I am looking for a chemist's shop. I wonder if you can help me."

"The nearest to here is Boots in the High Street," he answered, and made to go in.

"But I'm looking for one particular shop," I persisted, "in this square. At least I thought it was."

He turned right round, one foot on the doorstep, and looked at me curiously.

"There's no chemist's shop in this square. You can see that for yourself," he said.

He spoke loudly, almost defiantly I thought. His tone rather nettled me, and I also raised my voice as I answered, "Then I'd like to know who gave me an injection here last night, because I haven't paid his bill yet."

The effect of my words was quite surprising. Trollope (or was it Barr?—I never found out) changed his expression all at once. Some of the colour left his cheeks and his jaw dropped. Then he said abruptly but very quietly, "We don't want everyone to listen to this. Come inside for a moment."

I followed him into the office, more puzzled than ever, and we went into his private room. There he sat down and said with the greatest seriousness:

"Now, sir, please be good enough to tell me how you come to be looking for a chemist's shop in this square."

I told him exactly what I have been telling you, and he never interrupted by so much as a syllable. When I had finished he said very quietly:

"There hasn't been a chemist here since Vincent. He

202

was where the tailor is now. Vincent. We acted for him, you know. Vincent."

He repeated the name in a meaning tone, as if it ought to convey something to me. I looked at him stupidly for a bit, and then I remembered.

"Vincent!" I gasped. We were both talking in whispers now.

"Yes," he answered.

"He—he killed his wife, didn't he?" said I.

"With a hypodermic syringe." His lips framed the words rather than spoke them.

We sat staring at each other for what seemed a long time. Finally I pulled myself out of my chair.

"Well, thank you very much," I said. "I must be going." It sounded absurd, but what else could one say?

"Can I help you in any other way?" said the lawyer, playing up in the same fashion.

A thought struck me. "Yes," I said, "there is one other thing. Have you by any chance a photograph of—of the man we have been discussing? If so, I should like to see it."

"Surely," said he. He took a book from the shelf. "He's been written up in the Famous Poisoners' series— I expect you know it. Here we are—quite a good likeness."

He was speaking quite naturally again, but I swear his hand trembled as he passed me the book. As for me— well, gentlemen, I'm sorry not to be able to end the story on a more elevated note, but the plain truth is that as soon as I'd set eyes on that photograph I spoilt the carpet of the leading solicitor in Gorblington by being very violently sick on it.

He stopped abruptly, and there was quite half a minute's silence. Each of us, I suppose, was absorbed in his own thoughts and none too anxious to give them voice. Finally Polkington spoke.

"And what is your theory?" he asked the commercial.

"Theory? I don't rightly know that I have one. I've thought about it often enough, of course. Perhaps I should say that I have a hope rather than a theory."

"A hope? What for?"

"Why, for him, poor devil. A hope that after all they did give him a chance to make amends for the life he took, by saving another one. Perhaps it will make things a bit easier for him there . . ."

Polkington turned to Hertford.

"What do you think?" he asked.

"I think," said Hertford with great emphasis, "that the story is worth another whisky all round."

The proposal was carried unanimously.

The Markhampton Miracle

William White, formerly Detective-Inspector of the Markshire Constabulary, and now the senior partner in White's Private Enquiry Agency, called by appointment at the offices of Mark's Football Pools two days after Boxing Day. He was taken at once to the room of the managing director of that famous and profitable concern, where he found a very worried and very puzzled man.

"I have called you in, Mr. White," the managing director explained, "to investigate in strict confidence, what appears to be the largest fraud that has ever been perpetrated in the history of this firm—I may say, in the history of Football Pools."

"Yes, sir," said White. If the managing director had not been so preoccupied with his own concerns he might have noticed that White seemed rather downcast at his opening words.

"The fraud relates to our Ten Results Pool on matches played on Boxing Day," he went on.

"Quite, sir." White looked even gloomier than before.

"We have reason to think that some of the winning entries were faked."

"There was more than one all-correct line, then, sir?"

"Yes, more than one. To be accurate, there were"—he consulted some papers on his desk—"one correct line sent in from Middlesbrough, one from Redruth and fifty-three thousand six hundred and nineteen from Markhampton and its suburbs."

"*How* many, did you say, sir?"

"Fifty-three thousand six hundred and nineteen."

"But that's impossible, sir."

"Exactly. In the whole country outside this city there were just two correct entries out of approximately three-quarters of a million. The Markhampton figures speak for themselves. It is a fraud on a colossal scale. How was it done! That's what I've called you in to find out."

White was silent for a moment.

"Well, sir," he said finally, "you know as well as I do that there are just two ways in which a fraud on the Pools is attempted as a rule. Either you fake the date stamp on the envelope containing the entry, so as to make it appear that it was posted before the matches were played, when in fact it was posted afterwards——"

"That's quite out of the question in this case. A single dishonest clerk in the post office might try it just once to win for himself or to oblige a pal, but it couldn't possibly be done on this scale. Besides, the winning entries came from all over the district. Every post office in the neighbourhood would have to be involved."

"The other type of fraud," White went on, "is, of course, an inside job. One of your employees adds the winning line to an entry and slips it in among the others."

The managing director shook his head.

"You can see for yourself that that won't do," he said. "Even if my staff weren't honest—which they are—and I have a pretty strict internal security service, I may tell you—have you considered how long it would take to mark fifty thousand entries? Short of a conspiracy among half the girls in my office, it's simply out of the question. You'll have to think of something else."

"Well, at the moment, sir, there's nothing else I can think of. Except that by some extraordinary freak all these entries are genuine."

"Tcheh!" said the managing director.

Mrs. White greeted her husband eagerly when he got home that evening.

"Well?" she said. Then her face fell as she saw his disconsolate expression. "Is there anything wrong?" she asked.

"Something funny's happened to the Ten Results entries," he said. "Mark's want me to look into it."

"Oh, Willie, isn't that just your luck? When you told me they'd sent for you I thought it meant something good for you. Emily will be so disappointed, too. She'd set her heart on something wonderful for you this Christmas."

White was staring absently at an old copy of the *Markshire Herald* which lay open on the kitchen table. He read the headlines automatically. Then he said:

"Where is Emily? I want a word with her."

"She's playing next door with Susan Berry. Can't it wait till she comes in?"

"No time like the present. Besides, I might have a talk to Susan too, while I'm about it."

White went next door. He had his talk to Emily and Susan and to Mr. Berry also. He extended his enquiry to his next-door neighbour on the other side, and then to various houses further down the street. Next day he pursued his investigations among his friends and acquaintances, and outwards in an ever-widening circle. All the people he questioned were married men with young families, and everything he heard served to confirm the wild surmise that had come into his mind when he had glanced at the newspaper headlines.

Finally he paid two additional visits—one to the offices of the *Markshire Herald*, the other to a dignified old house in Markhampton cathedral close.

Within three days he was back in the offices of Mark's Pools.

"I have investigated the matter you complained of, sir," he told the managing director.

"Yes?"

"One person is responsible for the winning lines in the Ten Results Pool for Boxing Day. I interviewed him last night, and he admits everything."

"Who is it? I shall prosecute, whoever it is."

"As to prosecuting sir, I'm not so sure. The man in question is the Reverend Canon Furbelow."

"Canon Furbelow! Mr. White, are you trying to make a fool of me?"

"Not at all, sir. He is the culprit, though he admits that he would not have been as successful as he was if he had not had the assistance of a journalist who writes for the *Herald* under the name of John Straight."

"But this is preposterous! Canon Furbelow is against pools or betting of any sort. Why, I'm told he's been known to preach sermons against them."

"Quite so, sir. A very powerful preacher is the Canon. It seems that it's his preaching that's at the bottom of the trouble in this case."

The managing director mopped his brow with his handkerchief.

"One of us is certainly mad," he said. "Possibly both. Will you kindly explain?"

"Canon Furbelow," said White, "conducted a series of children's services during Advent. They were very popular, and the cathedral was crowded for each of them. He has a wonderful way with children, has the Canon.

My little girl, Emily, went to them. She was very much impressed by him."

"Confound your little girl Emily!" said the managing director rudely. "Will you kindly get to the point—if you have one?"

"I am just coming to it, sir," said White calmly. "His last sermon on the Sunday before Christmas was particularly eloquent. It attracted a good deal of attention. The journalist I mentioned just now happened to be in the cathedral on that occasion, and he made it the subject of a very striking article, which was read and commented on all over the city. Luckily the national newspapers didn't take it up, or the damage would have been even greater than it was. I have a copy of the article here, sir, if you would care to see it."

The managing director waved it angrily away.

"Unless it forecasts the results of the Boxing Day League matches, I don't," he said.

"It doesn't mention the football, sir. What the sermon and the article dealt with was the beauty of unselfishness. Canon Furbelow reminded the children that at Christmas time they would all, quite rightly, be looking forward to the good things they were going to get—their presents and parties and so on. But, he told them, these were not the things they ought to ask for when they said their prayers. They should ask for things for others, and especially for those nearest and dearest to them. What a wonderful thing it would be, he said, if on Christmas Eve every child in Markhampton were to kneel down and pray that their parents should have their dearest wish granted to them. He drew a beautiful picture of all those innocent, unselfish supplications floating up to heaven together at that holy time of the year. The Canon has a great faith in the power of prayer, sir, and a great gift for imparting his faith to others.

"And the children did what he told them, sir. And thanks to John Straight his words went all over Markhampton and reached thousands of homes where the people didn't go to church. The children's prayers were heard and their parents got their heart's desire. And fifty-three thousand six hundred and nineteen of us had set our hearts on the Ten Results Pool," he concluded a little bitterly.

The managing director was silent for a time. Then he said, "You don't believe all this stuff, do you?"

White shrugged his shoulders.

"I don't know what else there is to believe," he said. "Canon Furbelow believes it, anyway. By the way, sir, he was asking me—how much will the dividend on the Ten Results work out at?"

"Two shillings and fourpence."

"I told him it would be round about that figure. He said there was a moral in that. I believe he means to make it the theme of his sermon next Sunday. Good day, sir."

A Very Useful Relationship

Recently, I delivered a lecture on detective fiction in a village hall in the West of England. The chairman of the literary society which had invited me, who was also the leading local solicitor, was good enough to put me up for the night. We were enjoying some sandwiches and drinks after the ordeal was over when he observed:

"I've noticed how fond you detective writers are of making your principal suspect a nephew or niece of the deceased. It really becomes quite monotonous. Why is it done so often?"

"It's a very useful relationship for our purposes," I said, defensively. "The family circle provides an ideal field of suspects. From one point of view a son or daughter would do equally well, but the public might boggle at anything so horrible as patricide."

My host said nothing for a moment. Then he asked abruptly, "What did you think of our village hall?"

"I was rather impressed by it," I said. "Surprisingly ambitious for a place of this size. It must have cost a good deal to put up."

"Yes," he replied. "It did. And the way it came to be built is quite a story. I was reminded of it by what we were saying about uncles and nephews."

The village had been crying out for a hall for years (he said), but nothing had ever been done about it. We had

211

the plans, we had the site, but the project was at a standstill for want of someone to take the lead in organizing support and raising the funds. Until old John Pennington came along. John Pennington and his nephew Alec.

I never knew anybody enter so quickly into the life of the place as old Pennington did. He was a man of extraordinary charm and, for all his age, remarkably energetic. He hadn't been three weeks in the village before he made his presence felt. He had taken a furnished house for the summer, but he let it be known that as soon as he could find a place to his liking he meant to settle here for good. He was obviously fairly well off, and having reached the age of retirement he had time on his hands. As soon as I saw him I realized he was what the village had been looking for.

I mentioned the village hall to him, and asked if he could lend a hand. He was reluctant at first, but once I had persuaded him he took it up with enthusiasm. Before you could say knife, an Appeal Committee had been formed and things began to hum. Pennington started the ball rolling with a cheque for a couple of hundred pounds, I remember, and after that money came in at a remarkable rate. Long before I had expected, the subscription list showed enough in cash and promises to warrant my going to Tunstall, the local builder, and telling him to start the job.

We had all the local big-wigs on the Committee, of course—the squire and the rector and the rest. They made me chairman, but old Pennington was the moving spirit. My daughter did a grand job of work as secretary; and the treasurer—it seemed natural enough at the time— was young Alec Pennington.

Looking back on it now, I cannot understand how I failed to recognize Alec for the shyster he so obviously was. I think that we were all so blinded by the transparent sincerity and genuineness of the old man and his really touching affection for Alec that we were inclined to take the nephew at the uncle's valuation.

But there it was. We were one and all hopelessly taken in by the young rogue. Every penny we so painfully collected—much of it wheedled out of the most unlikely people by John Pennington's charm and personality—went into his hands. In the rather casual way these things are handled by amateur committees we accepted as gospel the financial statements he put before us at our meetings. Nobody doubted that the money was in the bank. Until, as it was bound to do, the balloon went up.

About a month after the work had started, Tunstall called on me in my office. He came to enquire when he was going to receive some payment on account. I was flabbergasted. The work had been going forward extremely well, and I knew for a fact that the architect had already issued two certificates for £500 apiece. There were ample funds to meet them—or should have been. And here was Tunstall, with tears in his eyes, threatening to withdraw his labour from the site because he couldn't meet the week's wages bill. Like all these small builders, he lived from hand to mouth, and he'd stretched his credit to the limit to finance the contract.

I did what I could to reassure Tunstall and got rid of him as soon as possible, with promises of immediate payment that I tried to make sound convincing. Then I got on to Pennington on the telephone and told him that I must see him and his nephew that evening. Luckily I was able also to make contact with the rector and one of the other committee men, Trelawney, the second biggest landowner in the parish. They came to my office and the three of us went along together.

Without beating about the bush, I told Pennington in his nephew's presence what Tunstall had said to me. It was obvious to me before I began that young Alec knew that the game was up. I was watching his weak sullen face as I spoke. As for the old man, his expression was so pitiable that I could hardly bear to look at him. It was like hitting a child. What made it all the worse was that I had the strongest impression that this revelation didn't come to him altogether as a surprise but rather as the dreadful confirmation of what must have been a deep-seated, unavowed suspicion.

When I had finished, he said very quietly, "Alec, how much money have you stolen?"

The boy tried to bluster at first, but he broke down pretty quickly, and he named a figure. It was something over two thousand pounds.

Then Pennington, his voice still well under control, said, "You will now leave us. But before you go, fetch me my cheque-book and the long envelope in the top drawer of my desk."

Alec did what he was told and then left the room. I thought his face looked positively evil as he went. Only then did the old man look round at us. There were tears in his eyes.

"One thing I must ask of you gentlemen," he said. "And that is, that you will not prosecute."

I said that obviously that was a matter for the full committee. Speaking for myself, I could make no promises. We had to consider how we were going to explain matters to our subscribers.

"I was hoping that that might not prove necessary," said Pennington. He opened his cheque-book. "I am not a rich man, but this is my responsibility." Then and there he drew a cheque in my favour for the full amount missing and handed it to me. "I hope this may induce the committee not to proceed to extremes."

I was about to say something, but he had not finished. "There is another matter which needs attending to," he went on, and his voice now was quite hard. "Life at my age is uncertain and I should like it done here and now. Will you be good enough to draw up a codicil to my will?"

"Surely that can wait," I protested. "You will want to think things over, after a shock like that."

"Now, please," said the old man firmly. He handed me the envelope, and I took from it a will, dated some months back and drawn up by a London firm of solicitors. I glanced through it quickly. It was quite short. There were some bequests to various charities amounting to several thousand pounds, a gift of five thousand pounds to Alec Pennington, and the residue was left equally between Alec and his sister Elizabeth, of whom I had never heard before.

"What do you wish to provide by the codicil?" I asked.

"Revoke the bequest to my nephew, and give the residue to Elizabeth absolutely. And perhaps it might help the committee to take a merciful view of what has happened if I were to leave the five thousand pounds to the Trustees of the Village Hall as an endowment. Will that be a good charitable bequest?"

I hate answering questions of this sort off the cuff but I said, "I think so—yes," and so it was done. I drew up the codicil on the spot, and the rector and Trelawney signed as witnesses.

I was blotting the signatures when Trelawney said suddenly: "This is all very well, and I'm sure we're very grateful to Mr. Pennington for the generous way he has behaved, but there's still Tunstall to be considered. Tomorrow's pay day and he must have some cash. Your cheque's on a London bank, isn't it, Mr. Pennington? It'll take a week to clear it."

The old man looked utterly woebegone. "Gentlemen, I haven't five pounds in the house. I've done what I can," he said.

Then the parson spoke up. "Fortunately I can solve that problem," he said. "There is at the rectory at this moment the sum of £347 and some odd shillings, and pence, the proceeds of our very successful fête last Saturday in aid of the Village Hall funds. I was to have given it to our treasurer today, but——"

It was at this moment that the telephone rang. The call was for the rector, from his wife, who was, mercifully, a woman of some sense. Mr. Alec Pennington was at the rectory, she reported. He had called for the money from the fête. Was it in order to hand it over?

Somehow or other the rector contrived to explain to his wife that on no account was the money to leave his safe until he returned, and then we all looked at one another in silence.

"After this," said old Pennington at last, "I have nothing more to say. Let the law take its course. They can do what they will with my nephew—if they can find him. I don't think he will wait at the rectory for us."

He was right, of course. When we got to the rectory—in my car, for Pennington's garage was as empty now as Alec's room—he was nowhere to be seen. The money was safe enough, though, and the rector counted it out on the dining-room table.

And this is where I cannot forgive myself. I had seen Alec's face when he left his uncle's presence, but I still did not realize just how far an utterly unprincipled man could go. I was about to take up the money when Pennington stopped me.

"Let me pay Tunstall myself," he said. "He is looking to my nephew for his money, and it will come better from me. After all, someone will have to explain to him what has happened, and I had rather bear the burden of it myself."

And I let him go, with the money in his pocket, a mournful, dignified figure, walking down the rectory lane in the twilight of a summer's evening. It was only a few hundred yards to Tunstall's house, but even as he went I had a horrible presentiment, that he would never be allowed to reach it. It was all I could do to stop myself running after him.

It was only next morning that I heard what had happened. Alec must have parked his car just off the lane. The police were able to trace its tyre marks as far as the main road. They could follow Pennington's footprints to nearly the same point, and there they abruptly stopped. The car was found abandoned later on the moors, near some disused mine-workings. Something heavy had been dragged to the mouth of an old shaft, hundreds of feet deep. They spent days looking for the body, but they never found it.

My host fell silent, and I became aware that he was looking at the clock. I took the hint, and got up to go to bed.

"What a grim story!" I said. "I don't wonder that you find wicked nephews in fiction small beer. Did they ever catch him, by the way?"

"They did, in the end. It took them the best part of eighteen months, though. He was tried at Bodmin Assizes. Not that it was much of a trial. He pleaded guilty and got off remarkably lightly."

"Got off lightly! For murder!"

A Very Useful Relationship

"Who's talking about murder? Old Pennington got three years for fraud. The so-called nephew was never found. I must say it was a most ingenious scheme, and beautifully put over. Mind you, I think I should have seen through it if it hadn't been for that will. There is something about a will that is damnably convincing. I've got the thing still. Remind me to show it to you in the morning. Good night."

Sister Bessie or Your Old Leech

"At Christmas-time we gladly greet
  Each old familiar face.
At Christmas time we hope to meet
  At th' old familiar place.
Five hundred loving greetings, dear,
  From you to me
To welcome in the glad New Year
  I look to see!"

Hilda Trent turned the Christmas card over with her
carefully manicured fingers as she read the idiotic
lines aloud.

"Did you ever hear anything so completely palsied?"
she asked her husband. "I wonder who on earth they can
get to write the stuff. Timothy, do you know anybody
called Leech?"

"Leech?"

"Yes—that's what it says: 'From your old Leech.'
Must be a friend of yours. The only Leach I ever knew
spelt her name with an a and this one has two e's." She
looked at the envelope. "Yes, it was addressed to you.
Who is the old Leech?" She flicked the card across the
breakfast-table.

Timothy stared hard at the rhyme and the scrawled
message beneath it.

"I haven't the least idea," he said slowly.

As he spoke he was taking in, with a sense of cold misery, the fact that the printed message on the card had been neatly altered by hand. The word "Five" was in ink. The original, poet no doubt, had been content with "A hundred loving greetings".

"Put it on the mantelpiece with the others," said his wife. "There's a nice paunchy robin on the outside."

"Damn it, no!" In a sudden access of rage he tore the card in two and flung the pieces into the fire.

It was silly of him, he reflected as he travelled up to the City half an hour later, to break out in that way in front of Hilda; but she would put it down to the nervous strain about which she was always pestering him to take medical advice. Not for all the gold in the Bank of England could he have stood the sight of that damnable jingle on his dining-room mantelpiece. The insolence of it! The cool, calculated devilry! All the way to London the train wheels beat out the maddening rhythm:

"At Christmas-time we gladly greet . . ."

And he had thought that the last payment had seen the end of it. He had returned from James's funeral triumphant in the certain belief that he had attended the burial of the blood-sucker who called himself "Leech". But he was wrong, it seemed.

"Five hundred loving greetings, dear . . ."

Five hundred! Last year it had been three, and that had been bad enough. It had meant selling out some holdings at an awkward moment. And now five hundred, with the market in its present state! How in the name of all that was horrible was he going to raise the money?

He would raise it, of course. He would have to. The sickening, familiar routine would be gone through again. The cash in Treasury notes would be packed in an unobtrusive parcel and left in the cloakroom at Waterloo. Next day he would park his car as usual in the railway yard at his local station. Beneath the windscreen wiper— "the old familiar place"—would be tucked the cloakroom ticket. When he came down again from work in the evening the ticket would be gone. And that would be that—till next time. It was the way that Leech preferred it and he had no option but to comply.

The one certain thing that Trent knew about the identity of his blackmailer was that he—or could it be she?—was a member of his family. His family! Thank heaven, they were no true kindred of his. So far as he knew he had no blood relation alive. But "his" family they had been, ever since, when he was a tiny, ailing boy, his father had married the gentle, ineffective Mary Grigson, with her long trail of soft, useless children. And when the influenza epidemic of 1919 carried off John Trent he had been left to be brought up as one of that clinging, grasping clan. He had got on in the world, made money, married money, but he had never got away from the "Grigsons". Save for his stepmother, to whom he grudgingly acknowledged that he owed his start in life, how he loathed them all! But "his" family they remained, expecting to be treated with brotherly affection, demanding his presence at family reunions, especially at Christmas-time.

"At Christmas-time we hope to meet . . ."

He put down his paper unread and stared forlornly out of the carriage window. It was at Christmas-time, four years before, that the whole thing started—at his stepmother's Christmas Eve party, just such a boring family function as the one he would have to attend in a few days' time. There had been some silly games to amuse the children—Blind Man's Buff and Musical Chairs—and in

221

the course of them his wallet must have slipped from his pocket. He discovered the loss next morning, went round to the house and retrieved it. But when it came into his hands again there was one item missing from its contents. Just one. A letter, quite short and explicit, signed in a name that had about then become fairly notorious in connection with an unsavoury enquiry into certain large-scale dealings in government securities. How he could have been fool enough to keep it a moment longer than was necessary! . . . but it was no good going back on that.

And then the messages from Leech had begun. Leech had the letter. Leech considered it his duty to send it to the principal of Trent's firm, who was also Trent's father-in-law. But, meanwhile, Leech was a trifle short of money, and for a small consideration . . . So it had begun, and so, year in and year out, it had gone on.

He had been so sure that it was James! That seedy, unsuccessful stock-jobber, with his gambling debts and his inordinate thirst for whisky, had seemed the very stuff of which blackmailers are made. But he had got rid of James last February, and here was Leech again, hungrier than ever. Trent shifted uneasily in his seat. "Got rid of him" was hardly the right way to put it. One must be fair to oneself. He had merely assisted James to get rid of his worthless self. He had done no more than ask James to dinner at his club, fill him up with whisky and leave him to drive home on a foggy night with the roads treacherous with frost. There had been an unfortunate incident on the Kingston bypass, and that was the end of James—and, incidentally, of two perfect strangers who had happened to be on the road at the same time. Forget it! The point was that the dinner—and the whisky—had been a dead loss. He would not make the same mistake again. This Christmas Eve he intended to make sure who

his persecutor was. Once he knew, there would be no
half measures.

Revelation came to him midway through Mrs. John
Trent's party—at the very moment, in fact, when the
presents were being distributed from the Christmas tree,
when the room was bathed in the soft radiance of coloured
candles and noisy with the "Oohs!" and "Ahs!" of excited
children and with the rustle of hastily unfolded paper
parcels. It was so simple, and so unexpected, that he could
have laughed aloud. Appropriately enough, it was his own
contribution to the party that was responsible. For some
time past it had been his unwritten duty, as the prosperous
member of the family, to present his stepmother with some
delicacy to help out the straitened resources of her house
in providing a feast worthy of the occasion. This year,
his gift had taken the form of half a dozen bottles of
champagne—part of a consignment which he suspected
of being corked. That champagne, acting on a head
unused to anything stronger than lemonade, was enough
to loosen Bessie's tongue for one fatal instant.

Bessie! Of all people, faded, spinsterish Bessie! Bessie,
with her woolwork and her charities—Bessie with her
large, stupid, appealing eyes and her air of frustration,
that put you in mind of a bud frosted just before it could
come into flower! And yet, when you came to think of it,
it was natural enough. Probably, of all the Grigson tribe,
he disliked her the most. He felt for her all the loathing
one must naturally feel for a person one has treated badly;
and he had been simple enough to believe that she did
not resent it.

She was just his own age, and from the moment that
he had been introduced into the family had constituted
herself his protector against the unkindness of his elder

step-brother. She had been, in her revoltingly sentimental phrase, his "own special sister". As they grew up, the roles were reversed, and she became his protégée, the admiring spectator of his early struggles. Then it had become pretty clear that she and everybody else expected him to marry her. He had considered the idea quite seriously for some time. She was pretty enough in those days, and, as the phrase went, worshipped the ground he trod on. But he had had the good sense to see in time that he must look elsewhere if he wanted to make his way in the world. His engagement to Hilda had been a blow to Bessie. Her old-maidish look and her absorption in good works dated from then. But she had been sweetly forgiving—to all appearances. Now, as he stood there under the mistletoe, with a ridiculous paper cap on his head, he marvelled how he could have been so easily deceived. As though, after all, anyone could have written that Christmas card but a woman!

Bessie was smiling at him still—smiling with the confidential air of the mildly tipsy, her upturned shiny nose glowing pink in the candle-light. She had assumed a slightly puzzled expression, as though trying to recollect what she had said. Timothy smiled back and raised his glass to her. He was stone-cold sober, and he could remind her of her words when the occasion arose.

"My present for you, Timothy, is in the post. You'll get it tomorrow, I expect. I thought you'd like a change from those horrid Christmas cards!"

And the words had been accompanied with an unmistakable wink.

"Uncle Timothy!" One of James's bouncing girls jumped up at him and gave him a smacking kiss. He put her down with a grin and tickled her ribs as he did so. He suddenly felt light-hearted and on good terms with all the world—

one woman excepted. He moved away from the mistletoe and strolled round the room, exchanging pleasantries with all the family. He could look them in the face now without a qualm. He clicked glasses with Roger, the prematurely aged, overworked G.P. No need to worry now whether his money was going in that direction! He slapped Peter on the back and endured patiently five minutes' confidential chat on the difficulties of the motor-car business in these days. To Marjorie, James's widow, looking wan and ever so brave in her made-over black frock, he spoke just the right words of blended sympathy and cheer. He even found in his pockets some half-crowns for his great, hulking step-nephews. Then he was standing by his stepmother near the fireplace, whence she presided quietly over the noisy, cheerful scene, beaming gentle good nature from her faded blue eyes.

"A delightful evening," he said, and meant it.

"Thanks to you, Timothy, in great part," she replied. "You have always been so good to us."

Wonderful what a little doubtful champagne would do! He would have given a lot to see her face if he were to say: "I suppose you are not aware that your youngest daughter, who is just now pulling a cracker with that ugly little boy of Peter's, is blackmailing me and that I shortly intend to stop her mouth for good?"

He turned away. What a gang they all were! What a shabby, out-at-elbows gang! Not a decently cut suit or a well-turned-out woman among the lot of them! And he had imagined that his money had been going to support some of them! Why, they all simply reeked of honest poverty! He could see it now. Bessie explained everything. It was typical of her twisted mind to wring cash from him by threats and give it all away in charities.

"You have always been so good to us." Come to think

of it, his stepmother was worth the whole of the rest put together. She must be hard put to it, keeping up Father's old house, with precious little coming in from her children. Perhaps one day, when his money was really his own again, he might see his way to do something for her . . . But there was a lot to do before he could indulge in extravagant fancies like that.

Hilda was coming across the room towards him. Her elegance made an agreeable contrast to the get-up of the Grigson women. She looked tired and rather bored, which was not unusual for her at parties at this house.

"Timothy," she murmured, "can't we get out of here? My head feels like a ton of bricks, and if I'm going to be fit for anything tomorrow morning——"

Timothy cut her short.

"You go home straight away, darling," he said. "I can see that it's high time you were in bed. Take the car. I can walk—it's a fine evening. Don't wait up for me."

"You're not coming? I thought you said——"

"No. I shall have to stay and see the party through. There's a little matter of family business I'd better dispose of while I have the chance."

Hilda looked at him in slightly amused surprise.

"Well, if you feel that way," she said. "You seem to be very devoted to your family all of a sudden. You'd better keep an eye on Bessie while you are about it. She's had about as much as she can carry."

Hilda was right. Bessie was decidedly merry. And Timothy continued to keep an eye on her. Thanks to his attentions, by the end of the evening, when Christmas Day had been seen in and the guests were fumbling for their wraps, she had reached a stage when she could barely stand. "Another glass," thought Timothy from the depths of his experience, "and she'll pass right out."

"I'll give you a lift home, Bessie," said Roger, looking at her with a professional eye. "We can just squeeze you in."

"Oh, nonsense, Roger!" Bessie giggled. "I can manage perfectly well. As if I couldn't walk as far as the end of the drive!"

"I'll look after her," said Timothy heartily. "I'm walking myself, and we can guide each other's wandering footsteps home. Where's your coat, Bessie? Are you sure you've got all your precious presents?"

He prolonged his leave-taking until all the rest had gone, then helped Bessie into her worn fur coat and stepped out of the house, supporting her with an affectionate right arm. It was all going to be too deliciously simple.

Bessie lived in the lodge of the old house. She preferred to be independent, and the arrangement suited everyone, especially since James after one of his reverses on the turf had brought his family to live with his mother to save expense. It suited Timothy admirably now. Tenderly he escorted her to the end of the drive, tenderly he assisted her to insert her latchkey in the door, tenderly he supported her into the little sitting-room that gave out of the hall.

There Bessie considerately saved him an enormous amount of trouble and a possibly unpleasant scene. As he put her down upon the sofa she finally succumbed to the champagne. Her eyes closed, her mouth opened and she lay like a log where he had placed her.

Timothy was genuinely relieved. He was prepared to go to any lengths to rid himself from the menace of blackmail, but if he could lay his hands on the damning letter without physical violence he would be well satisfied. It would be open to him to take it out of Bessie in other ways later on. He looked quickly round the room. He knew its contents by heart. It had hardly changed at all since the day when Bessie first furnished her own room when she left school. The same old battered desk stood in the corner, where from the earliest days she had kept her treasures. He flung it open, and a flood of bills, receipts, charitable appeals and yet more charitable appeals came cascading out. One after another, he went through the drawers with ever-increasing urgency, but still failed to find what he sought. Finally he came upon a small inner drawer which resisted his attempts to open it. He tugged at it in vain, and then seized the poker from the fireplace and burst the flimsy lock by main force. Then he dragged the drawer from its place and settled himself to examine its contents.

It was crammed as full as it could hold with papers. At the very top was the programme of a May Week Ball for his last year at Cambridge. Then there were snapshots, press-cuttings—an account of his own wedding among them—and, for the rest, piles of letters, all in his hand-writing. The wretched woman seemed to have hoarded every scrap he had ever written to her. As he turned them over, some of the phrases he had used in them floated into his mind, and he began to apprehend for the first time what the depth of her resentment must have been when he threw her over.

But where the devil did she keep the only letter that mattered?

As he straightened himself from the desk he heard close behind him a hideous, choking sound. He spun round quickly. Bessie was standing behind him, her face a mask of horror. Her mouth was wide open in dismay. She drew a long shuddering breath. In another moment she was going to scream at the top of her voice . . .

Timothy's pent-up fury could be contained no longer. With all his force he drove his fist full into that gaping, foolish face. Bessie went down as though she had been shot and her head struck the leg of a table with the crack of a dry stick broken in two. She did not move again.

Although it was quiet enough in the room after that, he never heard his stepmother come in. Perhaps it was the sound of his own pulses drumming in his ears that had deafened him. He did not even know how long she had been there. Certainly it was long enough for her to take in everything that was to be seen there, for her voice, when she spoke, was perfectly under control.

"You have killed Bessie," she said. It was a calm statement of fact rather than an accusation.

He nodded, speechless.

"But you have not found the letter."

He shook his head.

"Didn't you understand what she told you this evening? The letter is in the post. It was her Christmas present to you. Poor, simple, loving Bessie!"

He stared at her, aghast.

"It was only just now that I found that it was missing from my jewel-case," she went on, still in the same flat, quiet voice. "I don't know how she found out about it, but love—even a crazy love like hers—gives people a strange insight sometimes."

He licked his dry lips.

"Then you were Leech?" he faltered.

"Of course. Who else? How otherwise do you think I could have kept the house open and my children out of debt on my income? No, Timothy, don't come any nearer. You are not going to commit two murders tonight. I don't think you have the nerve in any case, but to be on the safe side I have brought the little pistol your father gave me when he came out of the army in 1918. Sit down."

He found himself crouching on the sofa, looking helplessly up into her pitiless old face. The body that had been Bessie lay between them.

"Bessie's heart was very weak," she said reflectively. "Roger had been worried about it for some time. If I have a word with him, I daresay he will see his way to issue a death certificate. It will, of course, be a little expensive. Shall we say a thousand pounds this year instead of five hundred? You would prefer that, Timothy, I dare say, to—the alternative?"

Once more Timothy nodded in silence.

"Very well. I shall speak to Roger in the morning—after you have returned me Bessie's Christmas present. I shall require that for future use. You can go now, Timothy."

Line Out of Order

A small group of men sat at a long table in a room off Whitehall. It was the late afternoon of a warm autumn day, and in the sunshine that streamed through the window their faces looked grey and anxious. The man at the head of the table spoke.

"I am sorry to call you together at such short notice, gentlemen," he said, "but it is a matter of extreme urgency. There has been a leakage of information."

A tall, distinguished man with a shock of white hair broke the dead silence in which the words had been received.

"Do I understand you to mean, sir," he asked, "information of what was decided at our meeting this morning?"

"Yes. It seems impossible, but there is no room for doubt. The enemy—I may call him that, although a state of war will not officially exist until nine o'clock this evening—the enemy is aware that of the two plans of attack open to us we have decided on Plan A. He is making his dispositions accordingly."

"But how could he have found that out?" the questioner persisted. "Surely our security arrangements——"

"The proper authority is investigating that question at this moment. It would be a waste of time to discuss it here. The reason I have summoned you is to inform you that as a result this morning's decision is rescinded. We adopt Plan B. As you know, our arrangements are such that we can select either plan up to the last moment. The enemy

equally is in a position to guard against either plan—
either, but not both. Like us, he has to make his choice.
He will go to war tonight believing that we are committed to Plan A. He will be wrong. His mistake will lose
him the war, provided——" His eyes went rapidly from
face to face the length of the table. "—provided that this
time the secret is kept. That is all, gentlemen. You will
want to be getting back to your offices now."

In the street below, a little crowd had gathered to see
them leave. There was not much to see—merely a strip
of pavement kept clear by the police, and a file of figures
stepping hastily across it into the official cars awaiting
them. The tall, distinguished man came near the end of
the procession. As he was about to enter his car he paused,
produced his handkerchief and very deliberately blew his
nose—twice. A shabby figure detached itself from the
back of the crowd and sauntered up the street to the
nearest bus stop.

Big Ben was sounding six o'clock when the right bus
came along. The shabby man reached his destination at
6.20. There was not much time to spare and he was
seething with impatience, but he had been schooled to
control his emotions and it was with an almost leisurely
air that he walked round the corner and up the stairs of
the gaunt block of bachelor flats. At 6.25 precisely he
closed his front door behind him and almost with the
same movement picked up the receiver of the telephone
on the table in the tiny hall.

He dialled a number and the call was answered at once.

"Rockingham here," said a deep, cultured voice.

"Worcester speaking."

"Again? I thought I'd heard the last of you. What is
the trouble?"

"Everything's changed. It's Plan B."

"Dear, dear!" Rockingham sounded faintly amused. "They can't make up their minds, can they? But are you sure, my dear fellow?"

"Absolutely. I had it straight from the horse's nose."

Rockingham chuckled.

"Very prettily put. Well, Worcester, you have left it rather late but luckily not too late. Spode will take your message out tonight."

"You're sure you can get in touch with him before he goes?"

"Don't fret, my good Worcester. Spode will ring me up from the airport in half an hour from now for final instructions. I shall tell him of the change then."

"Thank God!"

"Thank *who*?" said Rockingham derisively. He rang off abruptly.

The man who called himself Worcester still had the receiver in his hand when another voice spoke over his shoulder.

"That will do," it said. "Best come quietly."

At the same instant two enormous hands descended on his wrists and his arms were pinioned behind his back. The receiver fell from his grasp and remained dangling from its cord. It was the last thing he saw as he was led away. He made no sort of resistance.

"We were too late, I'm afraid, sir," said the young constable, wiping his brow. "We had to go up the fire-escape and get in at the back. He's sent his message, whatever it was. The line's dead now, so there's no knowing who was at the other end. And he won't talk," he added viciously.

The inspector nodded. He eyed the slowly oscillating

receiver hanging from the table, as though it fascinated him.

"Ring up for a tender," he said. "No, not that telephone. Use the one in the porter's lodge."

The young constable was right. The prisoner would not talk. He sat dumbly in the inspector's office, his eyes fixed on the clock, with an expression of self-satisfaction that deepened as the minutes ticked away. Slowly the hands crawled round the dial towards the fatal hour of nine. And at two minutes to nine he spoke.

"It's too late now," he said. "Whatever happens, you're too late to do anything about it."

"Meaning?" said the inspector.

"My message has gone." A fanatic's smile was on his thin lips. "While you idiots were bullying me the last plane to the Continent was on its way out. It carried my message with it."

"That be hanged for a tale," said the inspector coldly. "The last plane out was the 7.30 from Hurn airport. There was no long-distance call to or from your flat today."

"You think you're clever, don't you, Inspector? Just listen. When the war is over you'll be interested to know what beat you. My message went to a London exchange— on the automatic system. You'll never trace it, and it doesn't matter if you did. The place is empty by now. At seven o'clock tonight somebody rang that number from the airport——"

"He did, did he? And what do you think happened then?"

The inspector grinned suddenly in the prisoner's face.

"I'll tell you," he went on. "Before you hang as a traitor, you'll be interested to know. He found the line was out of order. The number was unobtainable. Your

234

message never got through. Why? Because when you left your flat the receiver was off. It's off still. And that means that the other number is still through to yours. He can't call anybody else and nobody can call him. That's the snag of the automatic——"

He broke off abruptly. "Here, Bert!" he called. "It's just on the hour. Turn on the radio, will you? And take this fellow out. You'd better get Bob to help you carry him."

Dropper's Delight

To forge a passable Bank of England note is a job demanding high technical skill and a good deal of complicated apparatus. England, the mother of the industrial revolution, can still produce the craftsmen and the tools needful for this delicate branch of applied art. But, like other artists, the forger must bring his wares to market if he is to reap the rewards of his labour, and this is apt to prove a difficulty. He needs an intermediary with the world of commerce outside his studio.

The functionary whose mission it is to put forged currency into circulation is known technically as a dropper. Charlie Carstairs was working as a dropper at the Northgate dog races on the evening that he met Tim Bellew. He paid out the notes one by one, carefully dirtied and creased, at Tote windows, bought endless packets of cigarettes and pocketed the change. He disliked the job intensely. Not only was it a tedious and dangerous occupation, but it was beneath him.

Charlie belonged to the aristocracy of crime. He was in fact one of the ablest confidence tricksters in London; but things had gone against him recently. The supply of mugs had mysteriously dried up and he had found himself compelled to accept this sordid employment to tide things over until the next good proposition in his legitimate trade came along.

When he first saw Bellew he had a momentary gleam of hope that here was the proposition he was praying for.

Dropper's Delight

The boy—he was hardly more—had the innocent, silly face of the born mug. He seemed to be well supplied with ready money and he was losing heavily. It was only when Carstairs saw the look of despair on his face as the final race was decided that he changed his mind about Bellew and with it his tactics.

Bellew was in fact hesitating between thoughts of suicide and the slower torture that would follow if he gave himself up to the police when the affable stranger accosted him. He accepted a drink, then another, and before the evening was out had unburdened himself of the whole wretched story.

Carstairs heard him without any visible signs of surprise. He had guessed that Bellew had been gambling with his employer's money before he had ever accosted him. He had had some vague idea that a man in that position might be useful. It was when he learned that Bellew was in the appallingly vulnerable position of a bank cashier that a brilliant idea flashed across his mind.

"Let's see just how you stand, old man," he said easily. "You're a bit short in your till, that's the whole of your trouble, isn't it? How much exactly?"

"A hundred pounds," said Bellew hopelessly.

"A hundred!" Carstairs' lip curled disdainfully at the miserable figure. "Well, you want to put it back before the manager twigs it, that's all. When's he due to check your cash?"

"It'll be any day now. He checks once a month, you see, and the month is nearly up."

Carstairs nodded understandingly. No need to tell the mug that he had once worked behind a bank counter and left under a cloud.

"I'd had to borrow a fiver to pay some bills," Bellew went on. "I thought I could get it back easily on the dogs, but I lost £20 the first time I tried, and tonight——"

"Oh, forget it!" said Carstairs. "If I'd only met up with you sooner I could have put you on to something good. I made a packet tonight."

He paused to let this sink in, and watched dispassionately a look of envy superimposed on the blank misery in the other's face. Then he added:

"Suppose I lend you the money?"

"My God, sir, if you would!"

"I could, you know. Money of a sort."

He peeled a note off the wad in his pocket and flipped it across the table.

"Just take a look at that," he said. "Good enough for a manager taking stock, eh? I don't say it'll pass the half-yearly audit, but there's plenty of time between now and then. Have ten now to be going on with."

"Ten?"

"Yep. That's all you're having for now. You'll have to wait till tomorrow for the rest. Let's see, there's racing at Old Cross, isn't there? Meet me there and I'll see there's the other hundred and ninety waiting for you."

"But I don't understand," Bellew stammered. "I'm only a hundred short. Why a hundred and ninety?"

"Because, you young fool, you're going to bring me a hundred of the best out of your till."

That was how it began, and three weeks later Bellew, as he contemplated the money in his till, wondered for the hundredth time whether the whole thing had not been some horrible nightmare. But it was real enough—as real as the notes shoved away at the back of the till were false.

Since his second meeting with Carstairs at Old Cross the original two hundred had grown to five, and the story of their growth had been a tale of dogs that ran wide on bends, dogs that fell at hurdles, dogs that did everything but win.

Carstairs had never known such a run of luck, he said. It didn't seem natural. Sooner or later it was bound to turn, and till it did he could always advance the needful—in the same currency, and at the same price. He was very amiable about it—and with good reason, for from his point of view Bellew was the dropper's dream. His evening's work was over in a moment, leaving the rest of his time free for honest gambling. The return was steady and the risk was negligible. As he had foretold, Bellew's till had passed the manager's check, and the game could go on as long as it was worth his while, or until the inspectors arrived at the bank.

Until the inspectors arrived! It was the thought of that awful moment that whitened Bellew's cheek and made his stomach turn over. There were only two days to go and he had lost all hope. Up to the night before he had cherished the belief that one good race would put him right with the world and enable him to take those hideous forgeries home and put them in the fire. Then at North Gate he had met Carstairs as usual—and Carstairs had cut him dead. Not by a sign or gesture had he given the smallest impression that Bellew meant anything to him in the world. His whole attention had been given up to a distinguished-looking man with a dark complexion and curly grey hair with whom he seemed to be on the most friendly terms.

And Bellew, too miserable even to try his luck, had slunk home, the money borrowed from his till burning in his pocket, and cried bitterly.

"The manager wants to see you," said a messenger, and he started guiltily. Was this it already? He dragged himself from the counter and walked on leaden feet to the manager's office.

The manager found Bellew unusually stupid that afternoon and it took him nearly a quarter of an hour to drive home the perfectly simple matter of staff vacations which he wished to explain. When Bellew finally got back to his counter it was just on closing time. A tall man was just going out of the door, which the porter was holding preparatory to locking it behind him.

The cashier who worked next to Bellew leaned over towards him.

"That chap just going out," he said. "He's cashed a cheque for two thousand payable to self. All in pound notes. It cleared me out, so I borrowed five hundred from the back of your till to make it up. . . . I say, old chap, are you feeling queer or something?"

It was a very shocked and frightened Bellew that left the bank that evening after his day's work. The shock passed, but the fear was to remain to haunt him for long afterwards. The effect upon his future conduct was all to the good. It was just as well, therefore, that on his way home that evening he did not look into the café opposite the bank, where a distinguished-looking visitor from a Commonwealth country was waiting with the patience of his race for Carstairs to return with the money he had handed to him, to demonstrate his confidence.

The "Children": Monday's Child

"Monday's child is fair of face"

John Franklin, who was my contemporary at Oxford, invited me to stay with his people at Markhampton for the Markshire Hunt Ball. He and his sister were getting up a small party for it, he said.

"I've never met your sister," I remarked. "What is she like?"

"She is a beauty," said John, seriously and simply.

I thought at the time that it was an odd, old-fashioned phrase, but it turned out to be strictly and literally true. Deborah Franklin was beautiful in the grand, classic manner. She didn't look in the least like a film star or a model. She had never been a deb, which was just as well, for she would have made the other debs look more than ordinarily silly. I suppose her vital statistics were in order, but looking at her you forgot about them. It was the sheer beauty of her face that took your breath away.

With looks like that, it would be asking too much to expect anything startling in the way of brains, and I found Deborah, though amiable, a trifle dull. She was of course well aware of her extraordinary good looks, and was perfectly prepared to discuss them, without conceit, just as a man seven feet high might talk about the advantages and inconveniences of being tall.

Most of our party were old friends of the Franklins,

Q   241

who took Deborah for granted as a local phenomenon, but among them was a newcomer—a young man with a beard named Aubrey Melcombe, who had lately taken charge of the local museum. As soon as he set eyes on Deborah he said:

"We have never met before, but your face, of course, is perfectly familiar."

Deborah had evidently heard that one before.

"I never give sittings to photographers," she said, "but people will snap me in the street. It's such a nuisance."

"Photographs!" said Aubrey. "I mean your portrait—the one that was painted four hundred years ago. Has nobody ever told you that you are the living image of the Warbeck Titian?"

"I've never heard of the Warbeck Titian," said Deborah, which was rather letting the side down, for Warbeck Hall is near Markhampton and its pictures are famous, though of course only visitors go to see them.

"Truly," said Aubrey, "I dwell among the Philistines. But you shall judge for yourself. Lord Warbeck is lending the Titian to an exhibition in aid of the Cathedral Fund which we are organising in the spring. I'll send you a ticket for the opening."

Then he went off to dance with Rosamund Clegg, his assistant at the museum. She had a face which didn't distract you for one moment from her vital statistics, and was said to be his fiancée.

I did not care much for Aubrey, or for his young woman, but I had to admit that they knew their job when I came to the opening of the exhibition a few months later. They had gathered in treasures of every sort from all over the county and arranged them admirably. The jewel of the show was, of course, the great Titian. It had a wall to

itself at the end of the room and I was looking at it when
Deborah came in.

The likeness was fantastic. Lord Warbeck had never
had his paintings cleaned, so that Titian's flesh tints were
golden and carmine, in vivid contrast to Deborah's pink
and white. But that apart, the face behind the glass might
have been her mirror image. By a happy chance she had
chosen to wear a very plain black dress which matched
up well to the portrait's sombre garb. She stood there
still and silent, staring at her centuries-old likeness. I
wondered what she felt.

A pressman's camera flashed and clicked. First one
visitor and then another noticed the resemblance and
presently the rest of the gallery was deserted. Everyone
was crowding round the Titian to stare from the painted
face to the real one and back again. The only clear space
was round Deborah herself. People were manœuvring and
jostling each other to get a good view of her profile, without losing sight of the Titian, which fortunately was in
profile also. It must have been horribly embarrassing for
Deborah, one would have thought, but she never seemed
to notice them. She went on peering into the picture,
utterly absorbed, for what seemed a very long time. Then
she turned round and walked quickly out of the building.
As she passed me I saw that she was crying—a surprising
display of emotion in one so calm.

About ten minutes later Aubrey discovered that a pair
of Degas statuettes were missing from a stand opposite
the Titian. They were small objects and very valuable.
The police were sent for and there was a considerable fuss,
but nothing was found. I left as soon as I could and went
to the Franklins'. Deborah was in.

"Have you got the statuettes?" I asked.

She took them out of her handbag.

"How did you guess?"

"It seemed to me that your reception in front of the Titian was a put-up show," I explained. "It distracted attention from everything else in the room while the theft took place."

"Yes," said Deborah, reflectively. "Aubrey arranged it very cleverly, didn't he? He thought of everything. He even helped me choose this dress to go with the one in the picture, you know."

"And the press photographer? Had he been laid on too?"

"Oh yes. Aubrey arranged for someone to be there to photograph me. He thought it would help to collect a crowd. Not that I usually need that sort of thing to make people stop and look at me, of course."

Her coolness was astonishing. If her tone betrayed a hint of bitterness at the failure of the scheme, there was not a trace of remorse. The serene beauty of her face was as unruffled as ever. Even with the damning evidence of the statuettes in front of me I found it hard to believe that I was talking to a thief.

"It was a very cleverly concocted scheme altogether," I said. "You and Aubrey must have put a lot of work into it. I had no idea that you were such friends."

I had spoken somewhat harshly, and for once I seemed to have made some impression on her maddening calm. There was a flush on her cheeks as she replied:

"Oh yes, I've been seeing a good deal of him lately. Ever since the Hunt Ball, in fact."

After that there didn't seem to be much more to say. The picture was fairly complete in my mind, though why such a magnificent creature as Deborah should have fallen for a young pip-squeak like Aubrey was something that puzzled, and will continue to puzzle me.

"There's one thing I don't quite understand," I said

finally. "People were surrounding you and staring at you up to the moment you left the gallery. How did Aubrey manage to pass the statuettes to you without anyone seeing?"

This time there was no doubt that I had roused her out of her quiescence. She rounded on me in a fury of surprise and indignation.

"Pass the statuettes to *me*?" she repeated. "Good God! Are you suggesting that *I* helped Aubrey steal them?"

She looked like an angry goddess, and was about as charming.

"But—but——" I stammered. "But if you didn't, who did?"

"Rosamund, of course. Aubrey gave them to her while all the shindy was going on in front of the Titian. She simply put them in her bag and walked out. I'd only just got them back from her when you came in."

"Rosamund!" It was my turn to be surprised. "Then the whole thing was a put-up job between them?"

"Yes. She made no bones about it. They wanted to get married and hadn't any money, and she knew a dealer who would give a price for things like these with no questions asked and—and there you are."

"Then how did you come into it?" I asked.

Deborah's face underwent a subtle change. For a moment I could see what she would look like when she was an old woman—still like a classical goddess, but a goddess aware of the follies of mankind and a little weary of them.

"Aubrey said that if I posed in front of the Titian it would be wonderful publicity for the exhibition—and, of course, I fell for it." She laughed mirthlessly. "I've only just remembered. When Aubrey wanted to make fun of me he used to say I'd make a wonderful cover girl.

That's just what I was—a cover girl for him and Rosamund."

She stood up and picked up the statuettes.

"These will have to go back to the gallery, I suppose," she said. "Can it be done without too much fuss? It's silly of me, I know, but I'd rather they didn't prosecute Aubrey."

I made sympathetic noises.

"It was Rosamund's idea in the first place," she went on. "I'm sure of that. Aubrey hasn't the wits to think of anything so clever."

"It was clever enough," I said. "But you saw through it at once. How was that?"

Deborah smiled rather wryly.

"I'm not clever," she said. "But that old dark picture with the glass on it made a perfect mirror. Aubrey told me to stand in front of it, so I did. But I'm not interested in art, you know. I was looking at myself. And of course I couldn't help seeing what was happening just behind me. . . ."

Tuesday's Child

"Tuesday's child is full of grace"

The sermon was over at St. Mary's, Markhampton. The
congregation rose to their feet. The last hymn was
announced, and the worshippers began fumbling in hand
bags and pockets for the collection. It was at that moment
that a woman left her place at the end of a pew halfway
down the nave and walked rapidly to the west door.

George Gray, the verger, from his post just inside the
church porch, saw her coming towards him. He was an
old man, but he retained the keen eye for detail that had
been the pride of Detective-Sergeant Gray of the Markshire Constabulary. He noticed several things about this
lady that interested him. He slipped through the door in
front of her and intercepted her in the porch.

"Excuse me, madam," he said.

She made no reply and tried to brush past him. Gray
laid a hand on her arm.

"One moment," he said. "Are you sure that is your
handbag that you are carrying?"

Under her arm was a large, black handbag, fairly new
and obviously expensive. At Gray's words she took it
in her hand, held it up and burst into tears.

"Oh, my God!" she exclaimed. Then, thrusting the bag
at Gray, she went on, "Take it—give it back to her—only
let me go!"

247

Gray took the bag with one hand, while retaining his hold on her with the other.

"I'm sure you don't want to make any more trouble than necessary," he said quietly. "There's a policeman on the other side of the square, as you may have noticed. Now don't you think you had better come back with me into church until the service is over?"

The Reverend Arthur Meadows was genial, tubby, and bald. His shabby cassock reached almost to the ground, so that the movement of his feet was hardly perceptible and he seemed to roll about on wheels rather than walk. He listened in silence to what his verger had to tell him, and then turned to the elder of the two women who were with him.

"And is this your bag, Mrs. Widdowson?" he asked.

"Yes. Quite new, as you see, Vicar, and——"

The other woman interrupted her.

"Mrs. Widdowson!" she exclaimed. "You're Mrs. Widdowson!"

"What's it to you who I am, Mrs. Haines? You knew that bag was not your property. Are you going to call the police, Vicar? If not, I shall."

Mr. Meadows sighed.

"There have been too many thefts from this church lately, have there not, Mr. Gray?" he said. "It is not for me to stand in the way of justice." He turned to the other woman. "But first, I should hear what you have to say."

"I took it by mistake. It was on the seat beside me and I thought it was mine."

"In that case," said the priest equably, "your own bag should be there still."

He ambled gently up the church, followed by the others.

"This is your regular pew, is it not, Mrs. Widdowson?"

248

he said. "I don't see a lady's bag there, I'm afraid." He
pursed his lips, shook his head and went on, "Perhaps
we could discuss this more comfortably in the vestry.
Will you come this way, ladies? No, not you, Gray; I
want you to . . ." The rest of the sentence was inaudible.

The two women sat side by side on plain wooden chairs
not looking at each other. The parson stood facing them.

"Mrs. Widdowson," he said abruptly, "what was my
sermon this morning about?"

Taken aback, she stammered, "I don't know, I'm sure,
Vicar. I was so upset——"

"Odd. You have heard it several times before. My sermons have a habit of recurring every two years or so.
Can *you* tell me, Mrs.—Mrs. Haines, is it not?"

"Repentance and—and forgiveness——"

"Quite right. Don't snivel, woman. It doesn't help.
And why did you leave before the last hymn? Don't you
like music, or did you want to avoid the collection?"

Mrs. Haines said nothing. She only shook her head
miserably and dabbed her eyes with her handkerchief.

"Well, if you won't tell me, I must form my own conclusions. Now, madam," he went on briskly, "why
did you take this lady's handbag?"

"But I told you——" Mrs. Haines began, and stopped
abruptly as the parson cut her off with a gesture.

"I am speaking to *you*, Mrs. Widdowson."

Mrs. Widdowson rose. She was a tall woman, and looked
down at Mr. Meadows with an air of immense dignity.

"I don't come here to be insulted," she announced, and
stalked to the vestry door. She opened it to find Gray
on the other side.

"Have you found that bag, Gray?" the vicar asked.

"Yes, sir. Stuffed behind a radiator at the end of the
pew."

"Excellent! You identify your property, Mrs. Haines? I only hope there's a clean handkerchief inside—you look as though you needed it. Sit down, Mrs. Widdowson. You have failed to answer two questions of mine. Let me try a third. How is it that you know Mrs. Haines by sight, although she did not know you?"

Mrs. Widdowson remained silent.

"Quite an interesting little problem, isn't it, Mr. Gray?" said Mr. Meadows, rubbing his chin reflectively. "And I see that I'm going to get no help in solving it. Here is Mrs. Haines quite overcome by my very pedestrian efforts in the pulpit—and equally overcome at finding that her neighbour in the pew is Mrs. Widdowson. Here is Mrs. Widdowson, who on her side knows all about Mrs. Haines, and improves the occasion by taking her handbag. What is the link between them?"

Mr. Gray grinned and shook his head.

"Drawing a bow at a venture," the vicar went on, "could it be—Mr. Widdowson?"

Both women began to talk at once; but Mrs. Widdowson's voice completely drowned the other's.

"Let her deny it if she dare!" she shouted. "The adulterous hussy!"

"I see that I was right," said the vicar with great satisfaction. "Then you knew Mrs. Haines because you had been watching her?"

"Any wife would!"

"We'll confine ourselves to what this wife did, if you please. While Mrs. Haines was absorbed in my sermon, you removed her handbag, which was on the seat between you, and substituted your own. You wanted to look inside her bag, and nothing would be easier than to pretend that you had opened it by mistake when the collection plate came round. And when you opened it, you hoped to find—

what, Mrs. Widdowson? Evidence to humiliate your poor, weak sinner of a husband—letters, like those you are now trying to conceal in your prayer book?

"You were sorely tempted, Mrs. Widdowson, and it was perhaps excusable to open it. But for what followed there can be no excuse. When Mrs. Haines hurried out of church with your bag under her arm you decided to improve on the plan. You not only took your husband's letters during the last hymn—Thank you; I will keep them, Mrs. Haines—but you hid Mrs. Haines's property and accused her of stealing your own.

"I have only one more word to say to you, Mrs. Widdowson. Next time you decide to commit a crime in church, choose a parson who is reading his sermon. Mine was an old one which I knew by heart, so that my eyes were free to roam, and it's surprising what you can see from the pulpit!"

Wednesday's Child

"Wednesday's child is full of woe"

Mr. and Mrs. Wellstead entered the tea-shop together and stood for a moment gazing hesitantly round its interior, as though uncertain of their surroundings. They were a quiet, unobtrusive couple, middle-sized, middle-aged, middle-class, and, one would say at a guess, Middle West. There was certainly no doubt of their nationality even before either had spoken a word. Mr. Wellstead's shoes had not been bought on this side of the Atlantic, and his wife wore, planted squarely on her head, the pill-box hat that is the crowning glory of the American matron.

"Are you sure this is the right place?" said Mr. Wellstead, after a pause. "I can't see anyone——"

"But I can!" his wife rejoined. "In the far corner. Don't you see, Chester? She's waving to us."

She led the way across the room to where a young woman in black was standing beside a table, a wan but welcoming smile on her pale, rather haggard face.

"Marion Browning?" Mrs. Wellstead said interrogatingly. The girl nodded, and she kissed her warmly on the cheek. "Honey," she said, "I'm real glad to see you. You and me are going to have a lot to say to each other. Marion, this is Chester."

"Pleased to meet you," said Mr. Wellstead. He did not sound altogether so pleased as he might have been.

252

The Americans sat down, and there was an awkward pause. A waitress hovered near.

"Shall I order tea, Mrs. Wellstead?" Marion asked.

"Do, dear," murmured Mrs. Wellstead.

Her husband grunted, "Tea? Yes, I guess that's what we came here for."

"Chester, we didn't come here for tea. We came here to discuss a very, very serious subject."

"We certainly did. And there's one thing I'd like Miss Browning to know at the outset——"

"Her name is Marion, Chester."

"I want her to know that my son was a clean-living, God-fearing boy, and this news—this suggestion, I should say—has come as a great shock to me. I don't want to believe it, and until it is proved to me I just don't believe it."

The arrival of tea produced an interruption. Marion poured out with a hand that trembled a little.

"I'm not in the least surprised or hurt at your taking that attitude," she said calmly. "Danny was everything you say, Mr. Wellstead. I blame myself entirely for what happened. But as to proving things to you, I hardly know how to set about it. A girl who goes wrong doesn't think about collecting witnesses, you know. Rather the opposite."

"It's easy to talk like that, Miss, but just now I've only your word for it that you so much as set your eyes on him."

"Oh, Chester, how can you say that?" Mrs. Wellstead intervened. "Why, Marion's exactly like her photo. I recognized her at once."

"My photo? I didn't know you had one. I gave Danny my picture, of course, just as he gave me his, but I thought it was burnt with everything else when—when——"

"When the plane crashed and caught fire. Don't distress yourself, honey. That's not the one I mean. He sent us a picture quite a time ago—last July it was—and you're in it as clear as could be, only not quite so thin, perhaps. Look, here it is."

She produced from her bag a small snapshot. Marion took it eagerly.

"Yes, that's me," she said. "I'd quite forgotten it."

"You see, Chester?"

"Yes, I see all right. There are two girls in that picture. One of them's standing close to Danny and looking very friendly. That one isn't Miss Browning. The one that might be her is with another man altogether."

"That is quite correct." Marion's rather refined calm remained unruffled. "The other girl's name was Catherine Temple. She is married now and gone to live in Australia."

"Would that girl be the Kitten he mentioned in one of his letters?" Mr. Wellstead asked.

"Oh no," said Marion swiftly. " 'Kitten' was his nickname for me."

"It was funny he didn't say any more about you if you meant all that to him."

"Chester, need you be so cynical? I believe what Marion says."

"It's not being cynical to want to be satisfied. If Miss Browning—all right, then, *Marion*—if Marion can satisfy me that her story is true—why, then I'll face up to Danny's responsibilities. Neither she nor her child will ever want so long as I'm worth a cent. You know that. But I want to be sure. That's why I ask—why didn't Danny ever say a word about it while he was alive?"

"Because he never had the chance. Mr. Wellstead, you must believe me about this, even if there's only my word for it. He never wrote to you about me because there was nothing to tell you, until just before the end. We only discovered what we meant to each other a few days before he left to go home on vacation. He was going to tell you about our engagement when he saw you. He never lived to do it."

Marion took a handkerchief from her bag and wiped her eyes. Mrs. Wellstead patted her knee affectionately with her soft, plump hand.

"Don't cry, dearie," she said. "Tell me something. When did you say this baby of yours is expected?"

"The first week in September, the doctor says."

"And Danny was killed in that blizzard in December. You see, Chester, the dates fit."

"Oh, the dates fit all right. I've never denied that. I've never denied that this young woman is going to have a baby. It's just that Danny wasn't the only young man about in this part of the world last December, and, with all respect to her, this particular young lady doesn't strike me as being the type that would attract him, anyway. I may be wrong. I've got a kind of feeling that I'm in a minority of one at this party." He stood up. "That being the case, I think it would be advantageous to all concerned if I were to leave you ladies alone together for a while. Maybe something will emerge from your joint discussions which will convince even me."

"But where will you go, Chester?"

"I'm getting a little tired of the tea-shop atmosphere. I shall try a pub."

"They are not open yet," said Marion.

"That is a phrase which has become distressingly familiar to me since I arrived in England. In that case, I shall talk a walk round the block—if there is a block."

After he had gone, Marion turned to Mrs. Wellstead with an appealing look.

"You do believe me, don't you?" she asked.

"Why, Marion," said Mrs. Wellstead, "I guess I do. And the reason why is that I want to believe you. I want to think that Danny will have left a child behind him. I'd much rather that than that he should come to an end with nothing to show for his life. Chester doesn't want to believe. He's shocked. He's shocked at you, and he's shocked at me for not being shocked at you. But he'll come round. It would help if you could give him an excuse to change his mind, though. Haven't you anything to show him? No letters from Danny?"

Marion shook his head.

"He always telephoned," she said. "Danny wasn't a great writer."

"True enough. But, child, didn't he give you anything? No ring."

"He was going to buy that when he got home."

"His photo, then? I think you mentioned that just now."

"Of course! How silly of me to forget it. I've got it here."

From her bag Marion took a well-worn envelope and from the envelope a studio photograph. It was of a fresh-faced young man and bore the inscription: *"To dearest Kitten, from Danny, 7.12.56."*

Mrs. Wellstead's eyes misted over as she looked at it. "Danny!" she whispered. "It's a good likeness. His writing, too. And there's a date."

"It's not a date I shall ever forget," said Marion softly. "Just before he was due to go. He brought me this picture and sat in my little room and signed it. We were going out to the pictures that evening, but it came on to snow, so we stayed indoors instead, and—and—that's how it happened. . . . Why, Mrs. Wellstead, what's the matter? I didn't mean to upset you so much!"

Mrs. Wellstead was sobbing quietly and uncontrollably. She was still crying when the waitress came to clear away the tea. She was still crying when her husband returned from his walk, but by then she was alone.

"Where's Marion?" he asked.

"The low little gold-digger's gone for good," she told him.

"So you found her out? How was that?"

She showed him their son's photograph.

"Look at the date of that," she said.

"I'm looking. July 12, 1956—about the same as that little group we had. What of it?"

"Only that she thought it was dated the English way, and read it as seventh December, 1956. She told me a tale about being kept indoors by the snow the day he gave it her . . . The little rat! I guess you were right, Chester, and the other girl was Kitten, and Danny gave her the picture when the other was taken. We've had a lucky escape."

"Then what were you crying for?"

"Because I took to her, the worthless tramp!"

Thursday's Child

"Thursday's child has far to go"

"Is that the island?" Mr. Wilkinson asked.

"Aye. That's Cara right enough."

"Cara!" Mr. Wilkinson stood on the jetty looking out at the long, low shadow of the island, dark against the setting sun. Beyond it, he knew, the nearest land was North America. He was at the ultimate edge of the Western Isles. It was a supremely romantic spot, and he looked supremely ridiculous there, in his dark city suit, with his neat city brief-case under his arm.

"Cara!" he repeated. "A beautiful place, and a beautiful name."

"It's the Gaelic word for a corpse."

Mr. Wilkinson looked again. Seen against the light, the island did resemble a human body, laid out upon its back. He could distinguish the shrouded outline of a head, a waisted trunk, a pair of stiff, upturned feet. . . . He shivered. It was getting distinctly chilly down by the shore.

"I shall see you tomorrow, then?" he said to the boatman.

"Aye. The tide will be right about ten. If it's fine we shall be in Cara within the hour."

"And if it's rough?"

"If it's rough we shall no' be going." There was a flat finality about Dugald Macdougal's pronouncement that

258

precluded argument. "The sound is no place for a small boat when the wind's blowing up from the sou'-west. There was a man tried it last spring. He hired Rory Maconner's boat and went alone. Rory was lucky. He got his boat back. She came ashore three days later, bottom up. The other fellow wasn't so lucky."

The next day was bright and warm, with hardly a breath of wind. The trip to Cara was like a pleasure cruise. Mr. Wilkinson watched the island slowly grow larger. He could distinguish a few goats on the grassy slopes, but no other sign of life.

"Where does Mr. James Filby live?" he asked.

"On the other side of the headland."

"All alone?"

"All alone. He likes it that way. Maybe he won't want to see you."

"I wrote to tell him I was coming."

"There's no postal delivery on Cara. Your letter's still at the post office waiting for him to collect it. He's not been on the mainland for six months."

Dugald steered the boat into a tiny harbour and tied up to the crumbling stone jetty.

"I'll wait for you here," he said. "If you go up yon path, maybe you'll find him."

Wilkinson found him very quickly. He was waiting for him round the first bend in the path, a tall, bearded figure, not sun-tanned as might have been expected, but pale-faced, with bright, sunken eyes.

"This island is private," he announced, and advanced on the intruder. Wilkinson became aware that Filby was holding a very purposeful-looking cudgel in his right hand. He began to talk extremely fast.

"I know that I am on private property," he said, "and

259

I apologise most sincerely for my intrusion. But I have come all the way from London to see you, Mr. Filby, on a matter of very important business, and I do beg you to give me a few minutes of your time."

Filby stared at him in silence for a full half-minute. Then he said abruptly, "Ye'd best come into the house," turned on his heel and walked away.

Wilkinson followed him to the ramshackle cabin that was the only house on the island. Filby motioned him into the one chair and stood opposite him. Between them was a rough table that had evidently served recently as a chopping-block for meat. It was foul with grease and dried blood. Looking at his menacing figure, Wilkinson felt glad of even that protection.

"So you're on business from London?" said Filby. "You'll have known my brother Fergus in London, no doubt."

"I'm afraid not, Mr. Filby. It's a large place, you know."

"Did you not? He called himself Farnby in London, I'm told."

"Fergus Farnby! Yes, as a matter of fact I have—er—heard of him."

"And where is my brother now, do you know?"

"Mr. Filby," said Wilkinson, "I have not come all this way to talk about your brother. My being here is nothing to do with him. I have an important proposition——"

"Fergus came to no good, I have no doubt."

"He went to prison for fraud, if you must know. I don't know what has happened to him since."

"I see. That is very much what I would have expected. And now your proposition, Mr. Wilkinson?"

"I should like to buy Cara."

"It is not for sale."

"Alternatively," went on Mr. Wilkinson as if he had

not spoken, "to acquire the mineral rights for a term of years. The group I represent would pay very handsomely for the privilege."

"Mineral rights? Are you crazy?"

"Not at all. A month ago a friend of mine and a party from a yacht came on shore at a sandy bay on the west of the island for a picnic."

"I did not see them, or I'd have turned them off quick enough."

"My friend is a geologist. He found in the dunes above the bay a deposit of silicate sand."

"And what is that?"

"It is the type of sand used in glass manufacture—common in some parts of the world, very rare in Britain, consequently very valuable."

Filby's eyes were glittering.

"Where is this deposit exactly?"

Wilkinson took from his case a large-scale map of the island and spread it out upon the table. He pointed to the pencil marks which indicated the boundaries of the deposit, and Filby spanned the distance with finger and thumb. He chuckled softly.

"Fergus had to go to London to seek his fortune," he said. "And it was waiting on Cara all the time. That is what you might call ironical, is it not, sir?"

When Wilkinson's plane touched down at Glasgow airport it was met by two specially selected police officers. Quietly and unobtrusively they took Wilkinson in tow, and escorted him to a car. At headquarters his brief-case was taken from him and its contents examined by experts. While this was going on, two very senior officers—one Scottish and one from Scotland Yard—were questioning him closely.

Presently a plain-clothes man joined them. He had with him Wilkinson's map of Cara.

"This has Fergus Farnby's prints on it all right," he said. "I'm much obliged, sir. It's a good clear set."

"It ought to be," Wilkinson observed. "That table was greasy enough in all conscience."

"So he did get to Cara in Rory's boat after all," said the man from Scotland Yard. "He was one jump ahead of us all the way. What happened then, do you think?"

"There wasn't room on the island for two of them," said his Glasgow colleague. "Jamie Filby tried to turn his brother away, I have no doubt. The brother stayed and Jamie—disappeared. It's a grim thought."

"I had a quick look over the island before I left," said Wilkinson, "and there is a patch of soft ground near the house that might repay attention. Or possibly something will turn up when we start exploiting the silicate sand."

"You mean to go on with that, if you can?"

"Bless you, yes! We've been after the Cara concession for years. Filby would never so much as talk to anyone we sent to discuss the matter. This man was interested as soon as I started to talk business. I didn't need finger-prints to tell me he was your man."

Friday's Child

"Friday's child is loving and giving"

"Three-quarters of a gallon, please, Ada."

"Three-quarters?" The girl at the petrol pump had a puzzled frown on her honest, pretty face.

"That's what I said, darling."

"You had a gallon yesterday and half a gallon the day before. What's the idea?"

"I'm making experiments to see what the consumption of the old bus is."

Even to the guileless Ada the story sounded improbable. It happened to be the exact truth, but when Ray Meldrum told the truth he usually contrived to make it sound false. This may have been due to lack of practice. The romances in which he habitually dealt always rang true.

"You're not the sort that cares about his petrol consumption," said Ada.

It was the kind of opening that Meldrum responded to automatically.

"I'm the sort that cares about you," he whispered hoarsely.

"Oh, Ray!"

"If I get a gallon at a time I see you five times as often as if I get five gallons, don't I?"

"Oh, Ray!"

"What time do you get off work this evening, Ada? Six?

If I were to be along about then perhaps we could see a bit more of each other. What d'you say?"

The assignation was made and Meldrum drove off. In the emotion of the moment he had omitted to pay for his petrol. Ada put the money into the till out of her own pocket. It gave her a little thrill to be doing this small service for the dashing young man in whose eyes she had so unaccountably found favour.

Pursuing his researches into the petrol consumption of the old bus—an extremely smart car which only needed to be paid for to be a very pleasant possession—Meldrum found that after driving on a carefully selected route Ada's three-quarters of a gallon came to an end on a rather desolate stretch of road midway between Markhampton and Podchester. Near the top of a steep hill the engine coughed, spluttered and expired. This caused considerable satisfaction to him and the companion whom he had picked up on the way. The latter was a baby-faced, elderly man, known to his friends as the Duke, who might have been a bishop in mufti. He was in fact one of the dozen best confidence tricksters in Europe. Ray was one of the other eleven.

The two men discussed the situation in all its bearings, then replenished the tank from a can which they had brought with them and drove back. Meldrum dropped the Duke where he had met him and went to keep his appointment with Ada. He could not give her very long, because business had to come before pleasure. His more austere partner would have disapproved of any dalliance on the eve of a coup, but Ray was a fast worker and he was not the man to pass up a chance. Ada had no reason at all to feel neglected when he left her to spend the latter part of the evening in a more expensive part of the town with George S. Pocklington.

Friday's Child

The trouble about describing a confidence trick is that it is difficult not to make the victim seem very stupid. The plan by which Ray and the Duke proposed to relieve George Pocklington of some thousands of pounds was simplicity itself. But Pocklington was anything but stupid. He was a very shrewd man who had made a large fortune in the hardware business and looked twice at every cent before he parted with it. He was fond of horse racing but never gambled more than he could afford, and he was extremely suspicious of strangers. All of which makes it rather hard to explain why, within six weeks of stepping off the *Queen Mary* at Southampton, he should have been willing to drive with Ray Meldrum to Podchester races for the purpose of putting all his spare cash on a horse which was going to win the big race there at fifty to one.

The only people who could explain this in detail are of course Ray and the Duke, and they are not likely to do so. The measure of their success is to be gauged by the fact that on the morning of the race George Pocklington was firmly convinced that the whole expedition was his idea. It was he who had selected the horse to be backed, it was he who had chosen the route by which they were to drive and it was he who had insisted that Ray should carry the stake money which he was to distribute among the unsuspecting bookmakers. The presence of an American, George pointed out, would only put them on their guard and bring the odds tumbling down.

When, on top of all this, Pocklington offered to drive, Ray was delighted. It somehow added a touch of verisimilitude to the scene, when the engine duly petered out within a couple of hundred yards of where it had done at rehearsal, that he should be at the wheel.

"Out of gas, I guess," said George, who was not afraid to state the obvious.

"I'm afraid so. My fault entirely. I do apologize."

"I noticed the needle was zeroing, but I thought maybe——"

"The gauge hasn't been working for weeks. My fault again. I ought to have had it seen to."

"What do we do now? There doesn't seem to be much traffic on this road."

"I'm afraid not. That's the worst of these picturesque side roads. But there's a garage less than a mile on, I know. Even if I don't get a lift from anyone, I can walk there in twenty minutes. I'll be back with some juice in half an hour at the outside. Don't worry. We'll be in good time for the race."

In the language of the bull-ring, it was the moment of truth. The work of years of training, weeks of arduous preparation, here reached its planned, predestined climax. George Pocklington took his coup de grâce meekly and quietly. He sat at the wheel of the car beaming approval as Ray Meldrum and his money disappeared together round a bend in the road. He felt relaxed and happy. Only one thing was necessary to complete his contentment— a drink. There was a picnic basket on the back seat. He decided to investigate. . . .

"Hey, Ray!"

Meldrum stood speechless by the roadside, looking up into Pocklington's laughing face, as the car came to a standstill beside him.

"What d'you think? There was a can of gasoline under the rug in the back all the time! Yes, sir, a full can! Can you beat it?"

Still Meldrum did not speak. He had less than a hundred yards to go to where the Duke was waiting with his car for the getaway and there was nothing whatever that he could do about it. Another man might have attempted violence, but violence was not in his line. Resignedly he climbed back into the car, resignedly he allowed himself to be driven to Podchester. And every yard of the way he was haunted by Ada's last words to him of the evening before: "One of these days, Ray, I'll do you a good turn when you're not expecting it!"

The words persisted with him even while under George's eye he was putting the money on the hopeless outsider of his choice. They remained when after the biggest win in the history of Podchester races a grateful George generously presented him with £100 as commission.

Saturday's Child

"Saturday's child works hard for his living"

As Dr. Faraday drove to his surgery that morning he experienced some of the symptoms that had been described to him, times without number, by patients for whom the only proper prescription was a good, long rest. He had a hard day's work ahead of him, behind him a broken night's sleep; and behind and beyond the immediate present, stretching in both directions to infinity, it seemed, were the memory and the prospect of other laborious days, other disturbed nights. He was young and strong and competent, but he could not carry on indefinitely like this. There had been blackouts, and, even worse, temporary fits of amnesia, which told only too clearly of the strain.

Surgery that morning was mercifully light, and Faraday, as he looked through his list of patients for the day's rounds, reflected that with luck he should for once be able to get home in reasonable time for lunch. But at the last moment his departure was delayed by a caller who was not a patient.

Detective-Sergeant Pim was ugly, talkative and desperately civil. It was his civility that Dr. Faraday found most alarming.

"I'm sorry to trouble you, Doctor, knowing how busy you are, very sorry indeed. But I'm enquiring into a

268

burglary that occurred last night, and it crossed my mind that perhaps you might be able to help me."

"A burglary, Sergeant? Where?"

"At Pinewood, sir—Mrs. Baker's house. She is a patient of yours, I think?"

"Yes. She has been for some time."

"Very old lady? Very ill, would you say, sir?"

"She is a chronic invalid and requires constant care."

"Quite so. And you saw her last?"

"The day before yesterday. She is on my list of patients to be visited this morning. Which reminds me, I have a long round to fit in and——"

"Just so, Doctor, just so. I mustn't keep you. I'll come along in the car with you, and then we can talk as we go."

It was an altogether horrible experience for Faraday to be doing his round with this babbling policeman beside him. The conversation started from the moment Pim took his seat and seemed to range over every detail of the doctor's life and work, all with the most deadly politeness.

What a nice car he had—one of the new model Quaestors, wasn't it? With overdrive? That came a bit expensive, Pim supposed. He didn't expect he'd ever be able to afford one himself, unless he had a bit of luck with a Premium Bond. Oh, the doctor had drawn a prize from Ernie? Well, well, that was wonderful, wasn't it?

Terrible lot of burglaries there had been in the district lately. Quite an epidemic, one might say. The Fosdykes over at Downham, and Colonel Norris at Didford—he'd lost a lot. Both patients of Dr. Faraday? Sergeant Pim could hardly contain his sympathy.

Miss Baker had been the chief loser last night, it seemed.

All her savings, in bank notes, taken from under her mattress where she kept them. Of course, it could hardly have happened if she had been sleeping in her own room. It was the doctor's suggestion that she should sleep in her mother's room in case the old lady needed help? Very wise, Pim was sure, but unlucky as it turned out. Of course, it might have been just coincidence, for there was a lot of silver taken from downstairs too. . . .

All this and much more, sandwiched between visits to patients to whom he must dispense treatment, advice, encouragement. Dr. Faraday's answers became shorter and more and more at random. He was beginning to find it difficult to concentrate. And then came the question he had been expecting.

"And last night, Doctor, where were you?"

"I was called out at midnight to see a child with suspected appendicitis."

"Was that Mrs. Carr's child, at Pinewood Lodge?"

"Yes."

"And was it appendicitis?"

"No. Nothing but a mild indigestion. Mrs. Carr used to be a nurse, and should have known better."

"She used to look after Mrs. Baker, before she married the gardener and went to live at the lodge, didn't she, Doctor? Well, as that was all the matter, I suppose you got home quite early?"

Dr. Faraday was frowning in an effort at recollection.

"No," he said at last. "I got home after two."

"Dear me! Now what was it kept you, Doctor, do you remember?"

The doctor stopped the car outside the last house on his morning's round. He had driven there automatically and seemed hardly to realize that he was at Pinewood. His face was white and drawn.

"No," he said slowly, "I don't remember."

Pim came indoors this time. He had enquiries to make, he said. Haggard and miserable, Faraday went upstairs to Mrs. Baker's room and somehow contrived to attend to her. When he came down the odious Pim was in the hall. Faraday had the impression that he was trying to stop him, but he was past caring. Pushing past him, he opened the hall door to go out.

He stopped abruptly on the threshold. His hand was coated with some dark sticky substance which he must have picked up from the door handle.

"My fault, I'm afraid, Doctor," Pim was saying. "I tried to stop you. I was trying a little experiment to see if fingerprints——"

Faraday did not listen. In disgust he turned back, made his way to the bathroom upstairs and scrubbed his hand clean with savage intensity. When he came down this time Pim was in the car.

"Are you calling at the lodge, Doctor?" he asked.

"What for? The child is perfectly well."

"Just as well to make sure," Pim suggested. "It might help you to remember about last night, too."

Faraday called at the lodge. He felt deprived of any will of his own. Mrs. Carr seemed surprised to see him, and still more surprised to see Pim, who asked her some polite but sceptical questions about the child's health. At last they left. Pim accompanied him all the way home.

"Thank you for your assistance, sir," he said as he got out. "Let me know if your memory about last night improves. Before I go, may I look in the boot of your car?"

Before Faraday could stop him he had opened the boot. From it he took a loosely wrapped parcel that gave a metallic clink.

"Mrs. Baker's silver," said Pim cheerfully. "How do you think that got there, Doctor?"

Faraday could say nothing.

"I'll tell you, sir. Mr. Carr put it there while we were talking to his wife. He slipped out of the back door as we came in at the front. I'm going back now to pick him up and have a look for Miss Baker's money. Can you remember now what kept you so late last night, sir?"

"Yes, I believe I can. When I left the lodge I found I had to change a wheel."

"Right, sir! While you were looking at the baby with the stomach-ache, Carr was letting your tyre down. He meant you to be out late the night your patient was burgled, and he and his wife organized it between them. He forgot one thing, though."

"What was that?"

"You could have pinched Miss Baker's money easily enough because you knew your way about the Pinewood bedrooms. But how's a doctor to know where the silver is kept *downstairs*? When I dirtied your hand just now, you ran up to the bathroom to wash. There was a cloak-room within a yard of you on the ground floor. Good day, Doctor; and if I might presume to advise you, take a long rest. You look worn out."